STAR TREK 51:
BATTLESTATIONS!

STAR TREK NOVELS

STAR TREK GIANT NOVELS

A *STAR TREK*® NOVEL

BATTLESTATIONS!
DIANE CAREY

TITAN BOOKS
LONDON

STAR TREK 51: *BATTLESTATIONS!
ISBN 1 85286 361 7

Published by
Titan Books Ltd
58 St Giles High St
London WC2H 8LH

First Titan Edition September 1991
10 9 8 7 6 5 4 3 2 1

Printed and bound in Great Britain by Cox and Wyman Ltd, Reading, Berkshire.

BATTLESTATIONS!

This novel is dedicated to the man and the ship responsible for my sail training—Captain Joseph Maggio and the beautiful, hardworking Bahamian schooner *William H. Albury*. Their union proved to me that captains really do exist who feel the same intensity toward their ships that James Kirk feels toward the *Enterprise*.

AUTHOR'S NOTE

I must thank my editors for both Trek novels thus far, formerly Karen Haas and now Dave Stern, for their diligent personal attention. As the rest of us can only guess, sifting through piles of Trekkery to find quality worth presenting to the world is neither an easy nor a casual job. Now that Star Trek is in so many hands, the effort to keep it pure becomes more strenuous. So rich a medium as Trek is easily polluted, even by the best of intentions.

Special thanks to word wizard Mark Okrand for many Klingon minutes via land line. Prime stuff, I must say, in any language.

Another shout of thanks to Brian "the Scarf" Thomas for designing Piper's ship with the same flair as he used for the Arco and Tycho fighters. Let's hear it for guerrilla filmmakers everywhere. And to Gary "éy mate" Jones, here's to old times, new times, and accurate call numbers on scout ships. Thanks, guys.

I'd also like to focus briefly on Boris and Doris Vallejo. Boris is responsible for the breathtaking cover paintings and his work continues to dazzle me, especially the care given to my designs and my characters. For all the sheer talent running in the Vallejo household, these are the most gracious, charming, funny, and welcoming people we've ever had the pleasure of calling our friends. To both of you, a warm thanks from both of us.

And, as always—and never enough—credit well deserved to Gregory.

Fair weather,

Diane Carey

"You could feel the wind at your back in those days . . . the sounds of the sea . . . even if you take away the wind and the water, it's still the same. The ship is yours, you can feel her . . . and the stars are still there, Bones."
—The Ultimate Computer

Chapter One

THE ENEMY SHIP cut across our port bow, forcing us to heel off to starboard, but our captain gripped the forward rail and refused to give more than a meter.

"Keep her to," he said, the quiet of his voice somehow reaching us over the roar of the ship straining.

"Jim, this is crazy."

"Don't swing off, no matter what your stomach says."

Space overhead was bristol blue, the crashing sea even deeper azure and marbled by green swells and white foam. The older officers called it cadet blue.

"Stand by to come about. Piper, stand by the backstay. Bones, you take the foresheet. And watch your head."

"Don't worry. *My* head's not going anywhere."

Below and around us white hull and green deck tilted to a sickening forty-five degrees that buried the boom tips in brine and put us straight alongside a swift gust of wind. The bowsprit bobbed in thirteen-foot arches. We crashed against the waves, skating alongside our enemy's beam for a moment of reasonless risk.

I freed the backstay on the port side so it wouldn't be in the way when the big main boom swung about, then slid down the inclined deck to the starboard backstay and got ready to pull it up tight once the sail swung by. There, shivering, I awaited the order to come about. With the ship at this hideous angle, my thigh cut into the rail. I was almost lying on my side. Just over the rail, an arm's-length away, the tree-trunk boom dug furrows into the seawater with every long dip of the schooner. Arching out and rising away from the water, the mainsail's bright white canvas tightened with air and became stiff as cast rhodinium. This was drama of the highest order, and my heart thudded testimony to the pure insanity I'd gotten myself into. Of course, I couldn't exactly decline the honor.

This old ship had been bending to the winds for something like a century and a quarter on this planet, revived to splendor by the very fading of her own kind. Originally built as a nostalgic replica of a nine-teenth-century pilot schooner, she was a working ves-sel, not a yacht. That "y" word wasn't allowed on board. And there wasn't a winch to be found. Every line had to be hand drawn, no matter how heavy the load. The acres of canvas, caught to the masts by big wooden hoops and lashed with rope to the gaffs and booms, made a puzzle of stitched white overlapping rectangles and triangles overhead and together formed a great seagoing pyramid of sailcloth and rigging. Pretty. But sitting here in excitement's grip, with abused timber groaning under me and the booms biting the tops off eight-footers, it was hard to see the pretti-ness. Not even in the echo of ourselves as the other ship, a bluff-bowed ancient ketch two meters longer than our schooner, carved away from our starboard stern and came about for another match.

"Here he bloody well comes again," uttered Mr. Scott at wheel watch, his Scots rumble getting thicker as tension grew. He was standing at the helm rather than sitting, gripping the spokes of the wooden wheel tightly, and narrowing his gaze forward. His eyes narrowed to dark wedges. His dark hair, matted against his forehead by spray, was laced with the first hints of silver. He wasn't watching the sails, though.

He was watching the captain. And the captain was watching the enemy ship.

Amidships, Dr. McCoy squinted accusingly at the captain and held on tight to the foresheet. Wind tore at his hair and spray battered his face.

Our bow lifted high out of the water, coming into the air like some flying fish, until half her keel was clear of the sea. Almost immediately she crashed back into the chop like a descending guillotine, burying the fo'c'sle, burying thirteen feet of bowsprit and the whole bottom of the Genoa jib. I winced and drew my shoulders in.

Heeled to starboard, the other ship was a mirror image of ours, except that her mast heights were reversed, her fore-tops'l wasn't flying, and her bow was bluff- instead of clipper-curved. When our captain first started talking about the enemy, I'd thought he was saying "catch"; one of many visits to his aft cabin library had set me right. She was the ketch *Gavelan*. We were out to get her, and she us.

My hands cramped as I gripped the backstay line. Awaiting orders, I looked at the captain and wondered what he was waiting for. Full sail in this kind of chop was crazy enough without waiting until the last second to execute a tack.

He stood on the forward deck, his eyes hard and pinched at the corners. In a heavy brown sea jacket with the collar up he looked like a holo on a tour spool from some planet-pushing travel agency. His hair, sandy and shimmering on top, darkening at the sides, shone nicely but couldn't upstage that glare of his. I could see him trying to put his mind into the head of the other captain before making a decision. He wanted more than anything to *be* inside *Gavelan*'s hold, secretly listening to what the other skipper was saying—more, though, he wanted to know what the other was feeling, thinking, breathing. He thought he could get there if he stared hard enough.

"Come about," the captain said. "Now."

3

Dr. McCoy let go of the foresheet a moment too soon, forcing Mr. Scott to haul hard on the wheel to keep from losing the fores'l into the waves. I held on as long as I could, but the ship wheeled and bucked, reversing herself in the water and cutting a pie wedge in the chop as she tacked. The rigging whistled overhead, the timber groaned, and the hoops grated so loudly I thought they were going to shear right through the mast.

Bam—the fore boom clunked to port. The sail luffed, then filled and tightened. An instant later—and Mr. Scott ducked just in time to avoid a ringing headache—the main. The schooner twisted back in the water with the grace of a shorebird's glinting wing.

"Haul in tight," the captain called. "I mean you, Piper. Put support on that main, then bring the sheet in close."

I shook myself, skidded across the tilted deck and drew in the main until we were so close upon the wind that we threw up a sickle of spray with every dive of our prow. He was watching me. I could feel it. Oh, he was looking at the other ship, but he was *watching* me.

"Closer," he said.

I drew down harder, sacrificing three more fingernails and one knuckle's skin.

Plunging toward each other like two Gloucester packets of a different age, our two schooners glided through walls of spray. The tapered lines of the sails and weaving mastheads conjured images of wave troughs deep enough to hide entire ships. I leaned harder against the teak rail, plain scared. From two sides of an angle, we speared for each other.

"Jim, I didn't come out here with you to become a damned South Sea walrus!" Dr. McCoy informed the captain, clinging desperately to the fore hatch and glancing wide-eyed at the oncoming schooner.

The captain didn't respond. Even now, there was a

distant tranquility on his face. This was his blood and beef—another man's peace was this man's boredom. When he wasn't wrestling the imbalances of interstellar space and intersystem politics, he was here, tasting death in the same seas our mutual ancestors called their own interstellar void.

The captain of the other ship was no Rigellian slugfin either. Silver spume spilled over *Gavelan*'s rail as she held tight into the wind and rocketed through jumping seas toward us. We were both pointed at the same square foot of ocean, and we both wanted to own it. Overhead, rigging whined. Tension buzzed through the halyards.

I drew in a breath, held it, and closed my eyes. The captain said I should learn to hear the ship, so I could hear what was wrong when it happened. Sometimes he made me close my eyes and cover my ears too. *Feeling* what's wrong, he called it. Even times like this—especially times like this—could teach.

Sails moaned. Waves smacked the keel. Gaffs and booms creaked. The wind rushed inward, filling the main tight. On collision course, our two schooners sliced through the seas toward each other. When our ship's prow dug deep into the waves, met a trough that matched its shape, and plunged six feet deeper, the deck dropped out from under my feet. Only catching my elbow around the backstay kept me aboard. I heard Dr. McCoy yell something as my feet left the deck, wobbled on the rail for three hideous seconds, then skated off. Down I went for a ride across twenty slippery feet of green deck, on one knee, until the fisherman's sail-bag stopped me.

"All right, lass?" Mr. Scott bothered to call from the wheel.

I took a moment to nod at him while I rubbed my knee. It was the wrong moment.

"Get your feet under you, Piper," the captain snapped. "Prepare to come about."

5

"Again?" McCoy complained. "What are you? A blasted porpoise?"

"Lay alongside, Scotty," everybody's devil called firmly. "I'm not going to let him work our windward. Piper, bring in the jib sheet two pulls. You left it too free."

Always the cut. Always the barb. Why? Didn't he have enough laurels to sit on? Not ten people in a million had his status. Why pick on me?

But as I glared at the captain, ire mixed with a stab of sympathy for him. Most humans could afford to cloak their flaws. A starship captain—the captain of any vessel, I was learning—constantly had his flaws thrown up in his face, with nowhere to deflect them. Not only could he see them, but he must see them displayed before all who wish to look—a galaxy ready to criticize. That would beat anyone into humility. Anyone but the strongest.

If he could be strong, if he could bear his flaws and mine too, then I could at least haul my end of the halyard.

Gripping the ship's rail, I got to my feet and moved carefully along the high side toward the bow. Battered by salt spray, the rail had gone from a burnished ribbon to a chipped ridge. It spelled work for deck hands. Like guess who.

I loosened the jib sheet, cranked it in, feeling the pressure of the wind as we heeled deeply, and belayed it without another screwup. Just when I was breathing my sigh of relief, I made the mistake of looking at the oncoming *Gavelan*.

"What—!" I choked. The other ship was so close I could almost count the planks in her hull. Wreathed in spray, she was crashing toward us out of a nightmare. I couldn't breathe anymore.

The captain cupped his hand around his mouth. "Now, Scotty!"

Mr. Scott closed his eyes and cranked the big wheel hard, then took a dive for the backstay to free it. The main boom began to swing. The sails, towering above us like wings, luffed for only an instant.

The schooner hung in midair, shuddered as shock waves thrummed through her wooden hull, then dived like a seal. Her bowsprit carved across our enemy's bow and forced the other ship to fall off the wind.

No one but the possessed would try such a move.

The booms swung around and slammed home. Climbing the wave, the ship shook off a wash of green seawater, filled her sails tight, and heeled in.

The captain leaned back. If he'd had a pipe, he'd have smoked it. "Fall off," he said. Mr. Scott stiffly complied.

Dr. McCoy slumped down on the fore hatch. "Shore leave, my eye."

I panted silently and got my footing on the deck. A few breaths later my thoughts came out in a mutter. "All we need is an aft phaser . . ."

Gavelan was upright in the choppy water, fallen off the wind. Her sails luffed uselessly, flapping and shuddering, in search of air.

Turning to me, the captain raised both straight brows and queried, "Did I hear you say something, Commander?"

Still out of breath, I blinked at him and tried to look steady. "Not me."

His lips pressed flat. Kind of a grin, and kind of not. "Good."

I watched, numb, as he walked casually down the long green deck, unaffected by the angle, and took charge of the wheel. Slowly now, he brought the ship about in a stylish tack that hardly let the sails flutter: the last turn of the blade before coming abeam with *Gavelan*.

Aboard the other ship, the skipper's familiar Mid-

Eastern features glowed in the sun behind a dark cropped beard. "Brilliantly executed, Captain!" he called. "I concede the match."

"Accepted, Ambassador," the captain returned. "I'm looking forward to my lobster."

"And you shall have it," our former enemy returned. Behind him, his crew, an unlikely collection of individuals, watched us coast by. "The best available in the next port of call. And my liquor cabinet is yours to raid."

"Faster than you can moor a dinghy."

The ambassador roared with laughter. *Gavelan* caught the wind and fell in behind us. Finally, *finally,* we were back on course.

I watched our captain as he steered the ship with damnable leisure. San Francisco was long behind us and I still tended to stay on the other end of the ship from where he was. A respectful distance, it might be called. A little chicken was another way to put it. He always saw the imperfection, that halyard belayed one turn less than the others, the backstay not hauled up tightly enough, the rope tied in a granny knot instead of a square knot . . . and there was nothing in this galaxy more soul-galling than coming up out of a hatch in time to see James Kirk correct your little error.

James Kirk. An enigma in his midthirties. And here he was, commanding seventy-two feet of timber and sailcloth with every ounce the commitment he used to head up the multidepartmental city-in-space we call a starship. The whole scope of that became scarier to me with every minute I spent in his company. He wasn't an easy man to get to know. He guarded himself. Oh, he talked often enough, but he *spoke* little. Curiosity boiled up in me, enough to turn a Star Fleet command candidate into a petty snoop. Despite the integrity I was trying to imitate, I often found myself haunting the open aft hatch, hoping to—accidentally—catch a line or two of the conversation between him and

McCoy and Scott during one of those quiet personal sessions. I seldom got more than a sniff of kahlua and coffee. In fact, the silence said plenty. My curiosity remained intact. So did the sting of knowing I wasn't yet welcome in that inner sanctum. I hungered more for it with every passing wind.

And the mysteries about Captain Kirk seemed to grow deeper as I knew him longer. I looked away from him and leaned over the ship's rail for the dozenth time to see black letters outlined in hunter-green scrolls: *Edith Keeler*.

Letters no one would explain. I knew "Edith" was a feminine name on Earth, not very popular anymore. Since sailing ships had always been named after both men and women, knowing the name's gender narrowed my curiosity by 50 percent. The rest remained a darkness.

It was nearly three o'clock, Earth time. I seldom knew what time it was, but as I came below, through the aft cabin, I happened to glance at the old-style ship's clock that lay half-buried in navigational charts on the captain's desk. The clock I could read. The charts—well, I could read the clock.

The aft ladder was easier to climb with a tray of coffee mugs than the forecabin ladder, so that's the way I went. I came up on deck just in front of the ship's wooden wheel. Behind it, the captain was grinning at himself and steering *Keeler* through waves that seemed to grow calmer at his behest. What had been eight-footers had smoothed to a light chop as we stopped fighting them and continued sailing into the middle of the Caribbean.

I relayed coffee to Mr. Scott and Dr. McCoy as they relaxed amidships, then returned with one for the captain. He took it with a silent nod, settled back in the helm chair, and eyed me with those hazel-browns.

"Something on your mind, Commander?"

9

I stared into *Keeler*'s wake. Stark even in daylight, the sea's chop was blue-black in the troughs, green-white at the crests, and making a lick-whap-suck on the hull that I was finally getting used to. I still was, however, not at all used to being called "Commander." He probably did it deliberately.

He was waiting.

I hugged my coffee mug and turned so the wind wasn't blowing strands of layered honey-brown hair into my eyes. Weeks under Earth's bright sun had given it the same lights as flickered in Captain Kirk's regulation-trimmed locks. "Sir . . . don't you ever get tired of it?"

If the question sounded accusatory, it didn't show on Kirk's face. This was a different face from the one he'd used during the war game. This was a face of soft golden brush strokes. Two of the brush strokes went up. "Of what?"

"Battle. We're hardly out of the affair with the dreadnought, Star Fleet's churning on its ear, the Federation's tumbling in the wake of Rittenhouse's attempt to subvert it, and you're out here in the middle of nowhere, jousting antiques. You said we were going out for some quiet sailing."

He tipped one shoulder down in a motion I now recognized, adjusting himself in the helm seat much as he did in his command chair aboard *Enterprise*. "I never make promises, Piper, you know that."

"I do now."

A calculated sip of his coffee gave us a moment to think. "Well," he began then, "it's good for you. If I had my way, every potential starship commander would go to sea on a sailing ship. No, it's not an affectation. It's simple logistics. Before you can out-guess an enemy in three dimensions, you've got to be able to maneuver in two." Illustratively, two fingers went up in a V before me.

My whole anticipatory system—what command

10

candidates used instead of nerves—jolted when he referred to me as a potential starship commander. I didn't know if it was more exciting than horrifying, or the reverse. . . . so, I changed the subject.

"Mr. Scott did quite a job of outsteering *Gavelan*," I said. "He never struck me as a sailor before."

"He was just like you," Kirk remembered. "Had never been on an ocean, and took to it like a cod once he understood what made the ship move."

I blushed. Captain James Kirk did not hand out compliments arbitrarily.

He scanned the seas, glancing briefly back at *Gavelan* as Ambassador Shamirian raised a glass high in an exaggerated gesture. Kirk raised his coffee mug in return, and was smiling when he turned back to me. "Scotty's really just an old halibut himself, down deep," he continued thoughtfully. Now he looked forward to where Scott and McCoy were lounging on the foredeck, probably discussing the lunacy we'd just subjected ourselves to. Kirk's broad-browed face, with its soft curves, and his eyes, with those slightly pouched lower lids lending a mellowness to the reposing strength, always seemed to be layered with thoughts. Never one thought; always several at a time. He contemplated his old friends silently after that last comment, no longer sharing his feelings about them with me.

Sensitive, probably out of habit, to his gaze, both older officers turned our way, made a silent decision, and came toward us at a careful pace along the tilted deck. "Are my ears buzzing for a reason?" Dr. McCoy asked.

"Why, Bones," the captain said, "you look as though you've seen a ghost." His mouth was stretched into that victory grin again.

"There are no ghosts at sea, Captain," McCoy said, planting himself on the rail opposite me. "Only taxed imaginations."

11

"That sounds like something Spock would say."

"Oh, no, Jim. Spock would comment on the waste. You know, exertion and risk with no true gain. Can't you just hear him say it, with a 'most illogical' pinned on the end of it?"

Bidden as though by drug, I indeed heard Commander Spock's rough baritone cadence knitting those words into his own kind of commentary on races and contests.

"Now, Captain, there's a proposal I'd like to see worked on," Mr. Scott said, as he cocked one leg on the cooler and gripped the loops of rope that held the mains'l to the big boom. "Mr. Spock on board this kind of starship. I wonder ha' he'd look in a slicker."

"Earth's a water planet, Scotty," Kirk said, bemused. "One of very few. Sailing ships grew with our culture. Besides . . . wouldn't you hate to see Spock even greener than usual?"

The three men laughed, enjoying their moment of teasing bigotry at the expense of their absent friend, forgetting that although I was human, Earth was not my home either. I had no reason to feel envious, yet I couldn't laugh along with them.

"Where are we headed, sir?" I asked.

"We're supposed to rendezvous with the other flotilla participants at New Providence."

I waited for him to finish the sentence. Perhaps it was his tone, perhaps the flicker in his eye, or the fact that I'd learned to expect more from him than whatever was obvious. After a moment, I assisted. "But . . ."

McCoy's rooster-tail brows arched up. "Tell her, Jim. What are you saving it for? She's been looking at you like a suspicious cat for a week now, even if she doesn't know it."

I flushed again, but McCoy's hilarious glare made me duck my head and smile in embarrassment. One thing was for sure: we weren't going to New Providence.

That half-grin stretched one side of Kirk's mouth. He gazed at me from the corners of his eyes. "We're sailing toward your future, Piper."

"A banana republic," Kirk explained, putting one foot up on the rail, still fingering the ship's wheel lightly. "A quaint local epithet used to describe island settlements in semitropical areas here on Earth. The Virgin Islands, . . . Greater and Lesser Antilles, . . . Jamaica, the Caymans, the West Indies in general."

"Because of the banana trees?"

"Banana trees, banana vendors, a generally banana life-style is what you'll find there."

He gazed at the sea between McCoy and Scott. "I guess we taught Ben Shamirian a good lesson today," he said, enjoying the sight of *Gavelan* plowing along several ship-lengths behind *Keeler*.

"That you did, sir," Scott said. "And bonnily too. 'Course, Doc and I'll ne'r be the same for wear . . ."

"What, Scotty? Thinning out already, at your age? I'm dismayed."

"And I'm ocean-sick," McCoy drawled.

Meanwhile, I was itching to find out what he meant about sailing toward my future.

When I spoke, my voice seemed not to fit in among theirs. "Are you tampering with my future, sir?"

He nodded, dawdling through a sip of coffee. "Your first command."

He was teasing me again. Bad enough when I *did* know what he was talking about, much less when I didn't. I sat down on the rail and leaned back against the lifeline. "A lobster scow, right?"

Kirk shook his head, saying, "A space vessel." Through my astonished stare he continued, "With atmospheric *and* stellar capabilities."

The stare started to hurt. My eyes watered in the wind. Mr. Scott was chuckling.

"Are you . . ." I stammered. "Are you kidding me?"

"Commander, it's a Star Fleet-commissioned space-going passenger vessel, and it's waiting at Man-o-War Cay for you to take command." When Kirk saw my expression—if by any reach of terminology I still appeared human at all—he buried a flicker of amusement in a blink.

McCoy leaned forward on the rail, supported by both hands on either side of his legs. Those demonstrative eyes widened at me. "How hard did you think it would be to wangle a light command for the youngest person to receive the Federation Medal of Valor?"

"But . . . but . . . but . . . but *why?*"

My question started in McCoy's direction, shifted to Scott, and ultimately landed on Captain Kirk. After a moment, he said, "Oh, I've got a little mission for you. Call it a . . . mail run."

"Space . . . a space . . . a mission out in space?"

"That's right."

I took a deep breath, and shook the seaweed out of my head.

"Think you're up to it?" he asked.

"No!"

Captain Kirk chuckled openly. "That alone tells me you are," he said. "We'll be there by tomorrow afternoon. Start getting used to the idea, Commander. As of tomorrow, you've got a ship of your own."

Chapter Two

"Anything you might say has already been taken down in evidence against you."

—The Squire of Gothos

MY OWN COMMAND.

Gladiator. Excalibur. Odyssey. Mountaineer. Troubadour.

Since she would be acquired during my stay here on Earth, shouldn't my ship have a Terran name? This planet might be just a little squeak that started a big rumble, but Earth's history had plenty to offer. More so in plain gallantry and intrepidness than in many more, dare I say, civilized cultures. I was just beginning to appreciate that. Earth, planet of my ancestry, had been the subject of my fascination, my study, even my curiosity, but never my respect.

As Star Fleet hung in political suspension a few thousand kilometers behind us, subject to tense purges, and courts-martial, I contemplated the name of *my ship*. Had I earned this? I had fallen into a bad situation and forded it. That was Star Fleet's hope when they created the Academy to mine the crude ore of future command, wasn't it? The cost had been long and wide—the lives of a Star Fleet destroyer's entire crew; no, not my fault, but inevitable because I refused to give in. I felt victorious about the failure of Vice Admiral Rittenhouse's clandestine attempt to trigger the collapse of Star Fleet and set up his own intersystem republic, but I still didn't feel good about it. Victorious . . . good . . . too different for peace of mind. And now Star Fleet trembled in the wake.

I stood in *Keeler*'s galley, heating coffee on what seemed an archaic gas stove. Though I'd grown used to it, I still marveled at Kirk's purity of cause. Dr. McCoy had told me that when Kirk had purchased this ship, she'd been half-restored and in bankruptcy. He'd completed the restoration, rope for rope, halyard for halyard, binnacle for binnacle, keeping true to the old style. Hence, gas stove.

Maybe a feminine name, so everyone would know the captain was female. *Edna St. Vincent Millay.* Too long. *Summer Rain. Myth. Siren.* Or a famous name: *Zuriak. Boone. Philip of Macedon. James T. . . .*

He didn't seem worried about the tumult at Star Fleet Command. After all, here he was, one of only a handful of starship commanders, cruising his home planet in the slowest possible fashion. Shouldn't he be back there . . . helping? Weren't there decisions to be made? I'd bet that somebody, somewhere, was turning to his second and grumbling, "Damn, I wish Jim Kirk was here."

Thunderbird. Chimera. Cumulus. Egyptian.

The coffee wasn't even hot enough to send up an aroma when an unexpected whine shook me from my plans. The whine turned to a hum, then caused a faint but recognizable oscillation of air particles around my face and arms, where the skin was bare. My ivory cotton flight suit shielded the rest of my skin from the particle jump, but the cause remained perfectly identifiable, even if it was totally out of place. I must be delirious, imagining things.

A transporter beam?

The hum grew deeper. I dashed to the forecabin ladder and climbed up enough to get my elbows onto the deck, and froze in place, astonished. Three forms were indeed materializing onto the aft deck. The synthesis of old and new hit me like the smell of bad weather. Invasion.

"How rude!" I exclaimed. My breath was stolen by the wind flushing into the fores'l. Beaming down! What raw nerve!

Still hardly more than bands of shimmering light, the forms were steps away from where I'd left Captain Kirk and the others on the aft deck when I escaped to collect my thoughts. Kirk obviously wasn't going to divulge any more information about this so-called mail run he'd slotted me for and I'd seen no reason to gawk at him. So I came down to the galley, to gawk into the coffee.

But with people beaming onto the ship without the slightest announcement, I had another direction to gawk in. The affrontery of it held me to my place half out of the hatch, peering around the main mast.

Three Star Fleet Security Division uniforms distilled into being and stopped shimmering. Two men, large. And a woman, compactly built but still somehow imposing in her own subdued way.

Kirk got up from the helm chair, moving to them like a prowling ghar-tiger. Sharply he demanded, "Just what is the meaning of this intrusion?"

"Captain James Kirk?" a big goon of a lieutenant began. It was a formality only, the beginning of a recitation.

"Yes."

"Lieutenant Alexander, sir. Sir, I am instructed to escort you to Star Fleet headquarters regarding an inquiry issued by Star Fleet Command and the Federation Military Advisory Committee—"

"Why?" Kirk asked with typical bluntness.

"For questioning regarding the theft of special technology by a member of your crew."

Kirk's voice changed. "Which member?"

"Lieutenant Sarda."

17

I bumped my head on the hatchway in a bolt of shock. Sarda . . . only weeks ago my biggest concern about Sarda was helping him find a channel back into the Vulcan disciplines he'd been denied by his race's pacifist prejudices. Only weeks ago we were fighting side by side. How did he get himself embroiled in espionage while on shore leave? I gripped the hatch rim and dug my fingernails in, seized with a sudden need to talk to him, to find out why—

"What in the devil!" McCoy blurted.

Scott moved to stand beside Kirk, a united front. He glared at Lieutenant Alexander. "You'd better have your chevrons on straight for this one, lad," he warned. "Lieutenant Sarda is a recipient of the Silver Palm."

The lieutenant shrugged. "Anyway."

Mr. Scott bristled. "You don't just go about tossing accusations at Federation honorees."

Alexander took a breath, ignored him, and addressed the captain again. "I am authorized to escort you to Star Fleet Command Headquarters for questioning regarding this theft. If you do not choose to cooperate, I am authorized to place you under special arrest—"

"In other words, I go with you either way," Kirk finished, his eyes narrowing.

"Correct, sir." Alexander pivoted on one foot and faced Mr. Scott. "Chief Engineer Montgomery Scott?"

"Aye . . ."

"Sir, I am instructed to escort you to Star Fleet headquarters regarding an inquiry issued by Star Fleet Command and the Federation Military—"

"A' right, mister, I've heard it."

"I'm authorized to escort you to Star Fleet Command Headquarters for questioning. If you choose not to cooperate, I am authorized to place you under special arrest."

18

I ducked back into the forecabin. Even beyond the complete surprise and unlikelihood of this turnabout, I sensed a deeper wrongness. Slipping aft through the cabins, I hid at the bottom of the aft hatch and listened. Half expecting Alexander to have turned to McCoy with his recitation, I had to recalibrate when he turned instead to Kirk and said, "Sir, I must request that you inform me as to the whereabouts of Commander Spock, who has also been named in the inquiry."

There was a pause.

Kirk's voice was low-toned. "Mr. Spock is not aboard."

"Where is he, sir?"

"On leave. I don't know specifically where." His vocal timbre stiffened then. "Lieutenant, this is a gross breach of protocol as well as a serious accusation. I demand to know who's responsible for levying these charges."

"Sir, there are no charges. This is only an emergency inquiry. I must also request that you inform me as to the whereabouts of the following Fleet personnel, who have also been called in for questioning: Lieutenant Commander Hikaru Sulu, Lieutenant Nyota Uhura, Lieutenant Commander Piper."

While I crouched in the forward hatch, my heart shriveled up and ran into the fo'c'sle. I couldn't swallow anymore.

"I'm not in the habit," Kirk went on, very steadily measuring his hidden message, "of monitoring my crew's shore leaves. None of those people are here."

"Then if you and Mr. Scott will please gather your things, I'll signal the cruiser to beam us up."

The lack of immediate alternatives showed in Kirk's voice; though I couldn't see his face, I knew exactly what his eyes were doing. "Dr. McCoy isn't able to pilot this schooner alone, Lieutenant. You'll have to wait until we make port."

I ducked back another step into the aft cabin. His message was gaining poignant clarity, if not explanation.

"Yes, sir," Alexander said. "A Star Fleet low-atmosphere tug is on the way to take control of this vessel. The sailing plan you filed with the San Francisco Maritime Authority specified New Providence as your next port of call. The boat will be taken there, unless you specify somewhere else. We could have the boat beamed somewhere, if necessary, but it's officially impounded until further notice." I caught a glimpse of Alexander's gesture toward the sober female guard. "Yeoman Philotoff will remain on board until the tug arrives. She knows how to steer it."

Beam the whole ship? *Wow* . . .

"Now just a minute," McCoy interfered, blustering. "How can we be expected to supply any useful information, considering we've been sitting on this ocean, out of touch with everybody and everything? How do you explain that?"

"I don't, sir."

The sound of shuffling feet replaced the voices for a moment, then relented again.

"Captain," Alexander said. "I have here a warrant of permission to search this boat, the North American Maritime Registry vessel *Edith Keebler,* as issued by Supreme Congressional Judge Michael Riley, stardate 4720.2."

Kirk bristled. "It's *Keeler,*" he said, taking a nip at what little flaws he could find in Lieutenant Alexander's efficiency. Alexander had been handpicked, no doubt. Most security people would have been more intimidated by the monumental assignment of confronting the captain of the *Enterprise*.

"If you don't mind," Alexander continued. "Lieutenant Harsch and I will take a look underneath."

"Below," Kirk corrected. "And I do indeed mind,

20

Lieutenant. My privacy has been ruptured. No matter how stringent your orders, I doubt they included beaming without notice onto private property. Be assured I'll have a discussion with your superiors when we return to Command."

"Nevertheless, sir, I'm going to have to search the boat."

Rushing back into the forecabin, I spun around frantically. No, not the head—they'd look there. The galley cabinets were too small . . . the berths were military-neat, without any convenient piles of blankets or clothing to hide under. I might have been able to hide in or under a sail bag, but I couldn't get on deck without being seen . . . unless the fo'c'sle hatch was open . . .

Alexander and Harsch finally picked their way through Kirk's stubbornness and started their search of *Keeler*. In my mind, supplemented by careful listening and imagining how I would do it, I saw the Security men investigate the ship's tight little hold, the engine room where the now-quiet engine—of course, an old restored diesel—sometimes throbbed, the supply shelves in the aft hatchway, both heads, the forecabin closet, and every other nook they could find. I wished desperately for Vulcan ears as their slow footsteps scraped on the upper decks. Poking the sail bags, peering around the sea sides of the fores'l and jib, then finally the walking and poking and opening and closing stopped. There were voices, but I could barely hear them. My hands were cold, sweating. I bunched them up under my chin and tried to make sense of this. Was Kirk being framed? Had someone pinned these charges on Sarda in order to entrap Kirk? Or to distract from other crimes surfacing during the purge? A half-dozen members of the Admiralty had come under suspicion—two had been court-martialed, one actually jailed. Captains of other starships had been

21

dismissed—four of them! I'd made myself ready to accept almost any change at Star Fleet Command—but not this.

My skin tingled. The air around me vibrated ever so faintly. My ears buzzed for a long instant, then everything settled again. Only the sea wind hummed now.

I burst out of the larder, shoving upward against the wooden board that made a lower berth and a seat behind the madiera table in the forecabin. The seat cushion bounced off as I climbed out. I unfolded my legs and winced at the creases left in my thighs and sides by cartons and tins of stored food. I'd been on board *Keeler* weeks before I even knew that compartment was there.

I quietly gained the top of the forecabin ladder and peeked out, past the mainmast, rigging, and sails, to the helm. Yeoman Philotoff was at the wheel, scanning the blue sky. Looking for the low-at tug, no doubt. McCoy stood near the aft hatch, hanging onto a block-and-tackle, scanning the deck. He spied me. His head craned forward and his brows shot together, but he clamped his lips tight. With a roll of his eyes he told me to stay hidden. He, too, evidently understood Kirk's efforts to stall the search. Hide Piper, give her a chance to act. But act how? What did Kirk want me to do? Sarda was no thief, certainly no traitor, and if anyone knew it, I did. Kirk was giving me some kind of advantage. The captain knew what he would do if Mr. Spock were in this position. Now I had to figure out what that was, so I could do it too. That was all.

The low-atmosphere tug appeared on the distant horizon, approaching rapidly. I ducked deeper into the hatchway. The tug was a flattish air/space vehicle with bumpers all around its turtle-shaped hull just below Star Fleet insignia and call letters. Typical of Security, the vessel had no aesthetic catalog name.

Arthurian . . . Culloden . . . Pioneer . . . Corinthian

. . . Versailles, America, Proxima—could I name a ship before I'd even seen it? I wouldn't want anyone to impound my ship; I wasn't going to stand by while *Keeler* was trussed up under Fleet red tape. She was going to the port her captain wanted her in.

My hands shook now as I heard the low throb of the tug's engines whine down to idle beside the schooner. I scoured my brain for some memory of the crew complement of a low-at—two or three, no more. Plus Yeoman Philotoff, above decks. I'd wait. I'd let them take us in tow. Then . . . phasers. There had to be phasers on board somewhere. Jim Kirk was a cautious man. Any sailor learned to anticipate pirates. I wouldn't leave my ship or crew without some kind of tangible protection; I guessed he wouldn't either. They had to be aboard—but where?

"This is Gavelan *calling* Keeler. *Jim, is there some problem aboard?"*

My heart took a dive. "Damn it!" I hissed. The com unit in the aft cabin! Ambassador Shamirian had no idea what he was doing if Philotoff decided to come below.

I was trying to crawl back into the compartment under the bench when I froze, hearing voices.

"Do you mind," McCoy was saying, "if I go down there and answer that? Our sister ship over there wants to know what's going on."

"Go ahead, sir," Philotoff replied. Her voice had a rough texture, but her tone was almost conciliatory.

The vision appeared before me of McCoy's brow rising in indignation. He grimly uttered, "Thank you." Caustic bitterness was uncloaked in the doctor's tone.

I met him in the aft cabin, but waved him to silence and motioned to the com unit. He picked up the transceiver and responded, "Ambassador Shamirian, this is Leonard McCoy."

"Yes, Doctor. What's happening? What has the tug come for?"

"We're . . . well, we're being impounded, Ambassador. Captain Kirk's been called back to Star Fleet Command for, uh, administrative reasons."

"Ah. I'm not surprised. Do you need help?"

McCoy shifted the question to me with a look. I shook my head, wide-eyed.

He swallowed, then spoke into the transceiver. "Not right now, Ambassador. We'll let you know."

"We'll be here, Doctor."

"Apparently so will we. McCoy out."

He replaced the transie and started to say something to me, but I pressed a finger against my lips. I opened my palms in an encompassing gesture and whispered, "Phasers?"

The sharp blue eyes grew huge. He stared at me as though I'd grown cauliflower ears. With a paranoid glance up the hatchway, he exaggerated a shrug and his eyes got even wider. Evidently it hadn't occurred to him to rupture the flow of events planned for us by Star Fleet security.

Above decks, we heard voices:

Someone hailing from the low-at: "You know how to steer this fossil, Yeoman?"

Philotoff answering: "I can keep it on course, but I don't know how to change course. It's a museum-quality relic, but it sure is slow."

"Can you fold up those membranes?"

"They're called sails, Vallo. And . . . we could try it. I'll need help. I've never seen anything like this before. I'm used to automatic sail furlings."

"Stand by."

Keeler rumbled as the low-at pulled up alongside, hovering at a pace so slow as to strain the heavy-duty tug engines. We heard a "thunk" as the tug officer dropped onto the aft deck. "All right," he began, "how do we do this?"

"Doctor!" I hissed from the bottom of my throat. "Phasers!"

McCoy touched his mouth in thought, paused through a few long moments, then whispered, "If I know Jim, they'll be near his own bunk." He pointed broadly to the captain's berth.

We went through every drawer and cubbyhole, expanding our search away from that focal point, until McCoy stifled a little yelp of victory; sure enough there were phasers—hidden nicely in a dull wooden box in the aft cabin head. In the head, of all places. Knowing Kirk, he probably asked himself where anybody who knew him would guess he might keep phasers, and he went immediately in the opposite direction.

I crossed the cabin in one step. McCoy watched, wordless, as I separated the gun-handle unit from the power pack of one phaser and stuffed it into the pocket of my flight suit. Good thing it had been a little chilly during my wheel watch this morning, or I might have been wearing a water suit or shorts and not been prepared for this at all. As it was, I could barely assimilate what had happened and what to do about it in the time I had.

"What do you—"

"Shhh!"

He lowered his voice considerably. "What are you going to do with that?"

"I'm taking this ship, sir," I told him. "The captain had something like that in mind . . . do you have any idea?"

"Me? I'm a doctor, not a spy. Nobody tells me anything. It does look like he left the ball in your court, though."

At that, I stared at him and gushed, *"What ball?"*

"Are you going to take over the tug?" the doctor asked.

"And leave it behind, yes."

"Wouldn't it be faster than *Keeler?*"

I nodded, struggling with shaky fingers to set the phasers on heavy stun, and explained, "But they can track the tug. Once we're in crowded Bahamian waters, the schooner becomes just another ship in the flotilla. Stay here," I told him. With a second phaser, the complete gun, wrapped in my clammy fist, I slipped through the ship's innards to the fo'c'sle, a dark and cramped quarter in the pointed bow. Above me was an open hatch, with no ladder. Beyond that, bobbing high aloft, was the foremast. I would have to climb out just right if the sail was to hide me. The dangerous moment would come just as I surfaced, for I would have to balance myself and had little option of ducking to one side or the other. *Turbulence . . . Counterattack . . . Identity Crisis . . .* the S.S. *Nerve Pinch . . .*

I straddled the fo'c'sle, one foot on each bunk, and hoisted myself up and out in a single motion, my head low, coming out straight up so the mast itself would hide me for a moment.

I crawled forward, squirming along the green deck, keeping the big sail between myself and the invaders.

The ship shuddered and faltered. A loud scraping noise filtered forward through the wind. I couldn't see, but I felt the mains'l drop, felt the slackening of control over the wind. I winced, thinking of those two security clods trying to furl the main. Getting it to drop was easy enough once the ropes were tracked back to their sources, but folding up all that yardage of sailcloth was something I hadn't come close to mastering even under Captain Kirk's tutelage. Not unexpectedly, Philotoff started yelling obscenities, both at the sail and at the tug crewman.

The phaser pistol was warm in my hand. Within its power pack, restrained compressed energy kept the whole weapon warm even when not in use. It doubled the sweatiness of my palms as I arranged it in police position, one hand holding the phaser, the other steadying that wrist. I backed as far to the schooner's bow as I could get—right up against the jib—braced

26

my buttocks on the rail, and aimed at the position where one of the men would have to stand in order to drop the fores'l.

"It's good enough," Philotoff was calling. "We can fix it later."

"I dunno . . . you really want to leave Captain James T. Kirk's float looking like that?"

"I'm not so sure it isn't *supposed* to look like that. And it's a boat, not a float."

"Okay, okay."

It's a ship, my tense mind corrected. Typical security inertia for brains.

Several more seconds I went on like that, brewing up animosity for them, for their churlish intrusion, and their offhanded treatment of *Keeler.* I gathered every last annoyance into a lump and sat on it until my teeth gritted and my finger itched on the phaser trigger. By the time the fores'l began to drop, I hated security people from the bottom of my . . . bottom.

The sail dropped. Wooden hoops scraped the mast. Sailcloth luffed and piled up on the boom. The ship fell out of the wind altogether. Soon the gaff was at my eye-level. I tightened my grip on the phaser.

The gaff settled as two sets of hands pulled it down from the other side. Then—two faces.

They gaped at me for an instant. Then Vallo went for his phaser.

I hunched my shoulders, and fired.

Chapter Three

"Sailor's luck, Mr. Spock."
—Amok Time

A PHASER IN full fire is a hot thing. All that energy so tightly contained causes flushback into the phaser casing, making it warm to the touch. The weapon reminds the user of the power in hand. A weapon with a conscience. My hands sweated as the beam propelled Vallo backward down the deck. He collapsed against the rail, then tumbled to the deck. I didn't mind using the phaser, but using it without a clear reason took me down with my prey.

Perhaps it was guilt that made me hesitate. Caught in the complexity, I held my breath as Vallo crumpled, and gave Philotoff the time she needed to react. I saw her phaser come up in my periphery, even saw the infinitesimal glow as the beam gathered inside the tiny muzzle perforation, and I would have loved to take credit for the response of my nerves. Maybe Star Fleet trained me better than I remembered or maybe primeval responses took over, but I found myself shoulder down on the deck as the blue beam lanced over me.

Footsteps vibrated through the deck wood and I knew she was coming around to find me. Scrambling like a puppy on ice, I somehow made it to the foredeck and hid behind the jib, the only sail still flying. The schooner's forward movement had slackened to almost nothing when the fores'l luffed and went down, and the jib was doing little more than providing some stabilization as we bobbed in the choppy lapis seas.

"You're just making things harder on yourself, Commander," Philotoff called as she circled the foremast and carefully came toward the bow. "Come on. I know who you are. Kirk cooperated, so why don't you do the same?"

I didn't answer. I held my phaser close to my chin and stepped carefully in the tight deck area on the pointed bow. There was no place to go but overboard. On a ship this size, even that wouldn't hide me. The rope netting under the bowsprit provided no solutions either. I would have to stay on board.

On the canvas sail I saw the ominously clear etching of Philotoff's silhouette kindly provided by Earth's vulgar yellow sun. She wasn't built so much differently from me, except that she was a little shorter and her hips were rounder. She looked well trained and strong in that silhouette, a uniform-bound power pack just like the phaser she carried. She was about to come around the sail. Her phaser was preceding her. Her hand caught the edge of the canvas. The sail started to luff.

Philotoff snapped the sail out of her way. The boom waggled. I moved—fast. I caught a glimpse of the phaser bolt as it struck out and sizzled into the sea beyond the starboard rail, and I was pinched with a sniggering little regret that I didn't hang around to see the look on Philotoff's face. I heard her scrambling around on the deck as she searched frantically for me, heard her drop into the fo'c'sle through the open hatch, and heard her shuffle through the galley, the forecabin, the main cabin, and finally up the aft hatchway, but by then I had the advantage. When she popped up through the aft hatch and the sun turned her dun hair to umber, I was there and so was my phaser. A second later, Yeoman Philotoff was heaped over the hatch stairway, twitching and numb.

She wasn't alone; I was numb too. My arms ached from the stiffness as I held them locked before me, joined at the phaser in a tangle of fingers. I stared at Philotoff's limp form, and at Vallo still crumbled beyond her. If only I could know this was right . . .

"Freeze right there, lady."

By the time the new voice cut through me, I'd already lowered my phaser, and my guard. I'd forgotten the tug. I looked over my shoulder, toward midships. The tug hovered just above the chop off our port side, casting a jade shadow on the water. A burly guard hung his arms over the bumper rail, his shoulders hunched, and a phaser trained square at my heart.

"Don't turn," he said. "Drop the phaser."

Defeat swarmed over me. Evidently being at sea for so long had dulled my thinking processes more than I realized. I would have to remember this—for future shore leaves. My phaser thunked to the polished wooden hatch-top at my feet. Only then did the guard climb carefully onto the tug bumper and hop from there to *Keeler*'s rail, and finally onto the deck just port of the foremast. I stood on the aft hatch, helpless, my back still to him. I didn't turn, but I was watching the guard as he kept the phaser firmly raised. He knew better than to trust me. Kirk's face passed by in the shadows cast by the guard's bulk as he slowly crossed the green deck. What was I supposed to do? What did the captain want of me? Should I take these people down—that was out of the question now; the guard had a solid drop on me.

High above me, the mainmast groaned in a stern gust of wind over the ship, echoing my feelings. The guard was big; I'd have a hard time taking him physically, if he ever gave me the chance. Not likely. He was very cautious, approaching me with suspicious slowness. A few more steps and he would have my phaser.

All at once, the fores'l boom, with the sail sloppily

bracketed between it and the lowered gaff like a rumpled bedspread, swung hard over from the starboard side where Vallo and Philotoff had left it. The guard threw his hands up when he saw the heavy tangle of wood, rope, and canvas swinging toward him, but he was no match for the sheer weight. The boom and gaff thudded into his chest and knocked him hard into the blocks and tackles of the rigging that supported the mainmast. He howled his pain and anger, and the expression on his face told me he wanted nothing more than to have my right arm in his gritted teeth. His big body shuddered and recovered in spite of the deadly blow. Somehow he stayed on his feet and shook the boom off with a mighty heave. Swinging freely, the boom wobbled back over the forehatch.

But I hadn't waited. The phaser was back in my hand. I leaped from the hatch onto the deck for a clear shot, and took it. The stun beam caught the guard in the shoulder and raced through his body, its energy force knocking him onto the rail. He pivoted over it, his eyes wide with shock, and tumbled into a mild white froth.

My shoulders shook with tension as I straightened. I broke my stare from the floating guard as his body bobbed under the blue surface. I looked to starboard. Dr. McCoy was just getting to his feet, leaning on the raised deck amidships.

"I forgot all about you!" I blurted on a gust of relief.

He crawled under the lobbing boom and reached over the rail to catch the stunned guard's left arm as the body bobbed to the surface. I tucked the phaser into a pocket and rushed to help him. Using the loose jib halyard, I tied the guard to the side of the ship, ensuring that he wouldn't go under anymore.

"What are you doing?" McCoy asked.

I looped the rope under the guard's armpits two more times for good measure and said, "I'll be right back." I stepped up onto the polished rail and made a crazy leap for the tug—it was farther away than it looked. The bumper squeaked under my deck shoes and keeping my balance was a fight to be remembered. I wasn't going to be surprised again. In moments, the tug had been thoroughly searched and I could stop worrying about having another face pop up behind me when I wasn't looking. I climbed back onto the tug's turtle-backed deck and called, "All clear. Help me get those three on board the tug."

McCoy glanced at the waterlogged form of the guard, then back at Philotoff and Vallo, both still safely under stun on the aft deck. "Pull closer, then," he called in a frustrated tone, waving his hands in surrender.

By the time the doctor and I had wrestled the three security people onto the tug and dismantled the navigational beacon so the tug couldn't be tracked too soon, yet another forgotten presence had pulled along our starboard rail.

"What's happening?" Ambassador Shamirian called as three of his crew held the two ships together. *Gavelan*'s bumpers were over the side, squeaking with effort between the vessels. The ketch's sails were being dropped and her movement soon stopped altogether. We were adrift.

"Oh. . . ." I buried the phaser deep in my flight-suit pocket as I followed McCoy back onto *Keeler*'s boa-green deck. Quickly I crossed to the port rail and stepped up onto it, holding the rigging. "Ambassador, I need your help."

Shamirian was a barrel-shaped man with a scruffy black beard and ink-spot eyes, his swarthy complexion softened by the gentle way in which his features came together. A collarless yellow shirt flapped against salt-and-pepper hairs on his massive chest as he inhaled thoughtfully. He was an adventurous sort, as he had aptly proven in the constant tournaments with Captain Kirk over the past few weeks, but the adventurer was always hidden behind an innate father-liness. Lacking Kirk's presence, I needed someone like that right now.

He squinted his eyes in expectation, even a touch of amusement.

"You name it," he said.

We sailed for days and I counted every hour. My only respite came in the dream-dogged sleep Dr. Mc-Coy forced me to catch while I could get it, and there was little more to do while sailing a straight course. Ambassador Shamirian led the way in *Gavelan,* while two members of his crew and I shared constant wheel watch in his wake. Four hours on, four hours off. Frustration nagged at me, as well as the dreams that jarred my sleep, dreams of James Kirk nodding at me to follow him into a very black void. I keenly missed his easy gestalt with the ocean, that gourmet blend of sea and eye. For a while I thought I might be losing my high sense of trust for him, and that frightened me. If I couldn't trust Kirk, then who?

Frustration. . . . If we had the facilities and the cooperation, we could have beamed to our destination in a matter of seconds. Instead we plodded tediously up one swell and down the other, creeping along the Earth's wet surface like insects and there seemed no end to it. I plied Dr. McCoy with questions, suspecting that Kirk would have told him what was going on if he told anyone, but all I got was various versions of "I'm a surgeon, not a secret agent." After a while I began to believe him. Perhaps even Leonard McCoy was kept from certain information. That made me more ner-vous; what could be so touchy that Kirk wouldn't tell McCoy about it?

Shamirian's crew members aboard *Keeler* set my mind at ease more than anything. I hadn't wanted to admit to him that Earth's wind patterns sometimes deceived me, and the ambassador's offer to lend experienced crew had taken at least one of the rocks out of my stomach. Captain Kirk had told me I should be able to feel the wind's direction on my face. I never could. I wanted to.

By the time we swung into the quiet Caribbean cove at Man-o-War Cay in the Abaco Islands of the Bahamas, I felt like an old woman. I took no time to breathe in the pure air or enjoy the mixed scents of the settlement, or even to marvel that the tiny semitropical island had managed to avoid the touch of the dilithium age. This was *Keeler*'s home port, the place where she had been rebuilt and rerigged, a place where small sailing vessels had been built for centuries, as far back as the American Revolutionary War, Ambassador Shamirian told me. Blond settlement natives, still carrying the fair coloring of ancestors centuries removed who had been shipwrecked here, and a strain of Haitians still made up the population. Since space travel had become common and the discovery of marvelous off-world resorts whetted Earth folks' appetites, the tourist trade had fallen off to a trickle in the Caribbean side-islands. Now, Man-o-War Cay shuffled along her own peaceful way, serving passing travelers and repairing water vessels as she had for generations. So what was I doing here?

"What now?" Dr. McCoy asked as he straightened from helping me take the main halyards down.

My spine clicked as I straightened. "The captain said there would be a ship here for me. A space-going ship. There can't be that many of those on a dot of land this small."

He shrugged. "Let's find it."

I was glad he suggested that. I didn't want to seem like I was giving orders to Leonard McCoy. Though he was technically my superior, he was not an officer of the line—and he liked it that way. Captain Kirk had

34

left me holding the bag, and evidently McCoy was happy to let me keep it. The doctor seemed to understand how much I needed to get that bag by the throat and shake it.

We left the schooner in Ambassador Shamirian's care, took his good wishes, and went ship hunting.

Indeed it was a banana republic. There was even a doddering Haitian native bent over a wheelbarrow filled with bananas, hawking his island fruit. So there were we, Star Fleet officers both, meandering along the sand-crusted dock area, each carrying a bunch of bananas. We questioned our way across the island to another cove, where we were told there was a hangar used for space hoppers and air transport vehicles. Indeed Man-o-War Cay did have its area of modern contamination, despite first impressions. The hangar was large enough for several space-going shuttles. When we first walked into the square blue building we saw four Federation shuttles being worked on. Beyond them were two private hover-cars, and beyond those a huge, ugly, patched-up wreck probably being salvaged for parts. It took up most of the hangar area and prevented us from seeing beyond it.

"Maybe it's behind that wreck," I mentioned.

"We could just be in the wrong place," McCoy said. "I'm not sure the fellow who directed us here was actually speaking English. Or maybe Jim's connections didn't hook up."

"Let's at least look."

My heart sank as we stopped to get under the wreck's twisted nose, taking care not to be cut by jutting pieces of metal and fibercoil hull. From here on, the hangar was empty. I strode a few paces into the area, and sighed. Would the pieces of this puzzle keep backing out of my reach?

"Nothing," McCoy commented as he came to my side. "Maybe we should just contact Star Fleet and see if we can reach Jim."

35

My lips pressed tight. "Not yet. I assaulted Fleet Patrol officers to get here. I'm not leaving until I'm sure there's no ship here meant for me." I continued glaring, unseeing, into the empty space of the hangar as though to clear my head and let revelations pour in, but none came. The only interruption was a drawling voice of someone singing, and the corresponding clank of tools from inside the wreck behind us. At least somebody was enjoying himself.

"Hello ma baby, hello ma honey, hello ma ragtime gaaaaaaaal. Send me a kiss by wiiiire. . . . Baby ma heart's on fiiiiiiire. Hello ma baby, hello ma honey . . ."

I closed my eyes and moaned. "Oh, no. No."

McCoy moved beside me. "What?"

My head drooped. "I know that voice." Collecting every bit of self-control I owned, I turned around and soaked in the panorama of dented, mangled, patched, time-battered hullscape. With a deep breath and gritted teeth, I bellowed, "Scanner!"

There was a bump from within the coilplate under-belly and an illustrative "Ow! Goddang it." A face bloomed from a hatch in a place where no sane life form would put a hatch. The familiar boyish features, brown eyes, and sloppy brown hair at once relieved and enraged me. "Piper!" rolled the Tennessee pro-nunciation of my name. "Ya'll're late!" He crawled out of the hatch head first, and I was there to catch him by the—orange and blue floral?—collar. Ignoring the tropical shirt where a Fleet uniform usually lived, I rammed him up against the scored hull.

"Why are you here?"

Scanner's smile dropped and he pressed back in my grip. Though I didn't have a man's strength, I had three things that worked on Scanner Sandage: five feet nine inches, a full clip of impatience, and his respect. "Now, whoa, Piper," he began carefully. "Don't cold

36

start your warp engines. I know what you're thinking."

"Then tell me."

"Mr. Spock said you might be surprised to have your own command all of a sudden, but I figured—"

"Spock was here?"

"Well, sure, for a while . . . when we installed the warp engines and the computer bank."

I let go of him to step back and stare in sinking disbelief at the ship. It was a piled design, but the original hull shape was lost in additions and modifications, each with its own shape and color. Only the original blunt nose and some of the starboard hull remained unfettered by extra equipment. It looked like a displaced prehistoric lizard, and the observation slits engineered into the sides looked like gills left over from a bad stint of evolution. I held my breath. "This lumbering, obsolete junkyard has warp speed?"

He touched his heart, flexed his knees, and uttered, "Oh, yeah! She'll go warp four!" He glanced helplessly at Dr. McCoy, then back at me. "Aw, Piper, have a heart. A ship hasn't even got any personality till it's at least twenty years old."

"Oh?" I shot back. "And what part of this ship is only twenty years old?"

Dr. McCoy followed, wordless, as Scanner took my elbow and escorted me slowly along the rutted hull. Names of people and projects were illegibly etched into dents and over patches, cut or burned in by whatever tool was being used at the time. "You got the wrong attitude," Scanner insisted. "When Captain Kirk asked me if I knew where there was a ship for a covert mission, I jus' naturally suggested this one. I got my pocket money when I was at the Academy by doing Federation construction jobs on this rig."

"You're responsible for this being my first command ship?"

"Yeah! It's got cutting lasers, it's got tractor beams tied right into the warp engines, it's got pinpoint disruptors for demolition, it's got a presser beam, it's got a containment field, it's got grapples, it's got a hull-tool bank, it's got passenger quarters, *and* it's got state-of-the-art computer capabilities that yours truly helped put in. It's got a full architectonics library and . . . *and* it's got Star Fleet registry." He poked his finger into the hollow of my shoulder with each of the last three words. "Federation-wide clearance."

"With Kirk's name all over it," I muttered.

He squared off in front of me, staging himself against the construction rig, and struck a dramatic pose, his brown eyes expressive and intent. "Remember the First Federation's giant tug? Doc, you remember!"

"Oh, yes," McCoy droned, rolling his eyes as the memory flooded back in. "The commander of that ship took a real risk. He bluffed us down and we fell for it. We could've bypassed his shutdown of our systems and blown that ship to bits with a few phaser shots. It didn't even have any shields or weapons. Just an incredibly powerful tractor beam." He shook his head and clasped his hands behind his back thoughtfully. "Jim was impressed by the theatrics."

"Right," Scanner said. "It was a supervessel designed to yank asteroids out of orbit and haul 'em in for mining purposes. All that power, and it turned out to be a giant space-faring truck. But think what we learned from it! Think of the mining boom after we set up relations with the First Federation! That's what this is!" He swung both hands endearingly toward the ship. "It's a *Fesarius!*"

"It's a barge!"

My head started to throb.

I backed off a few steps to see if the rig looked any better, and was greeted with yet another—as though I needed one—surprise. From the main air lock appeared a second familiar face, one which confirmed my guess that I'd been set up. I watched in silent astonishment as the slim young woman caught sight of me, narrowed her slightly tilted almond-shaped eyes, the only suggestion that she might be other than human, and strode down the long ramp toward us. Her short beige-blond hair was a shade or two lighter than the last time I'd seen it, a gift from Earth's relentless sun. My hair, too, bore a few streaks of extra gold after so long at the schooner's helm, but it would never reach the pearl shade of hers.

"Merete," I breathed, almost a groan, confirming what I saw as she came down the long ramp and approached us.

"Hello, Piper," she said. Her tone of voice told me that she knew exactly what was going through my mind. She reached for McCoy's hand. "Dr. McCoy, how are you?"

He took her narrow palm in subdued greeting. "Well, *I'm* just fine, Dr. AndrusTaurus. What are you doing here?"

She shrugged. "Medical duty. Or so I was told. I only recently started to doubt it."

That was enough formality for me. I rounded on her. "Do you know what's going on? All I've got so far is Scanner, this bizarre excuse for a space vessel, and a pile of unanswered questions. And I hope this thing really can fly, because I'm guilty of assaulting Star Fleet officers to get to it."

Merete pressed her delicately colored lips into a line and gave me a look of intense sympathy, but she plainly had no answers for me and, knowing that, declined to complicate my mood. As she had in the past, Merete AndrusTaurus gave me her best prescription: a steadying presence.

Scanner shook off my words and recalibrated. "Piper, it's a good ship. It's got heart. Here . . . look over here. See that dent? That happened when they

39

built the very first outersystem communications relay station. And this patch over here? That's from the superstructure for the Martian Colonies' Orbital Medical Center. And up yonder, that's what happened when they built the new docking bay for Star Fleet Command itself. *I* was there." He poked his own chest. "There's my name. See? Judd Sandage, light-etched right in. And there—see that name? Liex Muller? He died on that job. Piper, this ship . . . this is a memorial to construction projects all over the Sol system. It's an archive of local history! And it's all yours!"

His enthusiasm was almost pathetic. I backed away a few steps and leaned toward Dr. McCoy while Scanner waited anxiously near his prize.

"He loves the ship," I whispered to the years of experience beside me. "What do I do?"

Dr. McCoy folded his arms and rocked in contemplation. "Give him the benefit of the doubt. The ship is innocent until proven obsolete."

With a surrendering little nod, I tried to change the look on my face to give the impression I might be having second thoughts. "I . . . I see what you mean, Scanner," I said. "It does have a certain . . . uniqueness."

He nodded so hard his hair flopped over his eyes.

The massive blue hull, patched with various colors of coilplate, scored with Scanner's precious chronicles, stretched out across the hangar, begging for approval. Even the silly carnivorous teeth somebody had painted onto the bridge hull seemed to be trying to smile. I licked my lips, gazing across the veteran fibercoil. I had to clear my throat before I could speak. "Does it have a name?"

Scanner puffed up and squared his shoulders. With a nod he announced, *"Tyrannosaurus Rex."*

My nerves jarred against each other. I felt Dr. McCoy shift beside me, moving away. Must have been the steam coming out of my ears.

In a feeble attempt to shield my disappointment, or perhaps to shield Scanner from it, I ignored his hopeful expression and stepped past him, tersely stating, "Not anymore."

"This is U.F.P. Construction Transport S.S. *Banana Republic* requesting clearance for space access."

"This is Star Fleet Planetary Patrol, Banana Republic. Specify your registry code."

"MTK 4247, Patrol. It's a new code."

"We copy. That's not a new code, Banana Republic, it's a reissue. Please confirm and specify the old code."

"All right, confirmed. Scanner, take over."

Scanner leaned forward in the mate's seat beside mine as we sat in front of a slapdash control cockpit which bore the scars of having been overhauled and added to with each new phase of engineering science over its disturbingly long life. He tied his console into the communications link and said, "Patrol, this vessel was formerly registered as Construction Tug 87, S.S. *Tyrannosaurus Rex,* registry number MKT 1187." He leaned back as far as the newly installed command lounge would pivot. "You sacka wet socks."

I shushed him with a glance. "I don't want any more delays!" I hissed at him. "If we can get atmospheric clearance we can be at Star Fleet headquarters in fifteen minutes." Leaning closer to the com system, I asked, "Patrol, are we clear for space access?"

There was an annoying silence. They had no reason to hold us back but their own petty show of power over civilian vehicles. After a moment the same voice returned: *"Affirmative, 4247. Take a heading of point five seven seven by two six two. Have a good trip."*

"No thanks to them," Dr. McCoy commented from the passenger couch behind us. The foreman's cabin had been refurbished, storage compartments removed and altered for passenger seating. The renovations

41

were considerably more pleasant to look at than the conglomerated hull, with its damage repairs and its added chunks of hardware that had been tacked on with each new technical innovation. The construction transport looked less like any kind of ship than a collection of odd-shaped containers somehow welded together. Dr. McCoy had wasted no time in settling back into the cushions of the new pivot chairs and acquiring a professional slouch. Beside him, Merete AndrusTaurus gazed thoughtfully out the observatory gaps in the coilplate casing of the ship. Beside us, coasting through the clouds, flew a Star Fleet Planetary Patrol Cruiser. Merete waved at them, her slim eyes narrowing as she smiled in an attempt to smooth out anything they might have overheard. Merete wanted nothing more than peace of mind—*my* peace of mind.

"Well, Commander Piper," McCoy said. "Once we clear the atmosphere, you're officially the captain of a space-faring vessel. Quite an accomplishment, considering you've hardly been aboard a space-faring vessel long enough to change uniforms. If you don't watch out, Jim Kirk'll think you're upstaging his dazzling career." He was smiling, both arched brows raised in amusement.

I blushed, but not from pride. "Doctor, this wasn't my idea," I reminded him, burying my humiliation in adjusting a navigational mapping beam.

"Ah, but that's usually how it happens, Commander," he pointed out in his wise drawl.

Scanner nodded. "Sir's right, Piper. You know, in all the years ol' Rex has been alive, all the uncounted projects this ship hauled on, she's never had a captain before. She's had crew chiefs and construction bosses and foremen, but never *ever* a captain. You're the first one!" He slumped back in his chair, raised one foot high on the other knee, and stared at the mangled ceiling circuitry. "Captain Piper. Has a kind of a nice ring to it."

Perhaps the designers put too much pivot into the pivot chairs. I stood up, shoulders bunched beneath the cotton flight suit, and placed my hand on Scanner's chair. It gave a satisfying groan when I pushed it, and it reeled backward. Scanner yelped, hit the floor on his side, and rolled over, his face plastered with astonishment.

"What'd I do?" he bellowed. "What'd you do that for?"

I stood over him, one foot on either side of his sprawled left leg. For long moments I glared down at him, so intently that he dared not get up. McCoy and Merete were frozen to their chairs.

"Don't call me that," I said. I stepped over him. "Notify me when we're over San Francisco."

"Is it gone yet?"

The soft voice was consummately feminine. Nothing about it suggested its source might be other than human. There wasn't much about Merete that couldn't be human if she wanted to give up her Palkeo citizenship or heritage. The Palkeo Est people of Altair Four were one of the independently evolved cultures closest to humans so far discovered, at least in their habits and attitudes. Only physiological exceptions set them apart, such as genetic code differences, blood compounds, and certain nucleoplasms or some other biotechnical terminology that I could throw around. Merete's similarity to a human, spiced with that vestigial hint of alienness, comforted me somewhat, but unfortunately also reminded me of Sarda.

Sarda—a cultural foundling. A Vulcan, displaced by his own people, trying to dig a trench that would lead him back to the main river of Vulcan tradition from the separate pool fate had eddied him into. Had he broken under the pressure, the sorrow? Could a Vulcan deal with that kind of humiliation in the midst of personal honor and pride? Or would he reach a snapping point?

"Is your headache gone?" Merete asked again with her customary patience.

An added pressure on the heat cloth over my eyes let me know I was being touched.

I thought about giving her an answer and waited to decide if the pounding in my skull had receded. "Nope," was my conclusion.

Merete's weight tipped the edge of my bunk mattress. "I don't want to medicate you if I can avoid it."

"It's only a headache, Merete," I said. "I'll live." I pulled the heat cloth from my eyes and blinked into the dim light of the foreman's cabin. My cabin, now. It was a cramped and inglorious place. Constructugs simply weren't built for comfort, and room remained at a premium even when renovations were attempted. "It'll go away as soon as I get to talk to the captain. As soon as he tells me what's going on."

"You don't have any idea?" she asked, diminishing the seriousness by casually arranging the heat cloth in her medikit.

"I know Sarda's in trouble." I sat up, scooting back against the cold metal wall. "It's got to have something to do with that. Kirk deliberately made sure those security officers didn't find out I was on board the schooner. And I think he knew how I'd react once I found out Sarda had gotten caught up in espionage." I pulled at her wrist, forcing her attention away from the medikit. When she looked up, I asked, "Are you sure, absolutely sure, Mr. Spock didn't say anything about this so-called mail run?"

In deference to me, she took the time to think about it for a moment. Finally she shook her pale head and shrugged. "Not a word. He provided instructions for the ship, and for a while there were several Star Fleet technicians and engineers down here working on it.

44

Scanner and I didn't even know the ship was intended for you until a week ago, when the last of the Fleet crew left. I thought I was here to tend to injuries in the tech crew. I certainly didn't understand orders to stay behind. Then Mr. Spock told Scanner that you'd be coming. We assumed you'd beam in any minute after that. What were you doing on that sailing boat?"

I dropped back. *Good question, Doctor.* "It's Kirk's private ship. He offered to authorize shore leave for me aboard the schooner if I was willing to crew the ship during the Annual International Battle at Sea Flotilla for Masted Ships. War games. A collection of sailing buffs get together and try to outmaneuver each other. I thought it was a little primitive and silly until a couple of ships actually went over in the fervor for victory points. Smaller ships than *Keeler,* of course, but even we came close to being rammed a few times. They're pretty serious about it." I stared at my knees, suddenly unblinking, aware of little more than my own heartbeat. "Few more serious than Jim Kirk. I never saw such intent to win. He's a bedeviling man, Merete. He leaves me in awe . . . confused. . . . He tries to force me to figure out what he's thinking. He pushes the odds. This time, he miscalculated. Something went wrong. He meant to tell me what was going on, but he got pulled off the schooner before he could do it. I've got to find him, Merete," I told her, lost in conviction. "I've got to know what to do."

If she was unsettled by my intensity, she did a prime bedside job of concealing it. She nodded slowly, making sure I knew she had been listening. "You will," she assured. "We'll be there soon. It may all turn out to be much simpler than you expect. Just a mix-up of some kind. It may even be fixed by the time we arrive at Star Fleet."

"I hope so," I said. "I don't mind a struggle, but I can't stand not knowing."

An unfamiliar whine interrupted our conversation,

followed then by several clicks, and I knew somehow that Scanner was trying to shake the bugs out of the new intercom system. I was about to punch the transceiver button beside my berth when his voice frantically crackled through the hastily installed circuits.

"Piper! You better get up here! This danged ship is warping out of orbit all by itself!"

Chapter Four

"Make the most of an uncertain future."
—The Squire of Gothos

"STATUS!"

The command seat sighed as I angled into it and squared off before a band of flickering instrument lights.

Scanner was trembling slightly, but trying to conceal it as he frantically interpreted the readout screen. "She pulled out of orbit as soon as we reached the descent plane for the West Coast."

"Malfunction?" I asked as we reeled past the dazzling display of Jupiter and her moons.

"Naw, I don't think so. She's got a mind of her own. She's powering up to warp. Betcha the computer's behind it. Looks like this trip is going to take a lot longer than you thought. We might have to tote lunch."

The control panel was like the rest of the ship: a sloppy amalgam of new instruments shoved in wherever the old instruments could be moved or rearranged. I felt like a plebe as I tried to familiarize myself with the controls. "Get into the system. Countermand what it's doing."

"I tried."

"Well?"

He gave me a desolate look. "It's locked up."

A chill ran through me. I glanced over my shoulder to the passenger seats, where the two doctors sat in

47

expectant silence. Merete was noticeably stiff. McCoy appeared relaxed but wide-eyed. I felt uncomfortable under the sudden weight of responsibility for their lives, not to mention the self-consciousness of knowing how often McCoy had watched James Kirk perform under pressure.

No—I couldn't think about that now. I couldn't waste time and mental energy comparing myself to the captain. As I turned once again to the blinking control panel, I noticed with a shuddering apprehension that Jupiter was already far behind.

Scanner's face was patterned in blues and grays as he peered into the visual readout screen. "We're about to warp, Piper."

"Dr. McCoy, Merete, strap yourselves in, please."

"What's going on?" McCoy asked. "Why's it doing this?"

"You've been here all along, sir. You know as much as we do. Scanner, confirm that the computer has navigational control, or the warp could tear us up."

"Computer has full control," he responded. "Rex knows what she's doing, even if we don't."

"Stupid machine," I grumbled. "Project course and tell me where we're going."

"How?" he blustered. "He could go flyin' forever at warp speed. The computer's the only thing that knows where it'll stop us. How you gonna get it to tell you?"

We glared at each other for a long moment as I reviewed the fact that I didn't have any real answers. Something in Scanner's words had awakened the rebel in me. I shrugged. "I'll ask it." My hands lingered over the controls until I figured out which ones to push to revive the computer, or at least distract it. "Computer tie-in, command authorization."

The board began whirring and clicking as though it didn't have the slightest idea what I was talking about. Then the firm, resonant imitation of a female voice requested, *"Specify identification code for authorized command, please."*

I looked at Scanner. He blinked at me, then back at the computer console. "Ol' Rex has delusions of being a starship," he said, obviously taken aback.

"But it gives me some power," I surmised, "if it knows it was to answer to a particular person."

Dr. McCoy leaned as far forward as his safety straps allowed. "Let's hope it knows that person is you, Commander."

"Going to warp speed on automatic," Scanner said. To the instant, the stars before us blended into a segue of spectral color and we were at warp. A flush of helplessness caused silence on the cramped bridge. We waited to see if the ship could stand the strain.

"Warp two," Scanner advised. "Two-point-five . . . warp three. Entering cruise mode." He shook his head and sighed. "Well, here we are."

When my skin stopped crawling, I renewed my computer access and fed in my personal identification code. The gratifying result came almost instantly. *"Accepted. Lieutenant Commander Piper, Star Fleet clearance, Star Date 3988.1, command status acknowledged. Thank you."*

I took a deep breath and glanced at Dr. McCoy. "I'm alive," I told him. He looked a bit dazed, but said nothing. I tried to think clearly, readjusting my mind to talk to a computer. "Computer."

"Working," the gentle voice answered with just the perfect touch of question that invited me to continue.

"Release navigational control to the helm."

"Not possible."

"Why not?"

"Current navigational programming includes a preempt encoding which prevents change of program until destinational code is satisfied."

"Damn."

"At least we know it's not a malfunction," Merete pointed out. "There is a destination."

I cleared my throat. "Computer, specify destination."

More clicking. *"Tau Ceti Quadrant, Ciatella Star System, planet Argelius."*

"What?" McCoy blustered.

"The plot thins," Scanner drawled.

I sat back. "Argelius? Why Argelius? It's the sleepiest planet in the Federation! There's no place in the known galaxy where less goes on. Why would he send us there?"

All three of my hijacked "crew" blinked at me like a gaggle of curious birds. Then Merete and Scanner chimed, "Who?"

My brows lowered over my eyes in a scurrilous frown. "Who else?"

They backed off. Space was black, velvety, decorated, and ominous as we streaked through it, the old ship reveling in a mission that included no anchoring or pulling. For the first time in her existence, an ugly old tug had a chance to fly. Aside from a few shaking-down tremors, Rex took to the new warp capability with unexpected grace, maintaining her cabin warmth and keeping us all in quiet comfort despite the unaesthetic surroundings. I felt that, somehow, this old dog loved her new trick.

"What's our ETA?" I asked.

"Ninety-two hours," Scanner said. He watched the control board, his expression sunken, as though his old friend had betrayed his trust. In that moment of helplessness, when I could do absolutely nothing to change the situation, my senses finally opened up to someone's feelings other than my own.

"It's not a mistake, Scanner," I said mildly. "It isn't your fault."

He shook his head, brows knitted in perplexity. "I

wish I knew what was going on. I dunno what to say. I helped put in all this equipment. It wasn't pro-grammed, I swear it wasn't."

I slouched in the command chair. "You feel bad about being outwitted by Mr. Spock, and I feel bad about allowing myself to get dropped into this by Captain Kirk. I knew he had something on his mind, but I never had the nerve to ask until it was too late. If this is anybody's fault, it's mine."

"Yours?"

My lips pressed into a mockery of a grin. "Privilege of command."

"Aw, that stinks."

I shrugged. "But it's one thing they kept grilling into us at command school. Command is more than getting all the credit. It also means getting all the blame."

Scanner sighed and got to his feet, casting one pathetic look back at the computer console and instrument panel before saying, "I'm gonna get some sleep. Nothing else to do. Poor Rex . . . first space mission and all we can do is sit here like a buncha Dunsels."

My first command. I'd dreamed about it since entering my senior year at Star Fleet Academy, when I was offered the privilege of choosing whether or not I wished to go on to command candidacy. A singular honor, given to only a handful of graduates each year. Not just a chance for high rank, but a chance to command a Star Fleet space vessel. Then along came the mangle of events that had led me into the Rittenhouse conspiracy and finally to the Federation Medal of Valor, and I knew the meaning of being plunged into the unexpected. How long ago? How long had I served aboard *Enterprise*—a matter of weeks? It seemed like years. And I wasn't ready to have that feeling of years.

I glanced surreptitiously around the dull little command area of *Banana Republic*. I was alone now.

Merete had retreated to her cabin, McCoy to the one he and Scanner must share. The computer and instrument panels had settled down into a humming electronic euphoria of knowing exactly what they were supposed to be doing and quite simply doing it. Ninety-two hours. Almost four days before I would have any answers. Four days of being Dunsel.

Not exactly a command dream.

The hours crept by, each one ridiculing me, until I'd finally had enough and something snapped.

Scanner jumped about twice his height when I whacked him out of a sound sleep. "What—what? Red Alert? Whassa matter?" he babbled.

"Scanner, get up," I said. "We've got work to do."

He raked a hand through his hair and mumbled, "Are we there already?"

"Hardly," I said, trying to cut through his disorientation.

On one of the other berths in the crowded cabin, once part of a storage compartment, Dr. McCoy rolled to his feet. "Is something up?"

"Yes, sir," I answered. "My patience."

Scanner shook himself out and got up, wobbling slightly as he asked, "I hope you got a good reason for wakin' me up from that nice shore leave I was taking."

"I do. We're going to break into that navigational program. I want control of this ship."

If he hadn't managed to wake up completely, the shock of that statement brought him fully around. "You're gonna what? Are you fishin' in the right crick? The computer's been programmed by Commander Spock on Captain Kirk's orders!"

I straightened my shoulders, despite the low ceiling. "Well, you just get ready to unprogram it. He might be Captain Kirk," I said solidly, "but this is *my* ship."

I turned, strode out of the cabin, and stepped onto the interdeck ladder, not staying to examine the look of abject amazement the two men exchanged. It really wasn't meant to be a dramatic exit; I just wanted to get out of there in case they started laughing.

Scanner and Dr. McCoy followed me back to the bridge. As we passed Merete's cabin, she too realized something was up and hurried into the corridor. In a way, I was glad they followed. Their presence forced me to stay in the mode of defiance I'd reached, and gave me no opportunity to reconsider. I had to be in control of the ship. Suppose there was trouble? What if we were attacked or damaged? How would I live with myself if all I could do was shrug and say it was Kirk's problem?

I kept thinking about Captain Kirk, my mind dividing between trust and rebellion, obedience and insurgence. I respected him, certainly, but could I ever respect myself as much if I settled back and accepted whatever he or anyone dished out to me without so much as an explanation? Possibly I could have done so this time, if another element, deeper and harsher, hadn't been eating at me.

Sarda.

Lieutenant Sarda, recipient of the Silver Palm and Star for Conspicuous Bravery. Young Vulcan technical scientist, a weapons specialist. In fact, a weaponry pioneer, much to his own embarrassment. My fellow-classman at Star Fleet Academy. The only person who'd stayed relentlessly at my side during the dreadnought affair just weeks ago—I kept saying that to myself: just weeks ago, only weeks.

What was happening to him? Was this computer setting carrying me farther away from helping him? I had to know the entire truth. I couldn't get it here, on a space ship streaking toward passivity. My Vulcan friend had somehow strayed from the route back to the Vulcan teachings to one lined with suspicion. Theft of Federation-owned technology, the security lieutenant had said. Which technology? Sarda hadn't been working on any particular project that I knew of, not after the destruction of the dreadnought that carried the image projector he'd invented. That episode had been enough to drain the inventive urge out of anybody, at least for a while. Especially poor Sarda. He kept trying to turn his talent for weaponry to devices for defense, and Star Fleet Command, in its unending military wisdom, kept interpreting Sarda's inventions to be used aggressively if necessary. They kept giving him awards and commendations that did nothing more than shame him before his Vulcan culture. So far none of his inventions had been used punitively, except by Vice Admiral Rittenhouse. But Rittenhouse was dead now, and his dream to force galactic war was dead with him.

So what had happened? What had changed since I'd gone to sea with the intrepid James T. Kirk?

I forced myself back to the immediate present, jabbing a finger at the computer console. "I want to know how that thing's tied into the navigational system. I want every circuit examined until we find a way to interrupt the programming. You're the electrical specialist," I said to Scanner. "Start tracing. I'm going to get into the mechanics. I want control of this ship and I don't care how we get it."

Scanner gaped at me, hands on hips. "It must be autumn in Piperland, 'cause the leaves are dropping off your tree!"

I struck him with a cold glare. "I'm not joking, Scanner. I'm not going to be anyone's pawn. Not even Kirk's."

Dr. McCoy caught my arm as I stepped past him, on my way to the engine area. "Do you know what you're doing? The computer program may be tied into other things. Life support, engine control . . ."

"We'll have to find out," I said.

"But if Jim did this on purpose—"

"I'm not letting anyone dictate my command without an explanation. I'm going to get control of this ship's helm."

Scanner grasped the back of the command chair and shook it. "Piper," he whined, "don't you get it? This is Captain James T. Kirk you're dinkin' around with!"

If I ever doubted my decision, the last lingering regrets now dissolved away as I gazed into Scanner's desperate annoyance and realized that I had neither control of the ship nor control over those who were supposed to be my crew. To him and Merete, I was merely a fellow Academy graduate. To Dr. McCoy, I was a talented upstart. The obstacles before me grew as I began to perceive them. Control of the ship; respect of my crew. The weight kept my shoulders stiff as I squared them. "That's exactly right," I said coolly. "And he wouldn't let anybody do this to him."

By the look in Dr. McCoy's face, I could tell that I had hit upon an unmoving truth. I took my note of victory and escaped to the engine room.

For the next forty hours I drove them and myself to every physical and mental limit, making demands upon them that strained both their patience and my own. McCoy set himself up as Mess Officer, and, true to his word, that's what he made of the galley. We didn't eat well, but we did eat. At least we wouldn't faint from hunger—that is, if the broccoli with peanut butter sauce didn't kill us first. As the hours passed, we found out how the computer system worked, found out how the warp engines were tied into it, found out which circuits, foils, trip-joints, and conduits were responsible for the navigational lockup. I allowed them time for sleep, but only barely enough, and only on Dr. McCoy's insistence as senior medical officer. I catnapped, but only when he exercised his medical authority, and even then I did nothing but dream about which circuitry panel I was going to try next. I refused to believe the obvious: that we were trying to break an unbreakable program. The more obvious it became, the more determined I was to find that one flaw, that one backdoor that would give me access to control over the ship I supposedly commanded.

By the third day of this, we were all showing effects of the strain. Scanner, especially, since most of the pressure—and my wrath—landed on him. I wasn't a technical specialist, but I did have a way with machines, only because I didn't completely understand them and they didn't completely understand me. Deep down, I knew they were stupid, no matter how brainy they pretended to be. There was a way to wheedle into, out of, past, or through just about any system, any program, and if I had to force unprecedented performances, I would do it. There was a way to hack into that navigational programming and I would find it.

"If it kills me, you'll find it!" Scanner finally exploded when I muttered my intents as we both lay on our back under the dismantled bridge panel. He crawled out, unfolded himself, and got to his feet, primed for a tirade. His face was drawn and pale, his eyes ringed with exhaustion. Behind him, Merete had been trying to piece back together one of the circuit boards I'd picked apart. She paused to listen, but did not interrupt as the volcano bubbled up in Scanner's face. "We've tried everything we know. Logic override, process of elimination, systems confusion, drop-snag, memory-circuit jumping—I don't know what y'all want anymore! It's Mr. Spock's program! Where d'you come off thinking there's a flaw?"

I stood up and brushed several years' worth of construction dust from the legs of my flight suit. "Even Spock knows better than to design a completely impenetrable system, Scanner. You know he could get into it if he had to."

"*He* can. We ain't him!"

"I don't care. There's a way. I'm going to find it."

I stepped past him. My own momentum swung me around when Scanner clasped my arm and pulled me back to face him. I hadn't realized until then the extent of the frustration he felt. Nor, I think, had he realized the extent of my determination. We squared off, separated only by a circuit-drenched expanse of bridge space.

"Look," he said hoarsely, "I know you got Lieutenant Commander slashes on your sleeve. I know you're the youngest hoo-hah ever to get the Medal of Valor, and if you pulled my socks off and tickled my feet I'd have to admit you deserved it. But one big bang don't add up to eight or ten years of experience and if you scratch the surface you're gonna find out you're just like me and Sarda and everybody else, just fresh outa the plum tree, and we need help to do this! You can't just lolly in here and pop off orders to break programming by somebody like Spock, you just can't! You can't!"

His words grated on my bones. The truth of them, the spark within them, lit the burning need to establish myself beyond the boundaries that had been set for me, the cavernous desire to be worthy of Kirk's expectations, even beyond my own. And even beyond the deep humiliation of being told off by someone who was supposed to be under my command, there rose a special indignation. Closer and closer it came to the surface, until finally, in a rumbling, chilling tone of its own, it broke free.

"You hear me, mister." I narrowed the distance between myself and Scanner, hardly recognizing my own voice. "You can report status to me. You can tell me what's happening, and what might happen, and what happened in the past. You can tell me I'm sucking antimatter. You can tell me anything you want to tell me. But don't ever tell me what I *can't . . . do.*"

The words sizzled in the air between us. They had been hardly more than a whisper, the hissing voice of some command demon that had been dormant within me.

Scanner stared at me. Evidently he expected my reaction even less than I did. I'd never seriously exercised those commander slashes before.

He blinked slowly, and his eyes went down. For the first time both he and I understood the separation we must work within, and I genuinely felt—for the first time in my life—the intense desolation of command.

Rather than waiting for the situation to thicken, I turned and walked off the bridge. Merete was waiting in the narrow corridor as I stepped through. Our eyes met. Her tolerant expression manifested itself in a gentle tone of voice. "He's right, you know."

And the demon flushed back into power. My chin snapped upward. Wrong time, wrong mood.

"I'm in charge, Doctor," I snapped. "I'll tell you when he's right."

The desolation followed me as I made my way deep into the ship, trying to find a moment of peace in the midst of my obsession. I didn't like the sounds that had come out of me. I wondered if Captain Kirk had ever found himself in a situation like this, standing alone against the people he was trying to protect. What was it like for him? He had close friends too— Spock, McCoy, Scott—how did he manage to command them, order them around when he had to? Where did he draw the line? Where was the distinction between friend and commanding officer? Perhaps there wasn't any distinction at all. Perhaps the friendship had to be sacrificed altogether. Did I dare believe that? It seemed the easiest way right now, for me, if a lonely way.

The engineering circuit-boards to the steering mechanisms on the transport were spread around me as I lay on my side before an open access-chamber, drowning my insecurities in snapping voltage, when I became aware of a second presence. I didn't feel guilty, so it couldn't have been Scanner. I didn't feel any waves of sympathy, so it wasn't Merete either.

"Feel better now?" the tolerant voice began.

"I'm not sure," I admitted.

There was a shuffle beside me, and Dr. McCoy slipped into view as he sat down near me. I continued working. The beleaguered circuits crackled their fatigue.

"Are you going to tell me I'm behaving irrationally?" I asked him.

He shrugged, one brow raising into an arch. "Irrationally? Not yet. Obsessively . . . maybe."

"And obsession isn't irrational, sir?"

"Depends on who's displaying the tendency," he said casually. "Question is, do *you* think you're acting irrationally."

It might have been in question form, but something about it wasn't a question at all. I paused in my circuit junctioning and looked at him. "Defiance is a perfectly rational process," I said, hoping it sounded reasonable.

Now both brows went up. "New one on me," he muttered. Then he looked directly at me and asked, "Are you sure, really sure, that you want to break the captain's programming?"

I settled back to work, rather as a buffet around my answer. "Yes, I do."

"We'll be at Argelius in twenty-eight hours," he pointed out. "Maybe your answer will be there."

"And maybe it won't." I tried not to sound flippant. "Sir, you know Captain Kirk. You know he'd never allow this to happen to him. I can't help but think he expects the same from me."

He tipped his head calmly. "You'll tear yourself apart if you keep comparing yourself to him."

My hands, now scored with a dozen tiny electrical burns, felt hot and clammy inside the access chamber. I pulled them out, knowing I was fooling myself about gaining entry into the system by any mechanical route. I scooted out and leaned up against the bulkhead.

59

"I'm comparing myself to me," I told him.

McCoy pursed his lips and said nothing more about it, though I could see and sense him thinking deeply, possibly analyzing my mental state with his years of experience with deep-space psychology. Actually, I'd have relished the chance to talk to him, to sift out my conflicting feelings, perhaps even to ask his advice, but there wasn't time.

"Sir, you know Commander Spock. How would he program a system if he wanted it to be impermeable by anyone but himself?"

McCoy spread his hands out. "You're asking me? I don't even know how he makes the computer play chess with him. He'd do it logically, of course . . . one by one eliminating every possible flaw. He'd probably get the computer to help him set up the system in the first place. Double indemnity."

"But there's a way into any system," I persisted. "It's just a matter of—" I scouted for a better word, but there wasn't one. "Odds," I said.

He puzzled for a moment, then held up a finger. "Oh. You mean like if you fire an infinite number of shots at an infinite number of monkeys . . ."

"You'll eventually kill Shakespeare." A grin broke my frown and some of the tension flowed away.

"But you're overtaxing your resources, Piper," the doctor suggested. "There isn't the technical knowledge on board this ship to outguess a computer expert of Spock's level. From what I can see, you've already tried every possible way of getting into that system. You've exhausted your options."

As we sat on the floor, leaning up against opposite bulkheads, Dr. McCoy's untechnical presence and his obvious emotional empathy for my situation gave me a portal to slip through. In that quiet, sequestered place I found a clarity of purpose that had eluded me, no matter how directed my goals seemed, and a simplicity that just might be my salvation.

"All the options," I murmured on a sigh. A sigh of surrender, perhaps.

He too had been lost in thought, and now looked up. "What? Oh. Yes. At least, looks that way to me."

I stared into the access chamber. The circuits snickered back at me.

Scanner appeared, or shall I say peeked, through the narrow doorway, his fatigue-drawn face wearing its most puppyish expression. "Permission to come aft?"

I peered at him for a moment, then felt myself relax. "Granted."

He crouched near Dr. McCoy in the cramped area and sighed, hanging his head and not looking at me until he absolutely had to. "I thought about trying to cross-connect the spiral circuits into the computer bank, but I thought I'd better get your okay before I blow up the ship."

I dropped my gaze for a moment of private amusement, realizing the lengths I'd pushed poor Scanner to in his attempt to satisfy me. He seemed completely serious. He was that desperate. A faint shudder passed through me. Cross-fed spiral circuits. Brrrrr.

"Sit down, Scanner," I said. "Take a break. Believe it or not, I'm not out to wear you down."

He slumped onto his haunches against the bulkhead and waved a weary hand. "Nah, s'okay. I'm just the comedy relief."

McCoy shifted his legs on the cool metal floor and said, "I think we should all get some rest." Then he paused and regarded me soberly. "Assuming we've admitted we're going to Argelius."

My next words tasted bad coming up, but I let my pride slide away long enough to say them, for the sakes of the people I was responsible for. It wasn't desperation that was driving me, after all; I didn't have the excuse of trying to save lives or the success of my mission. It was, as Scanner had muttered at me a day ago, "plain cussed mulishness." Lacking any honorable excuse for my behavior, somewhat deflated by Dr. McCoy's accuracies about trying to imitate Kirk, I sank into remission and said, "We've done our best. Even Kirk couldn't ask more of us. We've tried every normal way of breaking the programming."

Scanner rubbed his eyes. "Everything but voodoo conjurin'."

My neck ached as I wearily nodded. I stared with unfocused eyes past my arms as they rested on my knees, past the circuit cleaver still hanging from my fingers. Aware of everything, I saw nothing. Voodoo, he'd said.

"Every normal way," I mumbled. I continued to stare.

Vague movements in my field of vision, McCoy and Scanner shared a glance, then looked at me again.

"Uh-oh," Scanner moaned. "Lookit that. I'm scared of that smile."

Maybe I was smiling. I wasn't sure. My fatigue-stiffened cheeks did feel tighter, but I wasn't paying attention. Inside my head a tiny schooner suddenly came hard about in the face of its enemy and slashed a new course across *Impossible*'s bow. My fingers began to tingle.

"We've been going about this all wrong," I said.

Scanner's head drooped between his knees. "I knew it, I knew she was gonna say that . . . I *knew* it . . ."

"Come on!" I got up and led the way back to the bridge, hardly aware of my own movements and the aches of strain and fatigue. They followed me, probably as much out of curiosity as to follow my order, and even Merete, who could sleep through a supernova, was awakened by the electric anticipation in the air. She came out of her cubicle and followed, groggy but aware that something was happening. We emerged onto the bridge amid the scattered mechanical debris of Scanner's second attempt to reroute the computer program through the main guidance system. I settled into the command chair.

"We've been sailing the wrong tack," I said.

Scanner shook his head, and his bangs fell over tired eyes. "What's a tack?"

McCoy and Merete crowded near us as I continued. "Instead of thinking about the programming, we should have been thinking about who programmed it."

Scanner grimaced in perplexity. "Spock programmed it."

"Of course. A perfectly rational program, impossible to break by rational means."

"What are you getting at?" McCoy asked.

"I'm going to force the machine to be irrational."

"You can't do that," Scanner argued. "This is a computer. You can't fool a computer."

"It's a machine, Scanner. Machines are idiots. They're marvelous tools, but they're stupid. You know why they don't put legs on computers? Because they'd walk off a cliff if you told them to."

Drained and now confused, Scanner dropped into the nearest seat and slumped. "Okay," he resigned, "but the only one who knows what's going on inside that machine is the machine itself."

"My thoughts exactly." I settled into the command chair and punched into the computer link. "Computer, identify my voice pattern."

"Working. Lieutenant Commander Piper, Star Fleet identification—"

"Now identify the commander of this vessel."

The instruments quietly hummed. *"Lieutenant Commander Piper, command status authorized Star Date 3374.4."*

"Verify my personal authority to engage Class A-1 priority command under master's voice pattern."

The humming took a little longer this time. *"Verified."*

63

"Good," I murmured. "Computer, establish Class A-1 priority command as specified."

"Working. Priority established. Please go ahead."

"Question: is there a way to countermand current navigational program?"

"Negative."

No surprises there. I pressed on. "Is there a way to bypass current programming and engage a new program in its place?"

"One moment, please." Click, buzz, whirr. *"Affirmative."*

"How?"

"Under Star Fleet Regulations for Emergency Command, Section Z-12, subparagraph B, current authorized command must declare critical emergency computer activation."

"Ah. Computer, this is Lieutenant Commander Piper. As commander of this vessel, I now declare critical emergency computer activation according to specified Star Fleet regulation."

"Acknowledged."

"Compute method for overriding current navigation programming and engaging a new program in its place," I said nervously, taking great care with my words. "Specify how to free helm to manual control."

"Immediate answer is not available. Will advise upon completion of circuit analysis." With that, the computer board settled into a happy whirr.

Scanner's lips fell open. "I'll be danged!"

It took the computer only four minutes to figure out a way around its own programming. Before any of us dared break the expectant silence, the pleasant female voice returned, rife with directions which Scanner and I carefully followed.

"Reroute navigational circuitry through CKC-Bank, sections 72R through 197X, via Dexter-Nelson noncontiguous file cluster. Arrange file allocation

along following index pattern." A long list of number bunches appeared on the readout screen. Scanner wordlessly, even numbly, fed them into the appropriate systems, one by one. It was clear by the way he did it, slowly and with nervous care, that he didn't really understand what he was doing.

"What's happening?" Merete asked quietly, as though she might disturb the computer's concentration if she spoke too loudly.

"It's telling us how to get helm control," I said simply.

McCoy shifted forward eagerly, with a strange enthusiasm that I didn't quite know how to interpret. "You're actually breaking Spock's programming?"

"No, not breaking it," I answered. "It can't be broken or stopped. He knew that's what we'd try to do, if we tried anything."

"Then what—?"

"It can't be stopped. But it *can* be replaced."

He gave me an amusing frown. "Sounds like rhetoric to me."

"Ah, yes, but Rex has never been taught the art of rhetoric. It can't tell the difference, so it just does what it's told. The computer has no reason not to help us override the programming, so that's what it's doing. Didn't I tell you? Stupid!" My delight actually squeezed a giggle out of me, but I was too pleased to be embarrassed.

"That's it." Scanner sat back. Fine beads of sweat glistened on his upper lip. "Now we wait."

We settled down. The computer console did everything but spit bubbles. Lights glowed, then flickered, then changed intensity. Numbers on the readout screens flashed by faster than human eyes could assimilate them, backgrounded by jangles, grinds, and general electronic braying.

Soft lights played across our faces. Faces of humanity itself, reestablishing the true wonder of our own

65

power. Think of a machine . . . design a machine . . .
build a machine . . . be carried into the farthest reaches
of space by a machine . . . yet still rule over it. Still
outthink it. Quite a partnership, quite a symbiosis. Our
lives were in the hands of the machine, and its in ours.

The patterns of lights grew pale. The clicking fell
away, leaving only a whirr and hum. The whirr
stopped. The hum faded. The readout screen went
blank.

Then, three simple words, flashing calmly, outlined
in red:

HELM IS MANUAL

The computer's firm voice echoed the words, once,
in simple punctuation, then fell silent.

My eyes drifted closed. My head drooped on aching
shoulders.

Behind me, Dr. McCoy and Merete shifted, sharing
looks of disbelief that confirmed our success.

Even Scanner, in his silence, radiated bone-deep
amazement. One hand reached for the readout screen
and tenderly touched it, in a silly human gesture. After
a moment, his face, bathed in the gently flashing light,
turned to me. "Well . . . you got control, Commander.
I never woulda bet on it." He clapped his knees to
renew the moment. "So, it's all yours. Where do you
want us to go?"

I forced my eyes to focus and stood up slowly,
gazing out over the beautiful elegance of space as we
cruised along at warp three.

"To Argelius," I said. "But on *my* order."

Chapter Five

"Didn't think I had it in me, did you?"
—The Changeling

I THINK SCANNER was plotting to have me assassinated. Merete was contemplating my mental condition, and Dr. McCoy was shaking his head a lot. So, after another smooth escape disguised as a dramatic exit, I spent much of the next day's travel tucked safely in my quarters, gazing into the computer access screen.

I'd been in there alone for three hours before anybody missed me during the next day-cycle. No surprise it was Merete who finally opted to peek in.

"Disturbing?" she asked.

My eyes flipped up from the computer screen—my only movement. My preoccupation held for a long moment as I gazed at her, then I moved my hand from its parking place against my lips and said, "No. Come on in."

She invited herself into the chair beside the bunk and looked at the screen. "Tech manuals?"

"Look at this," I said flatly, punching the controls on the side of the access screen. The screen went blank for a moment, then flickered with new data. "I've been through this a dozen times already and I still can't fathom it."

"What is it?"

"Vulcan training."

She inhaled, held it, and sighed. "Oh. Sarda's still on your mind. Any particular aspect this time?"

"Sarda's clan."

Her delicate eyes narrowed. "Sarda's clan specifically? How did you ever find data that obscure?"

I made a guttural sound to double the impact of her question. "Obscure is right. The Vulcans are notoriously secretive. However, Doctor dear, the Federation's liaison committee to the Confederation of 40 Eridani isn't without its muscle. They convinced the Vulcans to loosen their grip on cultural secrets at least enough that off-worlders could understand enough about them to respect them at a little less distance. I'll bet that day saw logic fly."

"Even so," Merete countered as she sat at the end of my bunk, "Sarda's clan isn't exactly the visible elite of ShiKahr City, like Mr. Spock's. Isn't Sarda from somewhere below the Vulcan equatorial zone?"

"He wouldn't tell me. I've been hunting through the library systems for weeks. Before I put out to sea on the *Keeler,* I left a search worm in the mainframe library computer at Starbase One. It's been picking through its indices, looking for information on Sarda and his tribe, or whatever they call themselves. All I had to do was key into that system from here to get the results of the search."

"So Mr. Spock's new computer for this ship is coming in handy."

"Sure is."

"What have you found?"

"I found," came the answer, "the Lyr Zor."

My revelation was lost on her. "Clan or region?"

Self-consciously, I clarified. "Clan. The region is called Lyr T'aya, as closely as the computer can put it into English alphabet. It's way south, in the Vuldi Gorge. The nearest city is Jia'anKahr. Does that mean anything to you?"

She nodded, eyes widening. "It means remote. I knew Sarda wasn't from the city clans who usually gravitate to Star Fleet, but I had no idea . . ."

I leaned forward. "Can you imagine the pressure it would take to force a Vulcan from a clan that remote to venture away from the planet? Do you realize how alone he must have been? And he knew he'd stand out at Star Fleet too. We don't exactly see fair-haired Vulcans every day."

"And all this is teaching you something," Merete prodded gently, probably thinking my state of mind was as delicate as Sarda's.

I took a deep breath. "I've found that Vulcan clans pretty much keep the teaching of their respective children as a private matter. Only when a Vulcan child reaches what they call *Norn-La-Hal* do they take on the blanket training of all Vulcans. So there's a planetary unity, but only after a certain point, if you get what I mean."

"I do," she assured me. "And you're angry at the Lyr Zor for their particular method."

This earned her a good long stare. How did she know? Was it etched so clearly in my expression? A passing flush of denial swept over me, a self-defense mode of pretending to keep an open mind—oh, what the hell. She saw through it anyway.

I waved her closer to the computer screen. "Well, look at that. Just look."

Together we read the rare data from Vuldi Gorge, the air around us heavy with implication.

TRAINING FILE UI-77. LYR ZOR CLAN, LYR T'AYA REGION, VULDI GORGE CRESCENT, VULCAN. CONTACT: SUNVAR, MAGISTRATE OF INTERPLANETARY RELATIONS, JIA'ANKAHR, VULCAN.

NEWBORN–4 YEARS. VISUAL MATHEMATICS, BASIC CALCULATION, BEGIN NEUROLOGICAL ORGANIZING. LYR ZOR IDENTITY MELD.

FOUR YEARS. MATHEMATICS AND SPECIES IDENTIFICATION, PHYSICAL COORDINATION, ALGEBRA, GEOMETRY, PHYSICS.

EIGHT YEARS. PRELIMINARY TELEPATHIC COMMUNICATION AND ETIQUETTE. LYR ZOR CLAN HISTORY. VULCAN ANTHROPOLOGY. CALCULUS. QUANTUM PHYSICS.

TEN YEARS. SUPPRESSION OF CORTICAL STIMULAE IN DOMINANT HEMISPHERE. VULCAN CULTURAL HISTORY. STUDY OF VULCAN RITES OF PASSAGE.

ELEVEN YEARS. PRESSURE POINTS OF MIND MELDING. MEMORY ACCURACY. INTERNAL-TIME COUNTING. INTRODUCTION TO LOGIC AND DEFINITION. PRINCIPLES OF ANALYSIS. CONCRETENESS OF THOUGHT. PHYSICAL DEPORTMENT.

THIRTEEN–FIFTEEN. FORMAL TRAINING BEGINS.

"Have you ever seen anything like that?" I blustered, deep in useless empathy. "That's what a Lyr Zor child goes through."

"Have you got that in Vulcan years or Earth Standards?"

"Earth Standards. But, my God, Merete, look at the pressure. Think about the incredible mental discipline involved. Not only that," I said, turning to her, "but notice how much of it involves social approval. Look . . . cultural history, physical deportment, no less . . . and that's supposedly *before* formal training. It's practically child abuse."

Merete leaned back in her chair, her medical training showing as she gave me both the benefit of the doubt and a moment to cool off. "You're right," she said patronizingly. "But don't forget they're born to it. Chances are a Vulcan child would be mentally unbalanced if those tremendous brains of theirs weren't given something to grasp, even early on."

I held out my hand to argue, then shook it and said,

"All right. Just keep watching and see what you think. Computer, continue rundown of Lyr Zor training."

The screen unit buzzed, then moved ahead with colored letters on the screen.

FORMAL TRAINING. *TAL T'LEE.* FIRST MEDITATION ASSISTED BY AN ADEPT OF LYR ZOR COUNCIL. CONTROL OF SUB-DOMINANT CORTICES. *DWEMISH NI-AN.* IDENTITY ISOLATION. BRAIN CONTROL WITH NUMBERS SYSTEMS AND EQUATIONS. MULTIPLICATION LEFT TO RIGHT. *ENOK-KAL FI LAR.* PROCESSES OF DEFINITION. CONCEPTS OF GIVENS.

SIXTEEN–NINETEEN. *AN-PRELE.* PAIN CONTROL MEDITATION WITH COUNCIL ADEPT. READINGS INCLUDE *ESSAYS OF DISCIPLINE* BY SURAK AND *ANALYSIS OF PSEUDODOXY* BY T'VEEN OF JIA'ANKAHR. LOBE SEGREGATION OF BRAIN.

"Piper," Merete interrupted patiently, "why are you doing this to yourself? Your becoming an expert on Vulcan training won't help Sarda."

"Won't it?" I countered. "As I understand it, Sarda should have already gone through the stage called *Venlinahr.* That's the stage a Vulcan should have finished by Sarda's age in Earth years. It's the stage of most Vulcan adults, and it's two stages ahead of—well, let me show you. Look. Here's the part about the *Katra.* Now just watch."

With reluctant tension, Merete looked into the screen. Its faint blue lights played across her skin.

TWENTY–TWENTY-FOUR. *THE RUNES OF T'VISH,* LOGIC PARADIGMS. BEHAVIORAL MODIFICATION. MULTIPLICATION RIGHT TO LEFT, DIAGONAL, AND CROSS-MULTIPLICATION. ISOLATION OF THE *KATRA.*

TWENTY-FIVE–TWENTY-NINE. *SELE-AN-T'LEE:* COMPRISED OF LESSONS IN SUBDOMINANT BRAIN ORGANIZATION, ADVANCED PHILOSOPHY AND LOGIC, MUSCLE COORDINATION, AND CONTROL OF WILL. FIVE STEPS. BELIEF DISCI-

PLINE, REALITY AWARENESS, SENSORY ACUTENESS, VISUAL CALCULATION, FACT ANALYSIS. READINGS INCLUDE *LOGIC AND DEFINITION* BY LYRAS, *THE INTERIOR* BY TAL LUXUR OF ROMULUS, *EQUATIONS* BY SCORUS, *SYSTEMS OF LOGIC* BY SURAK, *PURPOSE AS PRIME MOTIVATOR* BY SURAK. ALSO INCLUDES ADVANCED MIND MELD TECHNIQUES.

"Now, that's where Sarda was when he was trying to teach himself the Vulcan controls," I told her. "*Sele-an-t'lee*, he told me. Can you imagine trying to do all that by himself? It was probably tearing him apart. How was he supposed to learn the techniques for advanced mind melding if there was no one to meld with? And he was still two stages behind. No, don't talk. Read."

THIRTY–THIRTY-FIVE. *NORN-LA-HAL.* SUPERIOR CONTROL MEDITATION AND NEUROLOGICAL ORGANIZING. IMPORTANCE OF DIGNITY AND TRADITION IN VULCAN IDENTITY. CONTEMPLATIONS OF INFINITY. *VENLINAHR.* STATE OF MOST VULCAN ADULTS. MEDITATION BY INDIVIDUAL DISCRETION. FURTHER STUDY OF VULCAN DHARMA. ADVANCED READINGS OF THE MYSTAGOGUES SURAK, SCORUS, T'ENNE, T'VISH, PRISU, AND SELTAR.

"See?" I said, tapping the place on the screen with one cracked fingernail. "That's when they can relax. *Venlinahr*. That's when they're true Vulcans by their own standards. Sarda should have reached that by now. Then there's the next one, the real killer."

"I see it." Merete's voice was funereal. Just as the words on the screen were.

KOLINAHR. FINAL DIVORCE OF THE BRAIN, BODY, AND *KATRA* FROM ALL EMOTIONAL RESPONSES. IF NECESSARY, *KOLINAHR* WILL BE ACCOMPLISHED BY MEMORY ABERRATION.

LIST COMPLETE.

I leaned back. "Computer off."

The screen went blank. The blue glow was gone, fallen off Merete's delicate features like shimmering leaves from a scale tree on Proxima. The fleeting thought of home gave me no comfort today.

Neither of us cared to rupture the dangerous silence we'd fallen into. Only Merete's calm courage allowed her to finally bridge the deepening gap. "Rigorous," she commented, curbing her tone of empathy.

"Killing," I corrected. "There's no excuse for that. And even worse, what's the excuse for denying that training to someone who was born to need it? Why would they do that to him? A half-trained Vulcan could go mad just trying to fill in the gaps."

She looked at me, and I could see her mind working as she tried to slowly reassess the information that had flashed by us in truncated form. Years and years of relentless mind training encapsulized on a computer screen, yet every bit as burdensome as those big words and wide concepts implied. Merete tipped her head, feathery brows lowering. "Is that what you think might have happened to Sarda?"

Silence this time was a noisy answer.

"Piper, you saved him from it," she said. "You set him up with Mr. Spock, and Spock arranged for a Vulcan teacher for him. It's only a matter of time now."

"No, not now," I snapped. "Now is the whole issue. *Now,* he's in some kind of trouble, and it doesn't make sense. Espionage? That's not Sarda. Not a healthy Sarda, anyway. Maybe . . ." I paused, hunting for the hurt, "maybe I was too late. Maybe, when he went back into training with another Vulcan, it was too much. Maybe he snapped."

Instantly Merete got up and stepped out into the skinny corridor to the food dispenser and came back with two cups of steaming coffee, sweet, with cream. She pressed my fingers around one of the cups, then

73

sat down very slowly, taking every last possible second to let time slide between me and my paranoia. "Piper, listen to me," she said. "You could be right."

I looked up. "What?"

"You could be right." Her tone was tolerant, not patronizing. "But don't rule out another possibility. There are still many things about this that we simply don't know yet. And one run through the computer library about Vulcan training doesn't make either of us experts on Vulcans. We're not Vulcans. It may be as normal for them as learning to fly a skimmer is to us."

"Then why was it tearing him apart?" My palm connected with the bulkhead. In my other hand, the coffee sloshed. "What's he doing in the middle of this, Marete? Did he snap?"

She shrugged one shoulder and sipped her coffee. She swallowed deliberately, stalling for more time. Her rotten tactic was working too. I was starting to realize the truth in her words, and the damning fact that I would just have to wait.

"What do you think?" Merete asked after several long moments. "What do you really believe?"

More moments. They were beginning to sap me dry. Kill me, but don't make me wait anymore.

"I don't know," I murmured, staring. Coffee steam wreathed my face.

I was rescued from myself by the intercom whistle, and Scanner's voice coming on before I could respond.

"Piper, we've got a ship on scope. Approaching rapidly, no identification, no signals, won't answer a hail, and the design is unfamiliar. You want me to slow down?"

I dived for the intercom button and mashed it. "No! Don't touch anything. Does Rex have shields?"

"Kinda. Enough to put off maybe one phaser shot. We just didn't figure—"

74

"Put them up. Don't alter course or speed. I'll be right there!"

Whoever it was, they had a fast ship. In the few seconds it took Merete and me to skim through the Rex's walkways, the triangular gold and red shuttle had pulled alongside and was matching our speed.

"Anything?" I asked.

Dr. McCoy, who had been lounging in the captain's chair, wheeled out of it and out of my way in the same movement. "Not a peep. Yet."

"No classification on that design, Scanner?"

He looked nervous. "Nope." The communications receiver hung in his ear as he stared, shoulders hunched, out the portal at the large shuttle. "Beats me what it is."

"What they are," I corrected. Anticipation hung on me like sweat. No . . . that really was sweat. Sticky. A captain shouldn't be sticky. Damn. "Ship to ship."

"Channel open. Fire away."

I cleared my throat. "This is the S.S. *Banana Republic* requesting your identification and purpose. Translator is tied in. Please respond."

The board crackled on my echo. The massive gold wing dwarfed our main viewing portal, making us all strain upward to see it. It was imposing, and we felt adequately imposed upon.

Scanner stiffened. "Something . . . yeah . . . static . . ."

"Pull it in." I knew he was trying, but I still had to say it.

Merete and Dr. McCoy huddled together near the port viewing slots, peering out at the unidentified vessel, their silence an ominous reminder of the unavoidable dangers humankind had given to ourselves when we first ventured out into space. We could live in space, we could keep ourselves alive with the most basic of methods, but we could never be completely safe.

Scanner listened, lightly touching the audio receiver in his ear. "They're requesting visual contact."

I thought about it for a moment, then shrugged. "Visual on."

The screen flickered, an ominous instant of seeing the screen superimposed against the unidentified ship that hung half-visible beside our bridge portal. Then it settled down to a somber, elegant face, familiar in its saturnine reserve.

"Spock!" McCoy blurted. Yet I could tell he wasn't altogether surprised.

While Kirk's face was built on curves and McCoy's on squares, Spock's features were a montage of triangularities framed by trim black hair and those ornamental Vulcan ears. The flush of comfort I felt at the sight of him was banked by fresh thoughts of Sarda.

"Permission to come aboard, Commander," he requested.

"By all means, come aboard," I said.

"Thank you. I shall arrange hookup and be there momentarily. Spock out."

The screen went blank.

Merete reached over for a generous squeeze on my forearm. "Time for answers," she said quietly.

Scanner grunted. "Good, 'cuz we sure got the questions."

We waited with false patience as Spock organized his shuttle to dock with *Banana Republic*. His ship moved out of our main view, now visible only through the ribbed portals on the side of the ship. Rex moaned and bumped hollowly as the ships joined and the breezeway was sealed off and pressurized. By the time the starboard loading-dock door slid open, we were already there, waiting.

The doors parted. Commander Spock stepped in.

We gaped at him. He no longer wore his usual Star

76

Fleet colors. This was an altogether different Spock. A dun-colored cowl framed his jawline, his shoulders broadened by a burgundy thigh-length cape. His lean form was even further elongated by dark azure velvet—a belted tunic. Those, simple leggings, and calf-wrap boots made him look like a planet-traipsing vendor or someone out of a medieval story, depending on who was doing the imagining. Only his fluid dignity reminded us that he was who he was. That and the fact that he carried a handful of computer cartridges—cookies to feed Rex's new main frame library.

"Sir," I began, "you're . . ."

"Out of uniform," McCoy supplied boldly.

Spock looked at him with an almost quizzical twinkle in his eyes. "Astute reckoning, Dr. McCoy," he drawled. He strode onto my bridge, the cape swinging. "A gift from the Organians some time ago."

"Thought that getup looked familiar," McCoy replied.

"It proved convenient," Spock said. He obviously didn't care for his current apparel in lieu of Star Fleet issue. "Once on Argelius, we must not divulge our military attachments. Our mission there requires that we travel incognito."

McCoy frowned. "You mean I'm going to have to dress like that?"

Spock had been scanning the bridge controls as though to refamiliarize himself with them, but now he straightened and nailed the doctor with his gaze again. "Doctor, I am actually anticipating the spectacle."

I felt my eyes widen, and ridiculously squinted in an attempt to curb it. McCoy folded his arms and cocked his head, but said nothing more about Spock's unlikely raiment.

Spock deposited his computer spools on Rex's main navigational board and turned to me, markedly casual in spite of the circumstances. His presence, entirely unforeseen as it was, had a pronounced effect on me—

77

a rush of apprehension, curiosity, the sense of teetering on some tightly stretched wire just about to fall into a pile of very spiny answers. I might know soon what was going on, but I was ready to bet I'd come out with bruises.

"Sir," I began, "can you tell me what's going on?"

He frustrated me and entertained McCoy with a thoroughly Vulcan response: "Yes."

My palms started to get moist. I rubbed them against the ivory fabric of my flight suit and licked my lips. McCoy surveyed me, rolled his eyes, and murmured, "You'll get used to it."

"Thank you, Doctor," Spock said tersely. "I shall explain fully once I've released the navigational programming to Commander Piper's control. It will be necessary to have manual control to maneuver into orbit."

Scanner coughed and hid behind Merete.

I didn't have anybody to hide behind. Although I do confess to a quick glance around the bridge for any handy camouflage.

McCoy came once again to life, approaching Spock with a noticeable swagger. "Don't bother, Mr. Spock."

Spock rewarded him with a perplexed gaze and waited patiently for the explanation McCoy was bubbling to give. I think my feet were sweating by then, too, but they were too numb to tell.

"The controls are all freed up," McCoy said. A grin tugged at his lips.

Spock's brows lowered. "I . . . beg your pardon?"

"Free. Unlocked. Piper did it."

Any previous beliefs that a Vulcan couldn't be stricken speechless were quickly flushed. Spock held his gaze on McCoy for a moment of incredulity, then turned to the controls, spidering one square-fingered hand over them, and ran headlong into one of the snags of being Vulcan. Surprise flared, tempted him, pushed up one Panish eyebrow, then fled. "Remark-able," he uttered. When he turned to face me, he was in control again.

However, that didn't stop his expression from freez-ing my blood.

"I'm impressed, Commander, though mystified," he admitted. "How did you manage it?"

"She outhumaned you, Spock," McCoy crowed, delighted.

Spock appeared annoyed—and I use the word ten-derly. He looked one more time at the navigation board, as one looks at a pet who suddenly turned wild. After a steadying moment, he breathed deeply and said, "Obviously there was some element I failed to consider. I shall anticipate your giving me a full description, Commander, once our mission is com-pleted."

Whew! Lifted off the hook by the Vulcan sense of priority. I started to feel my feet again. "Yes, sir. Won't you sit down?"

It was clearly an invitation to do more than relax. Spock knew that, and swiveled his chair to face us all. I settled into the helm chair beside him, while the three others took passenger seats, and we became—pardon the pun—all ears.

"Captain Kirk was apprised of the current situation by Dr. Boma," Spock said, typically direct, "who, you'll recall, was involved in the science behind the dreadnought project."

"Believe me," I said with guttural inflection, "I remember."

"Doubtless." Spock nodded, and not without empa-thy. He spoke to me with an easy clemency he could only have learned from humans, and only have learned to express without Vulcan shame after years of hard experiences among humans. As he spoke, I was the one to be impressed. "Those involved with the dreadnought project were a select few," he went on.

"The late Vice Admiral Rittenhouse used only people he trusted or people whose expertise he could not do without. He tried to keep his choices to a minimum."

"And the minimum included Sarda?" I guessed.

"Yes," his voice rumbled, giving away his innermost regrets. "Lieutenant Sarda's innovative skill with weapons technology made him indispensable to a man who was trying to trigger a galactic conflict. Rittenhouse wanted Sarda's image projector. Along with Sarda, there were three others in the dreadnought's special science team who were not killed aboard Rittenhouse's ship when it exploded." He slipped one of the library cookies into the slot and touched the controls lightly. A picture blinked onscreen, a dignified black man with a longish face and cutting eyes, his age shown only by a frost of silver at his temples. "Dr. Samuel Boma, of course, who developed the dreadnought's actual hull material and structural design. Charges of conspiracy against him have been greatly reduced due to his cooperation with Star Fleet of late." Spock tapped the controls again and the face changed. A woman this time, human, midfifties. Her hair was pitch-black, short but shaggy, framing a translucent complexion and small blue eyes. She looked like she could be many things, none of them scientific.

"Professor Ursula Mornay of the University of Tarrigor, Altair Six," Spock introduced. "She perfected the theory for transwarp, and is one of the top theorists in the Federation. Professor Mornay is known for her unscrupulous behavior. We believe she is the key agent. The determinant."

"Of what sir?"

He swiveled his chair to face me again, shifting our attention from the viewscreen to his words. Everything he did, every movement, smacked of poignance for us who had been waiting. "The transwarp technology has been stolen."

He said it so simply that its full implication didn't hit any of us at first. Seeing that, he went on. "Mornay contacted Boma with an ultimatum. She said she and the 'others' were appropriating all information about transwarp and evacuating their lab."

McCoy leaned forward. "But why?"

Spock had anticipated the simple question and was right there with an answer. "Mornay is a subversive. She has never displayed loyalty to any system or person, and has accepted funding from dubious sources, intent only on her own personal advancement. She is known for her contempt of governmental systems."

"The Federation government?" McCoy asked.

"Any government, Doctor. She is not particular."

"Then why was she working on a top project like this?"

"Because, Doctor, she developed the theories."

"And nobody watched her more closely?"

With a Vulcan version of a sigh, Spock carefully outlined the reason. "Until now, she has done nothing overtly threatening. Therefore, she has enjoyed safe haven as a Federation citizen and scientist. She was, however, openly committed to Rittenhouse and his plan to aggregate the galaxy into one ideology. She fears for her life and status now that Rittenhouse is dead. This is her attempt to preserve that status."

I leaned forward, barely able to keep from clawing the arms of my chair. "She means to ransom the transwarp technology?"

"Virtually. And more. The scientists intend to throw it open for purchase by any bidder, knowing the galactic powers will welcome such opportunity and that the Federation dares not allow itself to be outbid. Unfortunately, Professor Mornay's understanding of politics is simplistic. If she succeeds in throwing the technology up for grabs, as it were, she will likely instigate something too forbidding for her to conceptualize. A cosmic scramble."

The phrase was unfamiliar to me, yet it hit me like the smell of bad weather. Sensitive to the glances of Scanner and Merete, who were taking all their cues from me, I squinted and forced myself to add up the sketchy evidence and paste it into something familiar. Galactic powers plus hot technology plus trigger-brained scientists equals. . . . "A feeding frenzy."

Spock pursed his lips and nodded thoughtfully. "An apt comparison. Cosmic scramble is a colloquial term, of course, but an accurate one. Mornay underestimates the severity of her actions. When cosmic scramble begins, individual lives and galactic peace are forfeit. Mornay is virtually sentencing herself and the other scientists to violent deaths."

"And Boma wants to head it off, but the other scientists wouldn't listen to him."

"In a word, yes. Boma approached Captain Kirk because—"

"For the same reason Paul Burch did when he wanted to foil Rittenhouse's plan," I guessed. "He knew Captain Kirk would be dependable *and* discreet. Right?"

"Correct. He also knows the consequences of cosmic scramble. A dozen petty wars could erupt that could pull down the structure of the galactic order as it now stands. If a hostile government gains the transwarp technology, the balance of power could shift drastically. Whoever has it could become a super-power, both economically and militarily."

"It's that special?" McCoy interrupted. "Isn't it just another form of propulsion?"

Spock frowned. "In simplistic terms, it is. However, the added complexity is this: Mornay and her team were spearheading special research for a process for the extreme refinement of dilithium into trilithium."

He stopped talking, his black eyes landing on Dr. McCoy. I watched the exchange in silence, as did Scanner and Merete, and recognized a sort of repartee going on. Spock remained silent, obviously waiting, punishing McCoy for his earlier jibes and forcing him to betray his own ignorance.

McCoy shifted uncomfortably, pursed his lips, and glanced around. He soon broke under the you-ignorant-boor treatment. "Well, all right," he blurted. "Go ahead."

"Trilithium," Spock said, hiding his victory and thus doubling it, "existed only theoretically until four years ago. It is the compound that allows the advanced flow of energy to be compacted into transwarp drive. Dr. Mornay managed to synthesize it in solid form, but it exists only in a matter/antimatter-flux environment. In other words, once the power source is turned off, the trilithium instantly degenerates. Last year, Mornay, Perren, Boma, and Sarda combined their abilities and devised the mechanism that would allow trilithium to retain its integrity for a workable period even when the system was not in flux. And that, Doctor, is far more than just another form of propulsion."

Spock spoke his words carefully, knowing the situation had become tangled. It was imperative that we understand; he knew that too. And because of the way he spoke, with concise eloquence, we accepted the cruciality. Slowly I began to understand. If the Klingons, the Romulans, the Orions, the Tholians, the K'zinti, or any of a handful of hungry governments thought they could get this new high science . . . truly a feeding frenzy. And the Federation would participate just to keep the science out of hostile hands. It would have no choice. Just as Rittenhouse had believed the Federation could win any war he induced, Mornay was probably making the same bet.

I licked my lips. "Her deal includes unconditional amnesty for herself and the others?"

Spock's chin went up a little. "How did you know?"

I shrugged. "It makes sense." I declined to tell him it was what a desperate human would do. I didn't need any more embarrassment.

Nodding slowly, Spock once again touched the control, and once again the face dissolved into a new face. The consummately human features of Ursula Mornay fizzled and reformed into the angularity of Vulcan features. Resisting those plaguing thoughts of Sarda, I forced myself to get familiar with the new person. He was a young Vulcan, though not as young as Sarda, and his hair was the same black as Spock's, but untrimmed. It hung almost to his shoulders, caught back only by Vulcan ears that were slightly more backswept than Spock's. His silver-gray eyes bore a glimmer of defiance—or was I imagining it?

"The third team member," Spock continued. "His name is Perren. He is a specialist in interspace physics. He and Mornay have worked closely for eight years on the science of transwarp. While Mornay is the theorist, Perren is the applied scientist. She refined the concept, and he developed the actual hardware for transwarp, the engineering itself."

"Another Vulcan working on an instrument of violence?" Merete asked.

Spock acknowledged her with a tip of his head. "The transwarp is not an instrument of violence in and of itself. However, you're correct in implying that Perren has deviated from approved Vulcan lines of morality."

"You mean he's like Sarda," I bridged. "Ostracized. He doesn't fit in on Vulcan because of his propensities."

"He is like Sarda," Spock agreed, "but only to a point. Sarda regrets his . . . divergence from Vulcan practices and is trying to mend it. Perren," he said, "makes no apologies."

*　　*　　*

I was only half listening as Spock explained our reasons for being at Argelius. That Mornay and her team had escaped to this distant planet, near the edge of disputed space, to use the passionless culture and neutral standing of Argelius as a fortress against everybody. Odd. The threat of cosmic scramble on the most sedate planet in the known galaxy. It was positively poetic.

"Even the Federation is not formally aware of the theft as yet," Spock was saying. "So far, Mornay has made no announcement, but time is of the essence. Boma wanted Captain Kirk to get here first. He wants the captain to convince the science team of the danger they're causing and find some other means of negotiation before the major powers go into scramble."

I straightened my back and it cracked. But I had to ask. "And me?"

"You, Commander Piper, are the captain's ace in the hole, as you say. Sending *Enterprise* to Argelius would be rather conspicuous—"

"Yeah," Scanner grunted, only then pointing out how quiet he'd been. "Like a battleship in a bathtub."

Spock paused, trying to visualize that, and finally opted to ignore it. "I will return to my shuttle and we will approach the city in question from two directions. Your assignment is to locate Lieutenant Sarda and separate him from Mornay and Perren. I will then attempt to isolate Perren, leaving Professor Mornay for Captain Kirk to handle."

"Divide and conquer," McCoy said.

"Essentially. Also, if the scientists are separated, they will be unable to give over the complete technology. The threat will be effectively cleaved."

The edge of my chair creased into my thighs. "But Captain Kirk is back on Earth," I protested. "He was yanked right off the schooner and taken under guard for questioning—"

"Captain Kirk," Spock said, "will be here when the time is right, Commander."

"But—"

His confidence in Kirk, even lacking the explanation I craved, squeezed away every last suspicion that I might be part of a plan that hadn't been thought out and carefully executed, with me playing the part of some cog in the middle of the mechanism. Spock's glare bored through me, and when it was disrupted by a slow blink, we both understood our concepts of Captain James Kirk.

I let it go. Part of command was learning to live with half the answers.

"Sir," I began slowly. "I know things look bad for him, but I can't—I *don't* believe Sarda is a willing part of all this. He's a victim of circumstance. I'm sure of it."

"Based on what, Commander?"

Now I froze. Had it been Kirk asking me that question, I'd have given him an unqualified "intuition." But this was Spock. Spock, who required all parts to all equations. Whose manner demanded precision from me. Why *did* I feel Sarda was innocent?

Finally I said, "He'd have no reason to run, sir. He's a Federation honoree. He's been on the 'right' side all along."

"And?" The steady eyes probed me, unfiltered and discerning, cutting straight through to the most human part of me.

So I said it.

"And I trust him."

Spock nodded, evidently satisfied by something a Vulcan shouldn't really understand at all. He slowly said, "I agree with you."

In my periphery, I saw Scanner's jaw slacken as he stared at Spock. Whether his awe came at my sudden credibility or Spock's almost human display of faith in

Sarda, I couldn't tell. Guilt stabbed me. Doubt came rushing back upon me from my conversation with Merete. Now that I'd spoken my piece, could I back it up? Or, more crucially, would Sarda back it up?

"However," Mr. Spock went on, "we must maintain our caution. You know of Sarda's struggle to become fully Vulcan, and of the intense strain he was under until you brought the problem to me. I must take partial responsibility for his welfare, since it was I who recommended a Vulcan tutor for him and bridged the relationship."

My skin bristled as I added up the infinitesimal clues in his tone. My teeth sank into my lower lip, and I tasted the dryness of complication.

Quietly I said, "Perren."

A deep silence fell behind my voice. Suddenly the situation took a dive for the intricate. Its entanglements shone in Spock's expression as he watched us all add it up in our minds, for he more than any of us knew the labyrinths of being Vulcan.

He shifted his long legs and started talking again. "Sarda and Perren knew each other already. Perren had the advantage of not possessing typical Vulcan prejudices against Sarda's talents. Yet, while he is a renegade in his own way, Perren is older than Sarda and had already advanced through Vulcan training. He was the logical selection." Spock fixed his eyes on nothing for a fleet moment. Was he apologizing, in his way? He knew we had both interfered with Sarda's life and, no matter the noble purpose, may have placed him in a compromising position. Or a position whose temptations were too much, even for a Vulcan.

Spock jarred me out of those gray thoughts when he asked, "May I speak with you privately, Commander?"

"Oh . . ." I glanced sheepishly at the others.

"Right." Scanner slapped his knees and stood up.

Merete and McCoy tried to disguise their curiosity in a casual stroll aft, and I longed for their presence once we were alone.

"Commander, this is rare information I must give you now," Spock began, steeping me in the elegance of his control. "There are certain things you must know before you can effectively deal with Lieutenant Sarda."

I nodded. "I understand."

This wasn't easy for him. I could see that. He evidently had put much thought into whether or not to tell me whatever it was. Finally he made his commitment. "Vulcan training methods are matters of great privacy. They are more than simple passings-on of information. They provide my only cause to question Lieutenant Sarda's part in this incident."

He was stalling. He might even be hoping I would come to those unspeakable conclusions on my own, to spare him the trouble of speaking them. In deference to him, I tried.

"You're saying," I began, "Sarda might be loyal to Perren in some way?"

My question made him uneasy. He gazed downward at nothing, saddled with a decision no Vulcan wants to make: whether or not to let a non-Vulcan in on the privacies they guard so dearly. Yet there was another perception pressing him, beyond just the rupture of Vulcan privacy; we both felt it. A human who could be friends with a Vulcan is an instant complication. The weight sat on me now.

Slowly he said, "The mental training of young Vulcans cannot be simplified, Piper. It cannot be reduced to a matter of mere words."

"But, sir, it's a matter of computer record," I told him. "I was just reading the library tapes—"

"The computer record," he interrupted, "is not Vulcan." Troubled by what he was trying to say, or not to say, Spock indulged in a sigh and sought for words

88

to explain what could not be explained. Something too deeply personal for words. "On the screen, there are words in print," he said. "There is no clinical way to convey the depth behind the words. It is the difference between a dictionary definition and the intimacy of personal interaction." He looked at me now to see if I understood, and his eyes no longer wavered.

I nodded for his sake. "You mean a kind of symbiotic relationship, beyond the learning of facts and controls? Something social?"

The eyebrows, their change of position on his stately face, gave me my answer.

"Vulcan training involves a mental endowment, tutor to pupil and vice versa. A . . . spiritual bond, if you will. And it is accomplished by meld. Under normal circumstances, I consider it illogical that Sarda would willingly take part in espionage. However, his liaison with Perren, at so crucial a time in his disciplines, does change the facts."

For the first time my doubts, my questions, about Sarda took body. To my shame, I had to fight through an ugly twinge of jealousy in order to think with a clear head. "A sympathetic relationship," I murmured.

Spock nodded. "And potentially dangerous now. Quite frankly, I am dubious of Perren's state of mind also. Ordinarily, a Vulcan would never condone the conditions Mornay has presented, would never so offhandedly gamble with countless innocent lives. If Perren's Vulcan attitudes have so completely contorted, there is cause for worry."

With a deep breath I concluded, "Meaning we have no idea what mental condition Sarda's in right now."

His tone of voice sank low. "Yes."

Chapter Six

"May we together become greater than the sum of both of us."

—The Savage Curtain

ARGELIUS IS ONE of a handful of planets bordering disputed space, relatively safe and unravaged on the edge of the Federation envelope. Relatively, of course, being the key word. These planets also tend to draw occasional undesired attention because of their proximity, and if there is some galactic incident it is quite likely to involve one or more of them. Most of those border planets handle their teetering rather well. Argelius, however, is a planet of insipid passivity. Its people, like the Vulcans, had once been warlike and snappish, but evolved, unlike the Vulcans, into a regressive society that stresses extraordinary complaisance. Its people, even its children, rarely quarrel even among themselves. They can't even work up a good brood. As a result, along with anger, out are ambition, growth, technology, a free-market mentality of any kind, and just about everything else that allow a society to depend upon itself. They are nice people, but they are helpless. They bring administrators in from other planets because they can't administer themselves, trade their location and benevolent hospitality for foodstuffs, medical services, in fact most necessary goods and services of any kind. They are a professional shore leave planet. It's all they do well.

The culture itself has its colors. The buildings are of

natural stone and wood, clothing reminiscent of Earth's Middle East during the classical period. Veils, slippers, turbans, belly dancing, mosaics, simple musical instruments, and so on. Several Federation anthropological studies had been made on the hypothesis that the Argelians are one of a handful of human-origin races scattered around the galaxy by a superior culture who'd sought to preserve them. The biggest fly in that ointment was a faint but definite telepathic ability that appeared hereditary in some of the women. But none of that was my problem. Even though Argelius has only three major population clusters that could be called cities, the clusters are disorganized and very old. Some streets—many, in fact—had never been named even in the hundreds upon hundreds of Argelian years they'd been in use. There are no class structures; everybody is poor. As such, there is no quartering of Yelgor City, no way to guess which end of town might attract a group of fugitive scientists.

So, here we were. Orbiting. We were waiting for Mr. Spock to devise a plan for finding the scientists. I suppose each of us assumed Spock would be the only one of us who would be able to solve the problem, a problem without many clues. As we watched him scan bits of new and old data about the scientists, trying to pick out some little propensity that would give a hint of where they might be hiding, we slowly digested the idea that even Spock, unfortunately, wasn't made of magic.

He knew that too. It showed in the taut lines of his jaw as he calmly, even hypnotically, pored over screen after screen of drab information about Mornay and Perren. When that store was exhausted, he unceremoniously began the whole process again with reams of data about Yelgor City and the huddled villages that surrounded it like a litter. Dr. McCoy and Merete confiscated Spock's information about the scientists and went to another terminal to go over it again, to apply their knowledge of human psychology. Maybe they could find something Spock missed. Meanwhile, Spock and I slowly analyzed the city itself. We looked for architectural styles that might be conducive to a band of renegade scientists, places that had multiple escape routes, natural shielding, seclusion within a populated area, that kind of thing. But it wasn't easy to try to think like a renegade scientist, mostly because I wasn't a scientist and Spock wasn't a renegade.

Scanner, meanwhile, bided his time watching the readouts of the planet while we quietly orbited. Normal fluxes of magnetic and heat energy that heave and sigh as a planet turns were enough to keep him satisfied. Come to think of it (which until then I hadn't) I'd never known Scanner to ask for more to do. So he had a hobby, and thus took his place as the least of my worries.

Only when Scanner suddenly stopped humming one of his obscure collection of folk songs and leaned forward did I realize how long we'd gone without uttering a word. His abrupt motion drew both Spock's attention and mine. Scanner's nose was almost touching his readout monitor. "What the blue peepin' hell is that?"

Spock turned in his chair. "Mr. Sandage?"

Scanner blinked, shook his head, grimaced, then shrugged. "Sir . . . I've never seen a wave like this before."

Spock keyed in his own viewscreen, giving us both a split-second glance at the computer's simulation of jagged waves streaking upward from a small portion of the planet's surface. The glance lasted only an instant thanks to Spock. He vaulted sideways, diving for Scanner's navigational controls, long fingers dancing over the board. His shoulder struck the chair, sending Scanner tumbling onto the deck. Just before Scanner would have struck the port bulkhead, the ship around us tilted violently away from the planet, yanking free of our orbit.

The engines groaned and wheezed. The artificial gravity lost its center of balance, giving our individual weights to the centrifugal force that sent us crashing into the starboard bulkheads. Scanner was thrown the whole width of the cabin space, and the side of his head hit the emergency door handle as he slammed hard into the bulkhead between McCoy and Merete.

I clawed at one of the passenger chairs, but couldn't hold on. I felt myself being sucked starboard. My shoulder hit the rim of the viewing portal and my own weight crushed me against Merete, who was trapped between my legs and the bulkhead. Dr. McCoy struggled against the crushing pressure to slip his hand under Scanner's bleeding head, but that was the best he could do.

Banana Republic's engines sounded like one of those old freight-train locomotives trying to drag an overload. Spock was still somehow holding himself to the control board, his cape flying across his shoulders, flapping toward the starboard side. Pure determination kept him clinging there as the ship wrenched herself and the attached shuttle out of orbit in a whine of strain.

My eyes watered. I forced them to stay open, trying to understand why Spock had inflicted such danger upon us. Just as the pressure began to slacken and the ship's gravity to regain control, a shock wave hit us.

It came from outside, down there. I felt its alienness with an almost psychic intensity and knew that it hadn't come from my ship. Nausea fluttered through me as wave upon wave rocked us—but these weren't just waves of energy. With them came distortion. Detachment from reality. Before my eyes the walls of the ship stretched and yawned, even faded to show stars of the wrong colors and placement. My arms changed length, shape . . . then reality settled again, for an instant. Then another wave.

A hull seam somewhere on Rex's outer skin suddenly ruptured. Loud hissing filled the cabin as the air spat out into space, then a sucking sound replaced it as the automatic sealants went to work. The ship, at least, was trying to take care of itself. But for us, the fabric of consciousness was fraying.

Between each wave was a moment of unsettling reality, as though the reality was the dream between waking times. Power waves, maybe. Dimensional tampering. Whatever it was, I hated it.

My nervous system buzzed. Everything in my body felt out of sync—heartbeat, breathing, everything—I lost count of the energy waves wracking us as we drifted just out of orbital distance. Even this far out, the waves shuddered through us, horridly potent. Through my sluggish mind came the realization that Spock had just saved our lives by getting us out of direct contact with the power waves.

Finally the last wave grumbled through Rex's shell, passed through our vibrating bodies, and passed out into space. We held our breaths, waiting for another wave, but no more came. I pushed myself off the bulkhead to Spock's side.

"What happened? What did they do?"

Spock straightened, then immediately bent over the readout screen. He was ominously silent.

McCoy knelt beside Scanner, helping him to sit up. "What did who do?"

"Mornay and the others," I said. "Nobody else on Argelius could create that kind of power emanation."

"Quite right," Spock confirmed. In a move particularly human, he looked over the computer readout screen and gazed through the big main portal at the serene planet, almost as though he only partially trusted the computer. He tapped the controls to test them, then asked, "Commander, I suggest we veer back into orbit."

I paused. "Sir, you're senior officer on board."

"Yes," he said, "but you misunderstand the nature of the conditions under which this ship was commissioned for you. Captain Kirk arranged a special priority command for this transport. No one, regardless of rank, can supersede your authority on this vessel."

My expression carried an unmistakable "you're kidding," but I forced myself not to say it. After a moment, I collected myself and asked, "What if I was killed?"

He tilted his head. "Obviously, the senior officer would have no choice but to take over. That officer would be authorized to command the ship, but not the mission. The ship itself is considered expendable. Your presence on this mission, however, is not. Shall I attain orbit?"

Dulled by his words and by his sense of courtesy, I simply nodded. I was about to ask again what had happened to us, when Scanner moaned and drew my attention. McCoy was probing the head wound while Merete ran a Feinberger over Scanner for vital signs.

I crossed the deck and knelt beside them. "Got bonked, huh?" I uttered sympathetically.

Scanner leaned his head back against the bulkhead as McCoy tended the swollen spot on his temple and dabbed at the blood. Though pale and disoriented, Scanner gave me a best-effort shrug. "I guess I'll just sit on the floor from now on. I keep endin' up down here anyhow. What kinda high-intensity flush was that? I never saw nothin' like that."

"It disrupted our autonomic nervous systems," McCoy said. "And if I'm not mistaken, attacked the brain thalamus too."

"It didn't seem real," Merete commented, still tensely running the Feinberger over Scanner. "No

95

concussion," she said to McCoy. "Dural contusion, and very slight subdural bleeding."

"I hope all that means 'headache,' " Scanner grumbled.

"Orbital status," Spock reported. He continued contemplating the planet below us, one hand still resting on the controls.

"Mr. Spock?"

"Commander?"

"Was it . . . unreality?"

"Perhaps," he said. "A crude description, but applicable." He leaned forward, puzzling over the readouts as they flashed before him. The ship's new computers were still waffling on what to tell him. Tensely then, Spock straightened. "It was the transwarp antimatter flux," he said.

Evidently that announcement, coupled with the distortions we'd felt during the attack, meant more to McCoy than to the rest of us. Or maybe he simply read something in Spock's tone that we hadn't yet learned to hear. "You mean they're down there tampering with the fabric of reality?" he said.

Scanner moved his legs gingerly and commented. "Reality's gonna have stretch marks."

Spock nodded thoughtfully. "I know comparatively little about the transwarp flux pattern," he said. "However, I do know that the energy requires sophisticated housing in order to be safe. I believe we have just experienced the result of an accident."

Stiff and cold, I murmured. "They must be trying to build it!"

Spock looked at me. The eyebrow went up in stern punctuation. "Undoubtedly."

"But they can't possibly have the right facilities on Argelius," McCoy said. "Not for something like that!"

"Why would they want to actually build a transwarp device?" Merete asked.

96

I clenched my fists and answered, "To raise their advantage. Now they not only have the technology, but they have the threat." I turned to Spock. "Unless the accident . . ."

Spock returned my stare, only to finally break it with a deep sigh. "Such contained antimatter power, engaged in a flux of that magnitude, could theoretically have obliterated the entire planet had it not somehow been focused out into space."

"Including whatever Mornay is using as a laboratory," I said. I didn't mean to sound accusative, as though I might be blaming him in my rush of irrational human concerns, but I couldn't help it. "It could've taken the whole lab with it, couldn't it? They could all be dead. Couldn't they?"

He saw the intensity of that thought tighten my face and knew what it meant to me that Sarda might already be dead, that all hopes to rescue him from a tangled situation might be nothing more than useless risks. Declining to give me the silly Vulcan statement that, yes, they *could* be, he pressed his lips together and lowered his eyes, assessing his long experience with humans and the honesty it had shown him how to use. He gave me the answer no other Vulcan might even have had the courage to:

"I don't know."

It was a long time ago. Maybe it wasn't really so long ago, when the shadows of memory start to fold with time. Like warp drive—a thought, and you're there.

The planetoid was hairy with jungle and brush. Inside that foliage lurked unspeakable danger. Enemies. Enemies who knew us, knew what we had and what we were capable of. We needed an advantage. Something they *didn't* know about.

I felt Sarda beside me, looking over my shoulder through a hole in the heavy ferns. We watched as a pair of our enemies passed through the ravine below, too far away for our weapons to be of any use. These mock phasers were only good at a distance of ten meters. We needed that extra advantage if we were going to survive.

"Any ideas?" I asked, crouching low.

Sarda crouched also, keeping his head down. His light, brassy hair stood out too clearly amid the greenery, and he was careful not to let it give away our position. "We are all equally armed and provisioned. If you and I are to gain some advantage, it will not be through our possessions. We must find some way to pool our knowledge. Our particular talents are the only things we have that they do not also have."

I sighed. "All right. What have we got?"

His amber eyes lost their focus for a moment as he analyzed us. Sarda and I had known each other all the way through Academy, but not particularly well. A greeting-in-the-corridor sort of association, along with a couple of terms as lab partners. And now we had been chosen as a team, pitted against the best of Star Fleet Academy. Even knowing each other better would have been an advantage, but we didn't have it to call upon. We had no idea then that the future would weld us together with a bond of ordeals.

And this would be the first. Contrary to belief, truly enduring friendships are founded not on time, but on trial. Lasting relationships have to be forged, not simply discovered. We had no idea that this would be our first trial, this random pairing off for the Senior Field Endurance Maneuvers.

It was an exclusive privilege to be recommended for these maneuvers. With only reserved amusement and even a little contempt, upperclassmen referred to these as "Outlast" games, and intimately as "the Outlast." That was the purpose, after all, to outlast the other teams. Not easy. These opponents of ours were the cream of Star Fleet's crop. Each participant had to be not only recommended, but actually sponsored by a ranking member of the Academy faculty. We not only carried our own reputations, but the reputations of the officers who'd stuck their necks out to put us here. The odds were by no means equal. Though each team consisted of one command candidate and one science specialist, that's where the equity ended. The command candidates could be anything from tactical geniuses to wizards of offensive improvisation. And each knew how to apply that specialty to incapacitate an enemy.

The science specialists filled an even wider spectrum: life science specialists in Earth or alien medicine, chemists, biologists and every other kind of -ologist, including neurophysiologists who could short-circuit a whole nervous system given the right circumstances, electrical experts, sound wave theorists, astrophysicists, speed/time people—anything beyond knitting, and sometimes they could even do that. And Star Fleet twisted itself into curls to keep any two teams from being alike during any one Outlast. There was no help, no planning ahead, no cramming for this test. Survive or don't. We would endure solely on our talent for guerrilla improvisation. How well we could use and merge our respective talents would tell the test.

The Outlast was not exactly the kind of honor anyone really wished to get. One thing, however, was sure: if you got it, you'd better not turn it down. You might go in scared, sick, or alone, but you go.

"I am a specialist in energy-wave direction and mechanics. You are versed in the history and application of strategy and tactics," Sarda began. "I am a Vulcan, therefore I have audio, visual, and muscular capabilities superior to those of our opponents. I can sense life form presence within roughly twenty meters. I have typical Vulcan sensory capabilities for estimating distance, volume, and speed. Since I am the only Vulcan participating in this particular Outlast, we may consider those to be advantages.''

"Okay," I agreed. "What else?"

"You are human. All of our other opponents are also human, with the exception of the Skorr entomologist in team six. We may assume that they expect you to behave in a human fashion. You are not an Earth native. Three of the other team commanders are also not of Earth. Of the three, we are aware of only Vesco's home planet, Altair Nine, which is primarily an ice planet. He will have no natural advantage in the jungles of this planetoid." Sarda tipped his head, then, and looked directly at me in the midst of his analysis. "You, however, come from Proxima Beta, which is a swamp and jungle planet. This environment is more natural to you. How well can you reconnoiter in this kind of terrain?"

"Well enough," I agreed. "I know how to move through thick growth without making noise. I know how to test the ground before putting my weight down. I know how to use plant organisms to make ropes, nets, camouflage, shelter, and a few other tricks." I shrugged, hoping it would all mean something to him. Immediately, though, I was dissatisfied. "It's not enough. We've got to have advantages, not tricks."

Sarda sat down heavily in a way that, for a human, could have been interpreted as surrender. "We cannot gain advantage against the unknown."

Then the rustling began . . . a sound both distant and near, as piercing as the Red Alert klaxon. Enemies!

Stunned, almost as though we'd forgotten, we stared at the gently waving ferns, then at each other, then scrambled for cover. It was early in the Outlast, a wise time to let someone else be the aggressor. Let them take each other out for a while and leave fewer teams for us to deal with. Of course, that also meant we would have to deal with the best teams.

But that was for later. For now—hide!

We squirmed backward, kneeling low, finally crawling on hands and knees. I caught a glimpse of one of our opponents, Gruegen, a honey-mouthed Norwegian who was much more clever than his demeanor signaled.

"Down," I whispered.

"We can ambush them," Sarda suggested, almost inaudibly.

"Not ready."

We flattened ourselves to the moss and let the ferns and cycads close over us. The rustling sounds grew closer, then began to fade. Soon we were alone again.

Sarda stood up cautiously to check the surroundings. "They've gone," he said. He turned to me sharply. "Why did you not attack them? They were perfect targets."

"I told you I'm not ready. I'm not going on the offensive without a plan of action. Gruegen's not the type to let himself be trapped that easily. The last thing I'm going to do is underestimate my enemies. Lesson number one in basic tactics at the Academy."

His response was caustic. "And lesson number two is not to allow opportunities to slip by."

"That doesn't make sense. We've got all the time it takes. There's no reason to rush into a confrontation that would give away our position before we have any advantage. When we do confront them, we don't want the odds to be equal, do we?"

Sarda's arms stiffened at his sides. "I would be satisfied simply to make a good showing during these games. Winning is an outlandish goal considering the odds. I find myself . . . wishing for early defeat," he murmured. The tone was quiet, weary.

I looked at him and frowned. "Don't you care whether we win or not?"

His amber eyes caught the deep greens of the ferns again as he met my glare. "I am a scientist, not a strategist. These games are of no use to me. I find them an unnecessary strain and can see no way for us to emerge as the superior team. Had I not been recommended—"

"But you were recommended," I snapped, slicing off his self-pity. "This is an assignment, Lieutenant, a mission. You might not care whether we win or not, but I do. You're not going to drag me down. I don't know how Vulcans feel about mission purpose, but if they're all like you, why do they bother to join Star Fleet?"

He bristled at my attack on his race, having no defense against my caustic, almost mocking tone, though he nearly shook with the effort to contain his feelings. The coldness returned to his face; the eyes dropped, shaded by drab russet lashes. Neat brassy hair flashed in a ray of sunlight filtering through the twisted trees overhead.

I stood up, fists clenched. "We're not under any time constraints other than the need for food and water. Eventually hunger and thirst will force us all to forage. I'm not going to wait. I'm going to build up a food store now, and we're going to hole up here and let the other teams take each other out. When only three or four teams are left, that'll be the time for us to take the offensive." I paced the mossy clearing, scanning the foliage and cultivating my analysis as I moved. This was my little bridge, the think tank of my ship. Here I would make my decisions and our "lives" would depend on them. This was the core of the Outlast. From here I would decide how we could take out the minimum two teams we would need to claim our superiority in the games, provided, of course, we were the last to survive. The two-team kill was required for good reason; to prevent the teams from simply hiding until all the others were down. It was a participation event, and I would indeed participate— later.

"Our strongest weapon," I thought aloud, "is information about the other teams. Rule number one: know the enemy. This high ground is a vantage point. We can see pretty well down into the ravines on both sides. Maybe we can get an idea of the tactics the others are using." I pushed down a puff of ferns and looked between them, scanning the lush, dark ravine below. All around us, insects and seedpods fluttered on the hot thermals. Eerie fingers of sunlight glowed with dust particles and tiny life forms. Behind me, I could feel Sarda's unenthused glare. "We'll wait here for a while. We'll hide."

"Hiding is not a very honorable tactic," he pointed out, sharply reproving me.

I twisted around. Revenge? From a Vulcan? I was right; I didn't know him very well at all. "I've got my reasons," I said. "I'm going after food. While I'm gone, you survey our supplies and see if there's any way to use them offensively."

His brow crinkled. "Offensively? Our supplies are not—"

"Just do it, all right? You can argue its logic with me later." Resentment rode my tone. Or perhaps it was nerves. Deep in my mind's basement I knew I was attacking him as part of a defense against my own apprehension. I really did want to win, and I also did understand the odds against it. I was blaming him for my own insecurities and disguising it in that I'm-in-command tone of voice. That tone . . . it could be quite a tool. For a moment there it almost convinced me. I hoped it convinced Sarda, at least that I was serious.

As I cautiously gathered nut clusters and wild fruit for our store, my disgruntlement with him slowly dissipated. Maybe it was my fault. As the command element, wasn't I supposed to be able to generate enthusiasm, or at least loyalty, in my crew? His attitude would be a reflection of my own success as a commander. Ouch—that was a chilly discovery. Could I be that powerful? Powerful enough to fire a Vulcan's sensibilities? Damn it all! It was tough enough to be on the Outlast, much less to be teamed up with a Vulcan. If only we were both Vulcan, or both human . . . our differences were too much of a burden.

I wondered what his problem was, why he resented his selection to attend the Outlast.

No. I wouldn't think about it. It didn't matter. Only winning mattered. One way or another, I would entice him to cooperate, even if I had to find some "logical" reason to dangle before him. Somewhere out there in theoryland, there had to be logic in the shape of a carrot.

Thus, we waited. We watched. The first three teams went down quickly, within the initial five hours of the Outlast. We actually saw two of the teams ambushed by others, saw their frustration when the dye darts hit them, and we knew the third had gone down when we heard the subtle hum of the transporter beaming them back up to the monitoring ship orbiting somewhere above us. Two more teams were eliminated just before sunset.

Sarda and I hid on our shaded escarpment, deep in the ferns and palmettos, trying to get a feeling for what we were up against. This planetoid had no moons, so after dark there was nothing but starlight to see by. Anyone with any common sense would settle down and not attempt to move about. Movement or light could only draw attention, and none of the remaining teams wanted that, including us. Night came, and was accepted. Even for command candidates, there is a time when rest is part of the strategy.

Morning dawned hazily over the five remaining Outlast teams. It was time for us to move out. At least two of the four other teams had to be ours.

For two hours we hunted our opponents, doing little more than homing in on their locations and movements. My classmate Vesco and his Skorr scientist were the most aggressive, setting some very creative snares while Sarda and I watched enviously. Why hadn't we thought of those? Vesco was a devious young man and he worried me. As we'd watched over the past hours, he had been the victor in three matches—one more than he needed to claim superiority in the Outlast for himself and his teammate. Now all he had to do was arrange for his team to be the last alive. But from what we could see, that wasn't enough for Vesco.

Nor was it enough for the Norwegian command candidate and his sultry science specialist. Those two had looked like a guy-and-girl advertisement for Alpine skiwear—*tight* skiwear—when we'd all met for the initial briefing before the Outlast. They hadn't seemed like they could discuss anything more complicated than their latest romp at the lodge, and I was taken down a notch when I realized they had developed a crude kind of communication system using the lights on their medical sensors. As I huddled behind a palmetto, the rough texture of the trunk scratching my arm, their code flashes deflated my creative ego as they arranged an ambush. I wasn't usually concerned with my own levels of femininity, certainly not at times like this, but I got a funny twinge of jealousy when I realized a woman that luscious could also be inventive.

Sarda evidently saw my shoulders sink. "Is something wrong, Lieutenant?" he asked.

"They're communicating," I groaned. "It's only Jacob's Elementary Light Code, but it's giving them an advantage."

"Why should that disturb you?"

"Why? Because I should've thought of it, that's why."

He paused, probably trying to assimilate my disgruntlement, but finally gave up on that and said,

"Communication is decidedly an advantage. However, theirs is limited to the distance from which the Feinberger light can be seen during daylight hours."

"Right," I admitted. "It also has another flaw."

"And that is?"

I held out a flat palm. "I just read it."

Sarda contemplated that revelation, then flattened his lips and nodded.

"It also gives away their position," I added. "We need something better. We need some way to pool our abilities and still put distance between us. We need a communicator that can't be visually read."

"We aren't allowed communicators," he said.

"Wrong," I told him. "We weren't *given* communicators. Nobody said we weren't allowed."

He shifted to one knee and balanced himself in the more comfortable position. "You're playing with words, Lieutenant. We have no private auditory means to communicate if we are separated. We shall have none."

"And you're being pessimistic," I accused. "Try opening your mind."

"Neither an open mind nor blatant optimism can change the facts," he countered irritably.

The irritation was catching. "For a Vulcan, you don't know how to think very well," I snapped. "There are alternatives. We just have to find them, or invent them, or something. I mean to win."

Sarda's expression hardened at the thrust of my words, and he icily pointed out, "The others do also. Determination is not in short supply during Outlast games, Lieutenant Piper. Your human obstinacy will gain you no ground here."

There were times when I hated the truth, and this was one of them. I hated him for telling me what I already knew. Yet something inside me refused to believe that I didn't have just that fraction more grit than anybody else in the Outlast, just that extra bit of

106

tenacity that would help me win if I used it right. He was a Vulcan. He'd never understand.

I dropped the issue.

"Let's add up our supplies," I said. "Maybe we'll get an idea."

"We have already done that."

"Let's do it again."

Frustrated, he glared at me before unrolling his landing-party kit. Before us lay the usual sparse provisions, things any ordinary landing party might have. There was a Feinberger mediscanner, an electronic match, Sarda's mock phaser, a hook and line for fishing or snaring, a standard emergency beacon, and a simple steel knife. No compass, no tricorder, no communicator. We each had one of those kits, but two times sparse is only double sparse.

"Nothing there," I muttered. I rolled the Feinberger in one hand, then plucked the electronic match. "Unless these mechanical components could be altered somehow. Could you build a communicator?"

"Without tools?" he answered. "Without a transtator/capacitor? Without—"

"Think in terms of 'withs,' not 'withouts,' " I demanded. "What's here that could be used to build any kind of communications device, anything that could allow us to separate and still keep in touch? Maybe the Feinberger sensors could be readjusted or something. Use your imagination."

Sarda glared rather corrosively at the useless collection of gadgets, fingered them, contemplated them, then continued staring them down. One by one he raised them for an individual look—the mediscanner, the match, the beacon—and put them down again. Eventually he shook his head and pressed his lips together. "I can see no provision here that would lend itself to the creation of any kind of sophisticated communications circuit."

I slumped down, shaking my head. "It doesn't have

to be sophisticated. All it has to do is relay and receive. Or even just relay. It doesn't have to be able to signal a starship, for crying out loud."

He frowned at my unfamiliar phrase, glowered severely, and tried once again to envision the impossible thing I demanded. After watching his battle, I plugged myself into the same circuits and tried to help. "This planetoid has the same basic geological makeup and energy fields as Earth, say, before the Industrial Age. What was on Earth then that we could use now?"

I really hoped he wouldn't start explaining it to me, but just apply whatever came up. Maybe if I tossed enough questions his way, one of the answers would strike a chord, preferably *before* we tore each other to bits. I'd never worked closely with a Vulcan before, yet I still got the idea that Sarda wasn't displaying the usual Vulcan level of patience. Instead of that elegant control, his was more of an induced frigidity. I kept sensing movement under the icy surface, a movement that frustrated him even more than my wild aspirations did. Sitting only inches from him, I now watched the internal fight tug at his stern expression and realized suddenly that, no matter what he said, victory in this Outlast meant as much to him as it did to me. I couldn't have substantiated that in a thousand years, but I felt it as surely as if he had engraved it on the skin of my hand. His lips tightened again, his amber eyes tinted green with the reflection of ferns, and his hand tightened on the Feinberger again.

Then the ferns flickered. No . . . the flicker was in his eyes. He gazed tensely at nothing, his lips parting in perception. He stared, no longer at the kit, but now into the ferns, yet not seeing them. He was listening.

I tensed. "What?"

Still longer he stared, now tilting his head slightly, raising his eyes until the amber in them was corrupted by the cloud-strung sky. "An approach," he said. "Very faint."

108

"Sure?"

"Yes."

The kits rolled into our hands as if by some strange kinetic force, and we sank into the dewy ferns. I drew my mock phaser and set it for close range. My shoulder shook, a giveaway of rookie tension as my fist closed around the weapon. If I was this nervous during Academy games, what would it be like some day on a real mission, when the phaser was set to kill?

Ignoring the nagging signal of my own inadequacies, I pushed Sarda behind me and listened. Now I too could hear the rustle of approach. One of the teams was near, growing nearer.

"Any hints?" I whispered. "Who is it?"

"No way to tell yet," Sarda responded quietly. "Could be any of them."

"I'm not ready to move on Vesco, but if it's the Norwegian or—"

The jungle parted.

Two people crept into view, weapons drawn. My heart sunk when I saw that they were wrapped in vines and leaves for camouflage. Should've thought of that, too. Everyone was getting the drop on me, and I was letting it go on. Something had to break, something . . . there had to be a way.

I aimed my mock phaser, carefully. The enemy team was moving toward us. They sensed our eyes and paused, then moved forward again, ready for us, somehow knowing we were here. Both were human, both male, one tall and wiry, the other stocky but light on his feet. The vines covering them made it difficult for me to take aim in the jungle's dimness, but I tried anyway. Somewhere between those heavy leaves were human forms to hit. I tried to estimate down from the filtered blobs of faces in the overgrowth, and fired.

A dye dart lanced away from me, swishing through the ferns. One of the faces dodged fast, and bright blue dye sprayed all over a palmetto.

109

We scrambled. Sarda went one way, and I the other, while the enemy team raced through the ferns trying to get to us before we got another clear shot at them. The jungle burst into pandemonium. Vines tangled around our legs as we plunged behind thick bushes and avoided stinger plants while trying to keep our heads down.

"Circle!" I hissed at Sarda. Just then, a dye dart whizzed by, just over my ear. I turned in time to see yellow dye smatter across a lichen-covered stump, and lost precious seconds staring at it and absorbing the horrible fact that I had almost been disqualified from the Outlast. In the same thought as my vow that they wouldn't come that close again came the awareness that I was entirely vulnerable to those dye darts. I took a broad dive for a wall of ferns just as another dart sang by.

I'd lost track of Sarda. Frantic, I risked standing up straight and trying to get a bearing on him. If he went down, that was it. Half the purpose of the Outlast was teamwork. We had to work together, protect each other, and jointly survive. Separating might not have been the best idea. Where was he?

The ground took a sharp dip without warning, and I slid down a bristly bank, just managing to keep control of my descent and land on my feet at the bottom. There, I paused and listened, crouching warily. Every muscle in my body quivered with anticipation, and I began to wonder if I could handle an actual survival episode, where lives really were at stake. After all, this was only a game. What would reality be like?

I shook off that thought and put my mind back in the present, where it belonged, remembering what one of my Academy professors had said about distraction being deadly. Sarda . . . I had to find him. If we couldn't communicate, separation could also be deadly. What if he'd already been hit? We could already be disqualified and I wouldn't even know it.

What if that happened? What if I'd been eliminated from the Outlast before I'd even made a single kill? What if—

Sounds . . . rustling . . . over there.

I crouched deeper into the ferns and crawled in the direction of the sounds. My legs ached as I moved forward, keeping my hand tightly around the mock phaser. Thorns caught my hair and pulled it, but I kept moving forward, letting them tear at me rather than adjust my position and give myself away. Only when I heard the voices, hissing at each other from deep within the steamy overgrowth, did I pause and realign my approach. They seemed to be moving away from me, but that could easily be an illusion of the jungle. I didn't trust it.

Good thing, too, because in seconds I was almost beside the rustling. With a howl I hoped was ferocious, I plunged from the protection of the rough cycads, aimed at the noise, and fired.

Instantly, a dye dart buzzed toward me and I plunged to one side. The ground came up to meet me, but the dye dart missed, splattering instead over the twisted roots and vines behind me. Blue paint flecked the shoulder of my uniform—blue? Blue!

"Sarda!" I burst out of the cycads again.

He was wide-eyed and waist-deep in some kind of brown and yellow cane growth, his mock phaser aimed squarely at me.

"What about the others?" I gasped.

"I thought—evidently I was mistaken," he said, brows drawn.

"They've got to be here somewhere! Get behind me!"

We joined forces and hunted. We found our prey, all right, and they found us. Dye darts flew, but none scored hits before one of us ran afoul of a trip wire strung across an open space, and down came a string of giant leaves brimming with stagnant water.

"Yuuuuuuuuck!" blurted one of our enemies. Gasping and sputtering, we split off in different directions, drenched in the most ghastly rank stuff a jungle could offer.

Sarda and I staggered back up our escarpment and rolled onto the moss, choking and definitely reeking.

"What the—what the—what is this stuff?" I gasped.

"A trap, obviously," he murmured, shaking droplets of stagnancy from his sleeves.

"Oh, *gaaack*," I choked, my nose shriveling. "This is . . . underhanded!"

"And obviously not set by that team."

"Somebody's playing practical jokes!"

As the echo of my words looped down through the ravine, Sarda cautiously advised, "Keep control of yourself, Lieutenant."

"But this isn't the time or place for practical jokes! The Outlast just isn't the time for jokes!"

Sarda grasped my arm to calm me down, only to let go when the sleeve squished and let loose a new waft of stink.

I gritted my teeth and clenched my fists tight, glaring off down the escarpment with an acid scowl. "Vesco! That *slug*. It could only be him. He used to do the same things to his dormmates at the Academy!"

Sarda sighed and looked at his drenched uniform. "I believe he has turned that particular epithet back upon us," he commented.

"Come on. We're going to take him out."

I struck off down the ravine.

"Piper! Wait!" Sarda chased me down the incline, catching desperately at my uniform parka. "Piper, stop before you give our position away."

Somewhere down very deep, I realized that I was losing control, letting anger get the better of me. Vesco and his tricks had prevented me from conquering the other team, and for no apparent reason. Why would he rig such a booby trap? Only when I started wondering how he'd known where we were clustered did I remember that his teammate was a Skorr and could fly. All this time, Vesco had had aerial reconnaissance at his disposal and we'd forgotten all about it. Anger hit me again. In my rage, I plowed right down the clearest areas of the jungle, just ahead of Sarda as he tried to force me to stop. Only when my feet sank into an unseen hole and I stumbled forward was he able to catch me.

I clawed at the ferns and pulled myself up. Honey. My boots were dripping with honey. I looked around, down. Yes, there it was . . . a neatly dug hole brimming with raw honey, covered with dead bugs. Now the honey, and the bugs, were all over my legs.

"That's it," I growled. "He's mine." The contaminated honey sucked at my boots as I pushed myself up and turned once again down the incline, but Sarda caught me and, this time, held fast.

He yanked me around. "Lieutenant," he began firmly, his pale eyes boring deep, "you must control yourself!"

"Vesco's not playing fair," I insisted, then accused, "You're not human. You don't understand."

Sarda grasped my shoulders and forced me to face him. "And if he were playing fair, you wouldn't be walking into his trap. We can beat him as you desire, but not if you let him conquer you even before there is a confrontation. If I can try to think like a human for a few hours," he said with quiet punctuation, "I ask you to think like a Vulcan."

Until he saw the fury fade from my face, he refused to let go of my arms. Determination narrowed his eyes. And in those moments of fire and ice, the trial that forged our relationship found its power of creation.

The moment drew itself out. How much real time passed, I've no idea. We read each other, communicated more deeply than words can manage, and made not a move until we both knew I had completely absorbed and accepted his pact. Think like a human; think like a Vulcan. The ultimate empathy—trade minds.

I nodded.

"You're right," I said. "You're right."

Sarda took a deep breath. Relief layered the determination in his eyes. For a few uncomfortable seconds he struggled to regain the stiff composure of his race. "I would estimate that Vesco has littered this area with such traps."

"I should've remembered. Vesco's specialties are reactology and reflexology," I told him. "He's out to rattle us."

"And very nearly succeeding," he said, his scowl putting me in my place.

I held my foot up so the insect-laden honey could drip off, then moved aside as carnivorous plants slinked out to lick at the vibrations of drops they hoped were blood. "Yeah . . . sorry. Well, Vesco's a psychologist. I should have expected he'd use it. Let's start using our own specialties."

Immediately, Sarda unrolled the kit and began proving that he hadn't been entirely unaffected by my earlier insults either. Evidently he had found his way through my bitterness to that faint ring of truth at its core. He'd opened his mind as I'd dared him to and discovered that he could readjust the receiving mechanisms on the mediscanners to read old-style carrier waves. A couple of hours work and *pop,* communication. Of course, it wasn't as easy as it sounded, but we did manage to arrange a rough kind of transceiver.

"It's called a radio," Sarda explained. "Very low gain vibrations, not very efficient."

"Efficient enough," I said, fondling the mangled Feinberger, now removed from its shell and hooked up with about a dozen spidery additions from pieces of uniform, parts of the electric match, and anything else we could jury-rig to our purpose. It wouldn't work very well, but it would work.

We put it to use almost immediately. Sarda took a place in a tree high on the escarpment, and I made my way down into the ravine, hoping against hope that the three other teams still remained for me to beat. If there was only one team left, I had already forfeited the Outlast.

From his high vantage point, Sarda was able to pinpoint the positions of the two-man team we'd just missed, and with his superior ability to judge distance he helped me zero in on them. In minutes, their uniforms were stained a satisfying bright blue. Defeat rose in their faces—I empathized, believe me—but they weren't allowed to utter a sound. They were "dead." According to the rules, they sat down right where they were and the leader engaged his locator beam. I watched, probably out of paranoia, as they were unceremoniously beamed up to the monitor ship.

Now . . . the Norwegian. And Vesco.

I had to wait, straining my patience, not to mention my courage, while Sarda tried to locate the two most dangerous teams. While on the bottom of the ravine, I ran into two more of Vesco's unfriendly little traps—one involving a sizable spider and the other layering my right arm with needleplants—but my promise to Sarda held true. I buried my anger and remembered: *Think Vulcan.*

"Piper!" the faint crackle of the receiver buzzed in my ear.

I twisted the two metallic fibers that would engage my transmitter. "Here."

"Piper, do you copy?"

I twisted the fibers tighter and brought the mangled unit to my lips. "Affirmative. I copy. Where are they?"

"I have spotted Gruegen and his teammate. Take a course bearing point-five degrees south. They are roughly 200 yards from you. Be on guard."

"Moving."

He kept me apprised of their shifts in position as I made my way through thorny, steamy jungle toward my prey. Finally, in spite of torn clothing and leftover needleplant spines, I spied the two blond heads, gathered my legs under me on a small moss mound, and drew my mock phaser.

In my ear came the faint sizzle of warning. "Piper, they're turning toward you."

I nodded to myself, not taking time to engage the transmitter. The fronds in front of me started rustling. They were coming.

I raised my weapon.

"Piper! Vesco and his Skorr are behind you!"

My skin prickled. Behind me! Damn.

"They're closing on you from both directions," Sarda warned, his concern coming through strained circuits. "You must retreat—quickly! Piper—"

I could feel them now. That unmistakable, indefinable sensation of warning ran up my arms as I tucked the mock phaser to my chest and hunkered down on the moss hill, glancing behind me at the bobbing heads of Vesco and the Skorr. Close enough to see. Not good.

"Piper!" Sarda hissed, his desperation breaking through that fragile Vulcan shell.

I tore the receiver from my ear and stuffed it into a pocket, then lay the mock phaser down on the moss beside me. Folding my legs, I sat down and arranged my hands in the most unthreatening position possible—hanging over my knees.

Vesco and his teammate broke through the ferns first. They stopped short when they saw me, frozen in astonishment for an instant. I made good use of that

116

instant; I shrugged despondently at them, then put one elbow on my knee and rested my chin in my hand.

Vesco's brow knitted. He glanced at the bird face of his companion, then grinned in a sort of deflected victory. As I hoped, he didn't bother to check me for dye-dart stains.

The jungle rustled like stiff taffeta. Vesco dropped his grin and stared. He drew his weapon. The Skorr took his cue and sank into a shadow, careful of huge golden wings.

Dark green jungle patterns gave birth to the muscle-man shape of Gruegen, soon followed by his shapely scientist. The Norwegian spied Vesco and drew his weapon with a shout just as a dye dart flashed between him and the woman. Everyone ducked for cover, except me. I sat quietly on my moss hill, head in hand, as dye darts whined in from four directions. It took every ounce of control I had in me to keep from reacting. I sat still, tense as drawn string, ignoring the whistles of darts ringing around me and splattering on the foliage and rocks. In my pocket, the muffled buzz of Sarda's frantic calls vibrated faintly.

A howl from my left accompanied the thud of a dye dart against a human form. Gruegen rose from the ferns, his shoulder and the right side of his face bathed in purple dye. His teammate came out from her own hiding place, staring at him. In a silent chorus, their expressions sank.

Misery crumpling his face, Gruegen wordlessly drew his locator and signaled to be beamed up. Vesco emerged from the bushes near me, followed soon by his scientist, and beamed his unabashed victory as Gruegen and the woman dissolved into bands of light and disappeared.

In his rush of triumph, Vesco never bothered to wonder why I too hadn't been beamed up yet. His shoulders straightened and he puffed up, believing himself the ultimate winner of the Outlast. He rubbed his hands around his mock phaser, rather lovingly, I thought, and grinned at his teammate. Striding fully into the clearing, he looked at me and opened his mouth to say something.

That's how he got ultramarine dye all over his teeth.

He blinked, and his eyes widened. Then widened some more. Arms spread, he dropped his gaze to the splotch of blue on his uniform. He stared at it. The Skorr stared at it. They both stared at my mock phaser, now firmly back in my hand.

I continued to sit rather sheepishly on my moss hill, my lips pressed tight. All's fair in the Outlast, after all.

Vesco started to shake. Pure rage rumbled up through his body. His fists balled up tight. Only the stern rules of the Outlast kept him from tearing into me.

Great golden wings drooped in despair as the Skorr scientist drew its locator and went to stand beside the rosy and rabid Vesco. Their last sight of the Outlast as they were beamed up was little old me sitting on my moss lump, quietly being the commander of the champion team.

I don't know. Three words a Vulcan hates. And I hated them too when they referred to Sarda's life. That friendship had been won on the Outlast, lost when I found out about Sarda's talent for weaponry and unknowingly humiliated him by making it known to Star Fleet, then finally won back when we had stood together against Admiral Rittenhouse's power-seeking campaign. I fought to absorb the idea that our relationship might have been cut off before its chance to grow. I fought not to be jealous of Spock as I stood near him on Rex's bridge. Spock had had years with Kirk to cultivate their unique mutual understanding. It seemed unfair that Sarda and I might be denied the same chance.

For all the pain it brought me when I recalled the Outlast, the privileges and honors and parties and advantages it gave Sarda and me at Star Fleet Academy, the vividness of that episode brought with it a glimmer of hope, a faint star of chance to brighten Rex's dim bridge and sweeten my determination. If Sarda was dead, I would make sure he hadn't died for nothing.

If he was alive, I now knew how we could find him.

I moved a few steps forward, to where Mr. Spock was tensely scanning the energy readouts of the fast-fading transwarp flux. "Sir," I began.

He turned his head. "Commander?"

"About locating Mornay and the others . . ."

Sensing something even I, in my numbness, didn't feel yet, Spock stood up and faced me. When he spoke, I knew he understood.

"You have a plan?"

Chapter Seven

"How fallible of me."
—The Squire of Gothos

"RADIO? YOU MEAN like . . . radio?"

"That's right, Scanner. Old carrier waves. Go ahead. Do it."

He gawked at me a moment longer, waiting for the punch line no doubt, then faced his sensor equipment, altogether dubious. He touched the console plaintively, and gave up before even beginning. Twisting around, he accused, "You say 'do it' as though all it takes is spittin' on a twig. I'm not even sure this kind of equipment can be tuned down that far. You're talking about a frequency that's lower than a hog in a waller, you know that?"

I pointed at the console's transmitting panel and said, "Try to aim them in the general vicinity of the transwarp flux, and when we beam down, we can continue to track them with tricorders."

"But I'm tryin' to tell yawl—"

"Lieutenant Sandage," Spock interrupted fluidly, "if you set your frequency balance at submedian, then gradually adjust the energy level according to the correct bands, you may find carrier waves accessible."

"It'll all have to be manual, sir." Scanner sounded apologetic. "Otherwise the computer'll tell us it can't be done."

"That's all right," I told him. "Just don't listen to it.

It's like flying an atmosphere craft and keeping altitude with throttle instead of wing angle."

Spock nodded. "Correct. If those frequencies are accessible with these sensors, it will be through energy power rather than actual adjustment of the wave bands."

Scanner threw up his hands. "Okay, okay. S'worth a shot." He settled down to the tricky adjustments, which had to be recalibrated every few seconds. "Do I have any idea what I'm waiting for?"

"Response," I told him. "If Sarda's alive and in a laboratory of some kind and picks up those waves, he'll know who's sending them."

"That's a lotta if's." Scanner sighed and wiggled his fingers before hunching over the sensor console and searching for the delicate balance of energy and wave output. So low they were affected even by our movements in the ship's orbit, those waves had to be chased by hand and eye. A starship's sophisticated computer sensors could have kept up with them, but Rex's ragtag system could not do anything so refined. Scanner sat there for an exhausting two hours, painstakingly sending low-gain waves toward the location of the transwarp flux. As the time passed, I grew more respectful of Scanner's talents with the sensor equipment as he made adjustments with his fingers that were even too tiny to show up on the screen. I soon gave up trying to follow what he was doing and simply sat back in amazement.

Below us turned the outskirts of Yelgor City. I was dying to get there, to get things going, to find Sarda and rescue him, or, if he was dead, to begin dealing with his death. Kirk would be along soon, ready to deal with Dr. Mornay, yet Spock and I hadn't even been able to begin our mission of separating her from Perren and Sarda. Time began to sit on me, smothering and prickly with responsibility. I'd expected the appearance of Spock to siphon the weight of that responsibility, but it hadn't. Less and less was I able to shift away the pacts I made with myself when I accepted the stone of command.

Frustration of this caliber, this feeling of sitting at the core of a storm yet being completely impotent to take action, drove me to confront Spock when otherwise I never would have. He was still trying to pinpoint the transwarp flux origin, even though the waves had long since dissipated, leaving only the faintest traces of disruption in the fabric of space. Speaking in a low voice so as not to bother Scanner, I began, "Mr. Spock?"

"Yes, Commander?"

"Where is Captain Kirk, sir? Is he on his way? Do we have any clues?"

Spock's honesty, both of word and expression, was easy to appreciate. "He may be," he said, swiveling to face me. "Even he was unsure of his moment-to-moment plans. I know he was reticent to bring *Enterprise* to Argelius at the outset. He did obviously intend to join us at some point, but he himself didn't know the point. Beyond that, I cannot say."

I nodded, staring at the floor, contemplating. "Thank you," I said slowly then. "That leaves me free to move."

At this, McCoy elbowed his way between us. "How does it do that?"

"It gives us two choices," I explained. "Either we sit and wait for the captain to show up, or we take action according to what we already know. The captain wanted us to do one of those, and it can't be the first choice because he apparently didn't know when he'd be able to get here. I don't think he'd expect us to make a decision based on an unknown, so we'll act based on what we do know."

McCoy's brows went up.

Spock pursed his lips. "Logical."

From the passenger seat on the port side, Merete

said, "Then it's our move. But what move do we make?"

She *had* to ask, didn't she? I licked my lips, hoping some revelation would slide out. "Well . . . make ourselves indigenous to the planet, I guess. Get down there and start looking. We're not getting very far sitting around in orbit. Sir, you said you have Argelian costumes for us?"

"Yes, aboard my shuttle," Spock said. "Mr. Sandage and I will remain aboard and continue broadcasting the signal. In the meantime, I shall use connections in the government of Argelius to arrange for a base from which you'll be able to prowl the area. The prefect is already advised of the situation. You should have no trouble."

The Argelian prefect's idea of a base was a squalid little alley cantina deep in Yelgor City's north quarter. Spock had also arranged jobs for us, so no one would wonder what three strangers were doing there. At least we would have a central core to start from.

I led the way, feeling conspicuous, as Merete and McCoy followed me through the streets according to Spock's directions once we'd beamed down in an unpopulated dock area. Through the narrow, foggy streets we walked, flanked closely by scowling Gothic buildings of wood and stone, passing natives and their guests, the latter consisting of Star Fleet personnel on shore leave, Klingons and Romulans likewise, and even the occasional nonhumanoid, though those were rare. Argelius simply wasn't conditioned to make itself comfortable to a wide range of life forms. Of course, even the serene atmosphere couldn't dissolve military prejudices, much less racial ones. The Fleet people watched the Klingons and the Romulans, the Klingons watched the Fleet people, and the Romulans watched everybody. I felt everyone watching us. It might have been my imagination. It might have been the veils and the beaded curly-toed slippers. Or the plume pants. Or the feathers. Purple and chartreuse just weren't my colors. Somehow I got the feeling the clothing didn't completely hide our foreignness.

"I'll get Spock for this," McCoy vowed, glancing over his shoulder at a passing group of Argelians who had just given him the curious eye. Self-consciously he tugged at the tight brocaded vest and cummerbund. Purple wasn't his color either, especially under the bright orange fez. He looked like an animated piece of tapestry as he adjusted the shoulder bag that carried our tricorders.

"I hope we're not far from this cantina we're supposed to go to," Merete said. "It's damp in the streets."

"Don't complain," I told her, briefly scanning her ankle-length blue robe. "You're the only one of us who's not dressed up like a tropical bird." I clutched the wad of flight suit and boots under my arm. Spock had suggested I leave them behind, but I couldn't reconcile the idea of staging a phaser raid on extortionists while wearing feathers and veils.

"This is it," I said, turning down a loud alley and into a low-slung doorway. Acrid and dim, the cantina was crowded with laughing patrons. Sagging curtains decorated each of five walls, their colors and fringes faded by smoke and time. The patrons squatted on cushions or lay on long, low couches, munching confections I wouldn't have touched with a field prod. Squeaky music twanged from one corner, where a clutch of musicians wavered to their own questionable melody, and on a velvet podium a young girl twisted and spun in some kind of dance.

We were barely inside the door when a fat, surly-looking man approached us, babbling in Argelian, and grabbed my elbow to drag me farther into the cantina.

"What?" I blurted. "What do you want?"

He shook his head in disgruntlement and switched

easily to English, practically on the attack for an Argelian. "You're late! I do a favor for Chamberman Yiri and what do I get? I'm expected to operate shorthanded on the first night of the Archtide. You . . . take this tray." He shoved a wide metal tray heavy with confections into Merete's arms and ordered, "Serve those Klingons over there. Keep them happy. And you," he said, gesturing to McCoy, "pour more drinks. Over there."

Within seconds, I was alone with this charming round curmudgeon and he was walking me through a sea of legs and pillows. "It'll be your turn soon. Do you know the *litika?*"

"I . . . might," I stammered, stepping over a sleeping Argelian. "Have you seen any Vulcans around lately?"

His hands waggled in the air. "Who can tell? Vulcans, Romulans, they're all the same." He led me to a shimmering curtain and told me to stand there until he came back, which was fine with me. I took the moment to slip behind the curtain and retrieve my communicator from the folds of the veils, which had sounded a lot easier when I'd told Spock and Scanner I could hide it there. The communicator chirped when the antenna screen flipped up. "Piper to Rex," I said quietly.

"Spock here."

"Any change, sir?"

"None as yet. I am continuing to send the carrier waves. Since only one of us is needed here, Mr. Sandage requested to join you on the planet, and I agreed. He has changed clothing and should be meeting you there within a few minutes. What is your situation?"

"I think we've just been hired on for the season. We won't be too conspicuous here. I'll be able to ask a few questions, maybe get some answers or a lead to follow. Sarda's alive and he's in the area—I can practically feel him."

125

There was a stern, reproving silence after my exu-
berant claim, a kind of logic-to-nonsense wrist slap-
ping, but he didn't make any direct comments. "Yes.
. . . Advise me if there is any change of plans. I shall
hail you in thirty minutes for a check-in."

"Affirmative. Piper out."

I tucked the communicator into the pocket of my
folded flight suit, dumped the whole wad behind the
shimmery curtain, then slipped back out into the cantina, only to get a faceful of chubby proprietor.

"There you are! I told you to stay here and where
did you go? Behind a curtain. Those cubicles aren't
meant for you. You stay out in the open and do your
job. Well? Go ahead!"

The music had stopped. The patrons were all looking at me. I blinked back at them.

"Well?" the proprietor urged.

"Yes. . . . Well. . . ." I straightened my veils. The
patrons started banging their hands on squat tables.
Finally I asked him, "What am I supposed to be
doing?"

"Doing? Dancing, of course! What do you think
you're dressed for?"

"Ah. Of course. Sorry."

"Don't 'sorry.' Dance!"

From across the cantina, McCoy's eyes became
very wide when I stepped hesitantly onto that velvet
podium. The podium, fringed with silver, looked fairly
nice from a distance, but up close I saw that the
threads were separated and rotting from years of being
trod upon. It felt mushy. I could barely stand on it,
much less dance.

Dance? Me, dance?

The pounding grew louder. A gaggle of faces leered
up at me in brutal expectation. Klingons, humans,
Argelians, two Mengenites in the back . . . not a very
promising group as audiences go.

The proprietor got impatient and clapped his hands

sharply. The band groaned to life. Their music once
again whined. The audience kept pounding the tables.

I raised one veiled arm and lowered it, letting the
veil softly fly. Then the other. Two steps left, two right
. . . dance, huh? Now I could see Merete also frozen in
place, staring at me with the same saucer eyes I was
getting from McCoy. And now there was Scanner at
the doorway dressed in a waiter's ecru shirt and red
vest and holding a tricorder. Wasn't this nice? What a
privilege to have my Star Fleet colleagues on hand to
watch my un-Fleetlike gyrations.

Whatever I was doing, I was doing it wrong. The
audience howled their complaints, and I tried to improve my twisting to imitate what I'd seen the other
girl doing earlier. Not to much avail. I simply wasn't
trained to move in those combinations. After a few
minutes of this, I managed to find the beat of the tune
they were assaulting us with and was able to improve
my act by making the veils and feathers fly. Eventually, the audience started to treat me better. It was
probably just sympathy.

The Klingons at the table to my left began showing
their appreciation by snatching at my veils, and succeeded in yanking some free before I got possessive
and yanked back. They hooted at my un-Argelian
defiance and raised their mugs of a favorite Klingon
wine involving distilled butterflies. The smell identified
it quite well. They took my reaction for encourage-
ment—as I should have guessed Klingons would.
Their sooty complexions shined in the torchlight, cut
by bright teeth and sharp black beards. One of them
grasped my ankle.

"For an Argelian woman, you're a supernova," he
snarled up at me. "Come down here."

"Can't," I said. "I'm working."

"You'll still be working." He stripped off my slipper, brought it to his face and started sniffing it while
he leered at me. *"tlhIngan Hol Dajatlh'a'?"*

127

I didn't know what he was asking me and wasn't about to get into a discussion with him anyway. I twisted my foot, hoping to break his grasp, but he held fast to my ankle.

"You're not much of a dancer," the Klingon said.

The only female member of the group threw her head back and laughed. " *'elaS-ngan ghaH.'* " Whatever she said, they got a roar out of it at my expense.

The first gorilla pulled harder on my foot. "Kyrtu calls you a woman of Elas. Is that why you fight? You don't look like an Elasian!"

More laughter.

Another male downed the last gulp from a dented goblet. "There are other things Argelian women can do, Gelt. She's not working in *this* place without qualifications."

I stopped dancing. I glared down at him, gritting my teeth to keep in what I was thinking.

Gelt laughed along with his companions, then turned that gray face up to me again and gave my ankle a rough tug. "Enough dancing," he said.

My eyes grew narrow. My voice rumbled across the cantina. "Let go of the foot," I suggested, "or you'll be wearing it."

The laughter faded. A moment later, the music.

"I will teach things to you," Gelt said. "Things of Klingon. Strong things. A salute to things of Klingon!" He raised his mug and addressed the others, still holding my foot. "May you die angry!"

After a group swig, they watched for my reaction.

My lips grew flat. "Not bad for somebody who just learned to walk upright."

He had no misconceptions of my meaning. The grip on my ankle tightened. In my periphery, the tavernkeeper had his fists clamped to his mouth in frozen panic. McCoy was poised for trouble. Scanner and Merete were out of my line of vision. This wasn't the time to worry about them. This was the time to kick the lard out of a Klingon.

There was no sense in trying to talk my way out of this; that was clear in the Klingon's eyes. So I closed them with my other foot—a good, clean, Star Fleet kick to the bridge of his nose. His hand fell away from my leg, but the blow that would've floored any human merely echoed briefly within the misshapen Klingon skull. Gelt collapsed backward, his face crumpled in astonishment, but he was soon clawing his way back to me through a forest of his companions, who were also grabbing for me. I felt myself going down in a sea of Klingons, and caught a glimpse of Scanner's body flying head-on into the clutch like a giant brown-haired torpedo.

Star Fleet self-defense tactics did their best to keep our heads above those slimy waters, but there were five of them and only two of us. McCoy was trying to reach us, but the flood of Argelians who were trying to escape kept him from making much headway. Merete, too, was lost somewhere in the rush for the door. A party of three human vacationers hesitated for a moment, then cast their lot with Scanner and me, smoothing out the odds a bit, but we still had that awful Klingon ruthlessness to deal with, as well as their superior strength. I heard a bone crack somewhere in the forest of arms and legs before I fully comprehended the Klingon bar-fight mode. After that, I quit playing Star-Fleet fair.

I pulled ears and gouged eyes and even took a bite out of a fuzzy forearm. Scanner flew by me at least twice, neither time in control of his course, and by now McCoy had discovered the art of smashing bottles over Klingon heads. But Klingon heads are hard, and the Klingon temper short-fused. Gelt was still furious and he kept me occupied. I could barely keep him from getting a grip on me much less worry about

129

helping my friends. I landed a few good blows, still kicking at that tender spot on his forehead where I'd kicked him before, and this dazed him. He was slowing down, though his copper-gray face was still screwed up with rage. Where moments ago this had been only a saloon free-for-all, something had changed. The Klingon sense of pride had taken charge. If Gelt got a good hold on me, he would kill me.

It was a lucky thing that Argelian edicts prevented the possession of any weapons while on the planet, or I'd have been dead already. As the Argelians scrambled into the alley, the cantina slowly emptied out, leaving only a tangle of humans and Klingons, and one petrified tavernkeeper who was frantically ringing an alarm bell. The sound of an alarm on Argelius usually translated into, "Run in the other direction," so if help was to arrive, it wouldn't be soon enough.

Gelt was circling me. I had managed to get the podium between us. Roaring, he dived over it, fingers waggling at my throat. I slithered clumsily to one side, feeling his scratch rake across my upper arm, and I tore one of the veils from the waistband of my plume pants. I jumped up onto the podium and for a frantic moment lost my balance. Gelt rolled over, but a solid slam on the ear rocked him back onto his stomach. I looped the veil around his neck, dropped onto his back, and twisted.

He clawed at me, scoring my wrists. I kept pulling. His throat grew taut against the veil, and he drew blood on his own neck in an attempt to free himself. He gagged and spat, then twisted around to grasp the veil near my hands. Neck muscles stiffening, he made me believe he wasn't going to let himself black out. So I snatched up the nearest stone jug and introduced it to the side of his head. He wavered under me, and at the first sign of recovery, I clubbed him again. This went on three, count 'em, three more times. Finally his eyes rolled up and he drooped back. As soon as I felt his struggle slacken, I let go of the veil and leaned over him long enough to be sure he was breathing. It was a ragged, throaty kind of breathing, but the job was done.

I rolled off the podium only to realize that I was wrong; the job was far from done. Scanner was being pummeled by a large Klingon, two of the human vacationers were trying to rescue him while holding off their own problems, and Dr. McCoy was grappling with the spitting Klingon woman—and losing. With a deep breath, I steeled myself for more.

Hardly had I drawn the breath when the ogling crowd at the alley door parted and the cavalry sailed in. Merete, followed by Mr. Spock, cape flying, and to my astonishment, Captain Cavalry himself—Kirk.

Though I was stunned with relief, McCoy knew exactly what to do. He grimaced with effort and shoved the Klingon woman straight at Spock, who was able to down her with a slightly modified version of the Vulcan nerve pinch. Evidently he'd bothered to learn how to numb a Klingon nervous system in his years of dealing with them. Handy data.

Kirk was not so subtle. He ran headlong into the fight, took a leap, and bodyslammed two Klingons right into the tavern wall. He was on his feet before they had a chance to shake off the surprise. He picked one, hauled him to his feet, and let fly a classic right cross that rearranged the Klingon's jawline. In spite of the victory, I saw the captain wince and shake his aching hand before turning to deal with the second Klingon. Number two was quickly dispatched, but it took an extra punch.

The cantina was littered with bodies. At every door and window, Argelian faces goggled at us, amazed at our willingness to defend ourselves and each other with physical force. This would keep their gossip lines buzzing for years.

Kirk rubbed his knuckles, surveying his happy hunting ground. A quick glance around the room gave him a head count, and he seemed satisfied when he turned to me. "Ah, Piper. On the job as usual. And looking dapper."

I turned red, quite aware of the torn veils, the one bare foot (which was almost as bad as the foot still wearing the absurd slipper), the filmy harem pants, and the scanty top. I would've told him it wasn't my idea, but that meant having to tell him it was Spock's idea, and I decided not to do that. Of course, Kirk wasn't in uniform either. He also wore some version of Argelian clothing: a simple toast-brown tunic, beige trousers, and Federation boots. Well, nobody's perfect.

Limply I said, "I think I blew my cover."

Captain Kirk raised his brows and blinked. "Yes, you do seem rather uncovered." He surveyed the clumps of Klingon. "Well, it was worth it."

Scanner stumbled to my side, holding his elbow. "Bet you're a fun date."

"Klingons!"

We all turned abruptly at Merete's warning call as she stood near the dockside window.

Kirk took a step toward her. "Where?"

"Heading this way," she told him. "They must've heard the noise."

McCoy joined her and leaned out the window for a better look.

The captain asked, "How many, Bones?"

McCoy pushed himself off the windowsill and blurted, "Too many!"

"Let's go. Move."

The captain led us out of the tavern and down the alley, stepping aside to herd us through a narrow doorway into the next building, then out again into the open Argelian night. He'd barely given me time to retrieve my gear, but we got away before the Klingons discovered us standing over their fallen comrades. Panting, we slipped behind a huge stone cistern and knelt there for horrible moments while a barrage of Klingons thundered past, looking for us and frothing for revenge. We held our breath as their hard-soled boots clattered down the docks.

Scanner slid to his knees between Merete and Spock and pressed his shoulders back against the cool stone. "Gawd-a-mighty. Klingons really give me the colly-wobbles. Ugly with a capital *ug!*"

"Predictable human reaction," Spock commented. I watched his expression and McCoy's double take and decided it was another of those odd Spock-McCoy barbs that I was only beginning to pick up on.

I stanched the scratches on my arm with a veil and turned to Captain Kirk. "Sir, we didn't expect you so soon."

He shrugged. "Professor Mornay won't expect me so soon either. That's our extra playing card. Besides you, of course."

"Weirdest game I ever seen," Scanner complained, wincing as he stretched his arm.

I pressed on. "What happened when they took you in for questioning?"

Kirk shrugged. "I answered them." His casual air deflated the bureaucratic web he'd probably had to untangle before making good his promise to meet Spock here. He hadn't said, of course, that the answers had been truthful—only effective.

"You could've told me what was going on," I said, facing the captain, surprised at my boldness and somehow urged on by it. In that moment of bald honesty, I was talking to the captain of my starship, the captain of my schooner, and the captain of my destiny. He knew what I was feeling. I might as well have the satisfaction of speaking the words. "It wasn't neces-

133

sary to leave me holding an empty bag out in the middle of an ocean on a ship I didn't know how to pilot . . . sir."

He nodded, one shoulder cocked and his brow furrowed. "I see. Anything else?"

I dropped the crumpled flight suit and started peeling off excess veils. "Well, I could mention something about getting stuck in a smelly tavern and being pawed by some Klingon with no neck and a face like a macaque . . ."

"But," he prodded.

"But . . . I think I'd rather know what you want us to do next."

"I want us all to fulfill our respective missions. Go ahead, Spock."

Spock shifted as he crouched beside McCoy. In his tunic and cape, he seemed forbiddingly natural to this guerrilla life-style, as though he only half fit in any kind of world. He addressed me directly with his serene Vulcan approach, and any other identity but that of science officer dropped softly away. "I was attempting to hail you when the captain beamed aboard unexpectedly from the ship that transported him from Earth. You were correct about Lieutenant Sarda and your carrier waves."

Scanner inhaled sharply and grinned. "Did we tree him?"

Spock hesitated, lost for a moment in the colloquial assault, then recovered and said, "Yes, we . . . treed him. Shortly before the captain arrived, I began receiving low-gain impulses from what is apparently an abandoned dairy farm on the northern outskirts of the city, just over that rise." He gestured to a shadowy ridge just behind a densely populated slum area. In the twilight, we could see it clearly. "The pulses were regular and definitely geared to be picked up by sensors attuned to radio waves. Logically, the sender could only be Lieutenant Sarda, since those waves are

134

tricky to broadcast. Congratulations on your guess. We now have a location."

I slumped back and closed my eyes for a moment. He was alive. Alive and answering me. Cold and still since the first transwarp waves had hit Rex, my heart started beating again. Merete reached over and squeezed my arm in much-needed reassurance. She was grinning that silent fairylike grin. He was *alive*.

"The *Enterprise* isn't here?" I blurted, turning to Kirk.

"Not yet," he said. "Too conspicuous. Scotty's in command and the ship is on its way . . . slowly."

"A decoy? Mornay thinks you'll be on board the starship?"

"Yes. And Dr. Boma is on board. He may be of some help when it comes down to the wire. He's worked more closely with these scientists than any of us."

I crouched between the cistern and a wooden building long enough to squirm out of the harem pants and back into my flight suit and boots. Ahhh, that felt right. "So we'll go ahead with our plan to split up into three teams and separate the scientists, sir?"

"They'll be easier to handle that way," Captain Kirk added. "But I'm also counting on your relationship with Sarda to shed light on Mornay's mental state before we try to deal with her. We don't want her pushing the wrong buttons in a panic. With any luck," he said, peering over his shoulder at his closest colleague, "Mr. Spock will be able to pull out his bag of Vulcan logic tricks with Perren and weaken Mornay's stand by taking away her support. Her possession of transwarp loses its potency if she doesn't also possess Sarda and Perren."

Fully dressed and loving it, I stepped out to put on my boots. "What if you can't reason with her? We have reason to suspect they're actually building a transwarp device—"

135

"Which makes them a thousand times more dangerous." He paused, driving home the seriousness of that one change. "Spock told me. We can't afford to wait too long," he said, his voice taking on an abrupt strength. "Every minute that goes by heightens the risk that other governments, hostile ones, might get word of Mornay's plans and descend on Argelius. We've got to shut her down before that happens. It's up to you to give that process a strong beginning." The captain's finger pointed at me in illustration, pinning the responsibility right back on my shoulders. "Mornay doesn't know you. That's an advantage," he said. "Use it."

"Aye, sir, I'll do my best." Of course, I was really saying that I would fake it to the best of my abilities. I hoped he took it as that kind of promise. Nothing was guaranteed.

"We'll go in teams," he said, calculatedly making eye contact with each of us as he spoke. "Piper, you and Sandage go first. Isolate Lieutenant Sarda and get him out of the red zone. That'll leave Spock and me free to move in on the others."

Charming. . . . I get to go first. "How are we going to pinpoint the location without the ship's sensors?"

Spock retrieved a tricorder from Merete, who had kept her presence of mind during our foray with the Klingons and made sure our equipment got out of there safely. Checking the tuning, Spock then handed the tricorder to Scanner. "These tricorders have been adjusted down to the carrier wavelength. There's insufficient power to send the waves, but the tricorders can now receive them adequately to home in on the source. The signal will be faint. You'll have to constantly tune in. It may be tedious."

Scanner shrugged. "They don't call me Scanner for nothin'." His eyes made a self-conscious flick and he added, "sir."

"We'll give you forty-five minutes to get into position outside their compound," Captain Kirk said. "At that point, Mr. Spock and I will create a diversion, giving you the opportunity to get inside unnoticed." His tone, abrupt and poignant, insisted on success. "It's critical that each of you understand. Don't underestimate the gravity of this situation. Those scientists . . . each of us . . . even this entire planet are expendable. Mornay has to be stopped, even if the cost is all of our lives. Understood?" He paused, a long, measured pause until he received the depth of awareness from us that he demanded. With a nod, he said, "Good luck."

The clock started ticking again.

Chapter Eight

"There are some things that transcend even the discipline of the Service."

—Amok Time

It took us almost thirty minutes to wind our way through the Argelian slums and up that rise to the dairy farm. A motley collection of old wooden shacks and stone-processing buildings, the farm also now possessed an incongruous sophistication: guards.

"How many?" I asked as Scanner crouched beside me in the nearby overgrowth.

He turned his tricorder and squinted at the screen. "Twelve or more. These buildings are armed with screens. Sensors can't penetrate, but I read twelve guards on this side. You think they're Argelian?"

I smirked at him. "Not if Mornay's worth her salt. Look at those phaser rifles."

"Yeah, so much for Argelian law. Those guys don't look very affectionate, do they?"

"They look like hired guns to me," I said. "Mornay must've scraped the bottoms of some seedy barrels."

"Tell you what . . . they got a sensor wall around this place that's steady as a docked ship. A butterfly couldn't get in without them findin' out."

"But it isn't a force field . . ."

"Negative, just sensors."

"We only have twelve minutes before the captain

138

and Spock make their diversion. Let's find a door to target."

"What kind of a diversion you think the Captain'll come up with?" Scanner asked as he followed me in a wide arch through the surrounding trees and reddish Argelian scrub growth.

"Who knows?" I answered. "He'll use whatever's at his disposal. The ship he came in, the ship Spock came in . . . maybe even Rex. Whatever it is, it'll be fast and sudden. We'll have to be ready."

"We're ready for anything," he said with a little snarl of confidence.

"This is a good place," I said, hunching down and scanning the farm area below. "On the far side from the city . . . only one door, and only three guards. See any others?"

"Yup, right behind that wall. Two of 'em."

"Where?"

"Next to that lopsided shed."

"Oh . . . I see them," I said, peering down the grade at the guards as they lazily paced. "Look at their clothes. All different. And they're all humanoid, too. Quick and good with hand-held weapons."

"Those scientists ain't takin' chances, are they?"

"No," I said, feeling the weight again. "They're not." I gazed over the buildings, plugging myself into the faint lights that shone from tiny windows. Those were probably set up as labs, probably set up quickly and without safety measures. Sarda would be in one of them, confined somehow. Each of those thoughts made me stiff with worry. If the scientists, in their rush to produce a transwarp device and up their ante, could have one "accident," then certainly they could have more. Sarda wouldn't be safe as long as he was forced to cooperate with them.

The three stone buildings were attached to one another with lath-ribbed breezeways covered with

139

some kind of tarp. The only opening on this side of the compound was a heavy wooden double door, warped by time and the elements, and guarded by two sentries with phaser rifles.

"Any time now," I breathed. *Captain, make it a good show for me.*

Soon phasers would lance from the sky, or perhaps he would use photon torps for a brighter effect. A distraction, he said. If I was in Kirk's position, I'd have drawn the guards away by hitting a target down the glen, near enough to see very well and far enough to get the guards out of my way. Nervously, I glanced at the sky.

"Are you ready?" I asked Scanner, more out of need for the sound of a voice, even my own.

The night was dead quiet. The two nearest planets in the Argelian system wheeled blue and pink overhead, conflicting with the two moons for attention. "Yeah, I'm ready," he whispered, also watching the sky.

"Any time," I said again. I licked my lips and pushed my mind right through that door. All I had to do now was join it. "Any minute."

"I'm still ready."

"Good . . . good . . . ."

"Wish we had phasers."

"Use your imagination," I scoffed. "What did they do before phasers were invented?"

He shrugged. "They used photons."

A smirk was the best I could manage for his comment. I watched the sky. It was time. Where was the captain?

Fleeting and horrible, the idea struck that Scanner and I might be in the wrong place, about to break into the wrong compound. Could that be it? Was I screwing up already? Frantically I started scanning the countryside, looking for the right compound or some signal of Kirk's diversion, but . . . nothing.

Besides, why would they have phaser rifles if this

wasn't the right place? Right, right, that made sense.

"Hey, Piper?"

"What?"

"You see what I see?"

I swung around to him. "Where?"

"Yonder." He pointed down at the compound and the slope behind it.

I squinted through the purple Argelian night, trying to home in on a strange snorting noise that was groaning its way up the slope. A moment later a score of fat animal faces popped up over the hill, followed by lumbering gray bodies, then more faces and more bodies. Resembling, more than anything, a cross between Earth rhinoceroses and those clodheaded mudpigs discovered lumbering around Rigel Four about a century ago, they were Argelian currbucks. Big, gentle, and clumsy, they shook their horns in confusion and gallumphed toward the farm. Nobody would ever have bothered to keep them around except that their milk made up about 90 percent of Argelius's export trade, considered a delicacy for its alcoholic effects without the usual hangover. The animals themselves were born with a case of industrial strength stupidity.

"Warthogs!" Scanner blustered. He watched in astonishment as three chubby Argelian shepherds frantically waved prods at the animals, evidently trying to get them under control, but to no avail. The currbucks, wide-eyed and snorting in panic, thundered over the crest of the hill and headed straight for the guarded farm area.

We watched, tense and unsure, as the currbucks lumbered right through the compound's sensor screens and set off the alarms. The night filled with flashing lights and whooping klaxons. One by one, the guards around the compound ran to help herd the currbucks away from the farm. Eventually, when it was clear the herd was out of control, when currbucks were running snout-first into the compound walls in

141

blind panic, even the guards at the rear door drifted away toward the scampering herd.

Scanner stared downward. "Was that it?"

"I don't know," I said quickly, tensed on bent knees and ready either to go or stay, or go . . . or . . . "What do you think?"

"I don't know. What do you think?"

"What do *you* think?"

"You're the one who's always tryin' to think like the captain. You tell *me!* Would he send hogs after us?"

"Maybe that's it."

"We can go if you wanna go . . ."

"Maybe we should go."

"But what if that wasn't it?"

"But what if it was?"

"You think it was?"

"Yeah. Yeah. Let's go."

We went. A diversion is a diversion. And 100 Argelian currbucks can be plenty diverting.

The mercenaries were shouting at each other, because with mercenaries there's usually too much ego to elect any one leader, and they made a silly spectacle trying to direct an impossible roundup. By the time Scanner and I reached the door, the klaxons and flashing lights had thoroughly terrorized the currbucks and the guards were sufficiently distracted with what they thought was just an accident from a neighboring farm. With a last glance over our shoulders, we slipped inside the wooden doors and closed them tightly behind us, locking out the flashes and most of the sounds.

The silence of danger closed in around us. My skin quivered with anticipation.

"Lock it," I said.

Scanner pulled the bolt with a shaking hand.

The hallway was simple, made of stone blocks, unadorned except for small filament lights that cast a cold glow.

"I can't believe that worked!" Scanner gasped. Until then, I hadn't noticed how nervous he really was. He gawked at me.

"What?"

"The bit with the hogs!"

"Well, it wouldn't have except that they didn't know we were coming," I said.

Only then did we sense the presence at the end of the hallway. We paused, looked at each other, then turned and stared into the muzzle of a phaser.

From the end of the hall, a soft voice emerged.

"Greetings, Commander Piper. Your presence is most gratifying."

There was no mistaking him. Even among his own kind, lost among the people who bred him and taught him so thoroughly to fish the ice patterns of the mind, he would have stood out. Only for an instant was he a stranger to me. Unfamiliarity lasted no more than a second. Suddenly, I knew him—personally, intensely.

He carried the gravity of the situation with polished Vulcan composure. His hair, a mass of soft ebony waves, was longer now than it had been in the photograph Spock had shown us. It fell over his shoulders, drawing attention down to a splendidly sculptured tunic of sage-green quilt, and up, to graceful backswept ears and canted eyes. The eyes—they were pale gray, almost silver, striking in raven hedges of lashes and upswept brows, and they held an undefined wildness. The deeper I looked into them, the more surely I saw that touch of self-indulgence, even turbulence. Vulcan ways could bridle him, but only to a certain point. He wore his attire, his long hair, his Vulcanness, and his independence like a crown.

Perren raised an arm in a beckoning gesture. Dolman sleeves on the surcoat, slashed with crescents of silver hiding between quilted green panels, immediately created the illusion of a cape. His beautiful

143

clothes might have seemed pretentious—he had obviously been well paid for his talents—had it not been for a bawdrick of platinum clasps sloped across his hips, enameled with the cool azures and greens Vulcans dream of as they mediate on their hot red planet. There were chips of semiprecious metals in the belt that caused a faint glitter, but all were very small and tasteful, providing subtle reminders of Vulcan heritage. Only the phaser in his left hand, held casually downward, but ready, jarred the image we saw before us.

Embarrassment made me resist Scanner's glance. A dozen questions flashed into my mind, all beginning with "how."

I swallowed hard, straightened my spine, and walked forward. Scanner stayed behind, his hand on the door bolt.

"I greet you, Commander," Perren said. "I presume you wish to speak to Sarda. I shall escort you to him. There are automatic defenses that will injure you if you go unaccompanied."

He raised his arm again and stepped backward, gesturing down a dim corridor. The phaser also came up just enough to maintain the subtle intimidation. Only his eyes spoke now.

In my defeat, so sudden and quick, I couldn't think of anything to say to him. What does prey say to its conqueror? My throat was tight with anguish. I pressed my lips and moved forward.

Perren herded us both into a small laboratory annex. High stone walls were lined with computer crates, discarded equipment, and storage boxes. Two sturdy folding tables held more equipment and stacks of computer spools.

"You will remain here," Perren said. "I advise you strongly against attempting to escape. This farm has been impregnated with rather sophisticated defense devices that will be unmerciful should you encounter them. You must be confined, of course, but I have no desire to see you injured."

Scanner turned his back on Perren and leaned toward me. "This is the bad guy?"

I cleared my throat. "We're only here because of Sarda," I said, hoping the lie couldn't be discerned in my tone of voice. With a little luck, I could deflect their attention from whatever Captain Kirk and Mr. Spock would be doing next. "I don't care about anything else. Where is he?"

Perren bowed his elegant head, tipped one shoulder, and punched a button on a portable communications unit. "Sarda."

Breath froze in my lungs. Beside me, Scanner tensed.

"Yes," came a voice that was chillingly familiar.

I stared at the com unit as though it had bitten me.

Perren spoke quietly, but with poignance. "Have you completed repairing the circuit usher?"

"Very nearly. I will need your assistance to recalibrate."

My chest tightened as I heard his voice. Mornay and Perren might have brought Sarda here against his will, but I knew very well there was no physical threat that could make a Vulcan work against his will. Perren knew that too. His eyes touched me as he spoke into the com unit. "Your visitors are here now."

There was a pause. My mind screamed in an effort to define that long moment. The communications unit beneath Perren's hand zoomed up and swelled to fill my field of vision. My eyes blurred.

"Very well," Sarda responded distantly. *"I shall be right there."*

It ended with a heartsickening click. Perren straightened and observed us coolly. I wondered if he could see my turmoil, the pain I felt as the idea rammed home that Sarda might actually be here voluntarily. He wasn't a prisoner . . . he was free to move around. My mouth clamped tight and my whole body went torpid. I was forced to stand there and add up the obvious. A trap.

A trap . . . a trap.

In my periphery I saw Scanner looking at me with concern, but I couldn't respond. I couldn't move. The deep wound burned.

There was a noise in the hallway. A faint shuffle.

He appeared. Amber eyes struck me like a hard wind. He wore only his standard Fleet uniform, the tenne gold fabric catching lights from his brassy hair, as though nothing had happened to spoil his right to wear it. His brow was slightly furrowed even before we spoke. He strode past Perren with familiarity that hurt me and stopped before reaching us. His lips parted.

Scanner burst out from behind me, clutched Sarda's collar, and rammed him backward into a wall. Sarda's arms flared outward, but he did nothing to resist the attack as Scanner growled, "You mule-eared son of a Romulan, I oughta pin you up like a fish!"

Perren took one step, then wisely stopped.

Sarda accepted Scanner's acid glare and hot breath with a calmness that said he had expected it. "Things are not as they seem, Judd," he said quietly.

"They *seem* dang plain to me, you rock-hearted rat," Scanner seethed.

Sarda shifted his eyes to me. With his Vulcan strength he could have thrown Scanner off like a snowflake, but he waited under that malicious grasp and did nothing.

I moved up beside them, making no effort to get Scanner under control. He was acting out my most frightening feelings, giving vent to a piece of myself I was just as glad not to see right now. Even with Scanner's fists jarred up against his throat, Sarda merely gazed at me, and I at him.

"We thought you needed us," I said. Obviously, I

146

was struggling. The quiver gave it away. I wished I could be Vulcan too, so I wouldn't have to feel this. But capped inside this human casing, the anguish bubbled to the top.

"There are things I must tell you," he said.

Scanner bumped him harder against the wall again. "You mean explain, right?"

Perren came closer. The phaser was raised now.

"No," Sarda said to him, bringing a hand up to his colleague, his mentor. "No need. Please leave us."

The phaser went down, but cautiously. The other Vulcan nodded once in acknowledgment of Sarda's right to privacy even above his right to safety. "As you wish."

When Perren left, closing the door behind him, the tension remained.

"Okay, Points," Scanner growled, "start tawkin'."

In a rare tactile moment, almost in relief, Sarda hung his hand on Scanner's arm. He was still looking at me.

Moments ticked by. The silent communication continued.

When it had done all it could, words had to come. I took a deep breath and swallowed. "Scanner."

"You gotta be kiddin'."

"Back off, please."

"Not till I get what I want."

"You'll get it. Back off."

He hated what I asked. Perhaps he even hated the fact that I wasn't really ordering him off, but just asking him, friend to friend. Somehow that made it different, more potent. With one more threatening bump against the wall, he let go and backed away. Suddenly it was almost as though Sarda and I were alone on a rock somewhere in the middle of nothing.

Sarda lowered his hands slowly to straighten his tunic. Still we gazed at each other in that uncomfortable knowing silence. The answer was there: he was no prisoner. If he started out that way, it hadn't lasted.

On top of the pain of having been betrayed by my friend came the hurt of being overshadowed in our friendship, being displaced by Perren. I'd been congratulating myself for a bond that might have already become secondary.

I dug deep, and found my voice. "Why did you answer our carrier signal if you knew we were walking into a trap?"

The complexity of the situation shone in his eyes. "It was not I who answered your signal," he said. "It was Perren."

"Because you told him."

Even through the Vulcan shields, he flinched. The misery now showed itself in his eyes, too, but for different reasons. With effort, he went on. "I would never have told him. I hoped you would know me better."

Guilt swarmed in. We both felt it, both felt victimized by the situation.

"There's no other explanation," I said. If I was wrong, at least the truth would have to come out now. Insult was a strong medicine.

He didn't respond immediately. He seemed embarrassed. With a momentary glance at the floor, he steeled himself to tell us things no Vulcan would ordinarily volunteer—unless the reasons were gravely important to him.

"Perren knew about you because he knows me," he struggled. "Through our training melds, he has come to know you . . . what to expect from you. When the stampede diverted our sensor system and the guards, he knew there was a 98 percent probability it was you."

The effort of saying that in front of Scanner, much less to me if we had been alone, drained him. For a moment his breathing was ragged. He quickly recovered, though, and contained his discomfort.

With a tremble of relief, I continued, "And the signal we sent?"

Fortified somewhat, he answered, "Perren also understands about the Outlast. He had no trouble interpreting the appearance of the carrier waves."

Behind me, Scanner slumped back to sit on one of the tables and hung his head, disgusted. He crossed his arms and heaved a rumbling sigh.

"We were worried about you," I said to Sarda. "I thought you'd been kidnapped. Are you all right?"

"I'm fine," he admitted, even though I got the feeling he would much rather have given me the answer I'd hoped for: that he'd been shanghaied at phaserpoint after a grueling ambush and beaten into cooperating.

"You weren't kidnapped," I concluded.

"Not precisely, no. I . . . elected to come. I am needed here."

"You're helping Mornay and Perren hold the galaxy hostage?"

He bristled. "I am not helping them, per se," he insisted. "I designed the correct containment equipment for transwarp energies. I alone know how to use the safety and backup systems properly. Mornay is attempting to build a transwarp device. Had I allowed them to build the device without my help, I would have been endangering countless lives on this planet. I could not . . . do that." The weight of responsibility was plainly still pulling him in two different directions. He was exhausted. "The experiment is too delicate for me to ignore. There has already been one slippage, but I managed to deflect the waves into space at the last moment."

"You bet you did!" Scanner exploded. "And we were right in the middle of 'em when they came through!"

Sarda stared at him. His face went ashen. He even stopped breathing. I hadn't quite realized the depth of the transwarp danger until he supported himself on the edge of the table and physically fought for control. He won, but he had to close his eyes to do it.

Even Scanner was affected by the sight. With a shake of his tousled head, he sighed, "Damn it, Points."

Sarda's brassy head dropped slightly. He gazed at the table, ashamed, yet committed.

"In other words," I continued, "you didn't elect to come at all. They blackmailed you. Your inaction would have cost lives, so you came with them."

"Yes," he said softly. He didn't look up.

Silence settled around us like fog. Without taking a step, we waded through it.

I was the first to move. I strode to the table, beside Sarda, turned and leaned against the edge. Now only inches separated us. When I looked up, so did he.

My words were careful, sincere. "I understand."

If there was anything more, any lingering regret or guilt, we beamed it out. If Sarda had betrayed us, I didn't want to know about it. There was no profit in repaying a mistake with another mistake.

He gathered himself with a solemn nod. "You're wise," he said. His gratitude was there, but sheltered. Neither of us made any attempt to uncover it further.

"Tell me about Perren," I asked. "What makes him tick?"

Sarda blinked, confused by the slang, then remembered what it meant and tried to find the best words to explain a complex individual. "You saw him," he said, as though that explained something. "He is supremely in charge of himself. He believes in the rationality of Vulcan philosophy, but he cannot abide the Vulcan tenet of not making moral judgments, even rational ones. Like Vice Admiral Rittenhouse, Perren believes there is an overwhelming moral difference between Federation philosophy and those of the Klingons, Romulans, and the handful of minor hostile powers.

150

He believes the illogic lies in ignoring the differences."

"Are you telling me he doesn't believe in the Vulcan philosophy of pacifism?"

Sarda's eyes flared in a wave of frustration. Maybe I didn't completely understand Vulcan ways, but now wasn't the time to chastise me for it. He realized that and continued, "Even on Vulcan, logic continues to evolve. Minor points in logic can extrapolate into vast differences in philosophy. Contrary to common belief, there are those among my people who do not accept the Vulcan system of pacifism. Things do change, Piper," he said, raising a hand to emphasize his point. "Even Spock was a renegade at one time. He disagreed with cloistered Vulcan ways. Since then, the Vulcan patterns of logic have grown outward to include our place as a major Federation contingent. Someday, Perren's ideas may be accepted, as Spock's have."

Scanner crossed his arms over one knee and argued, "That don't excuse putting the whole galaxy on the edge of a cosmic scramble, bud."

Sarda struck him with a deadly look. "No," he snapped, "it does not. But even pacifism has violent results when those who embrace it refuse to defend others' rights to peace." His tone was sharp, carrying echoes that defended himself as well as Perren. The flare faded then, quite abruptly, and humility returned. He was troubled; it was easy to see.

"You're saying he believes Rittenhouse was basically right," I said. "That moral unity has to be established, even by force. Right?"

"All Vulcans have the same basic beliefs," he went on, making it suffice as his answer. "But the right to individualism includes the right to disagree. Unfortunately, that also means there is disagreement on how to achieve the goals of peace. Perren's talents as an applied scientist have given him comfort all his life, and he feels an acute awareness of those who have no such opportunities because of their governmental systems. He feels a responsibility for the oppressed peoples of the galaxy and wants to bring down the governments that oppress them. He . . . thinks it will be simple."

I saw Sarda's embarrassment for Perren as he spoke, once again staring into the tabletop, unable to meet my eyes. This, however, was no time for delicacies. If Sarda had come here and was staying here out of loyalty to Perren, I would have to rupture that bond enough to get Sarda back. Our friendship, and the success of our mission—that peace he spoke of so reverently—depended on it. Time would come later for kindness.

"He's wrong, Sarda," I said, slicing across the lines of tolerance. "His mistake is assuming the Klingons and others will automatically give in when they're told the Federation will use the power of transwarp against them. He doesn't think they'll fight back against impossible odds. He doesn't understand irrationality. Am I right?"

Reluctantly, he admitted, "You . . . are correct."

"And Mornay. She wants power as much as Perren wants peace."

"Yes."

"And he doesn't see through Mornay any better than he sees through irrationality. He doesn't understand why anyone would simply want power, because it's an emotional goal."

"Yes . . ."

"And where do you stand?"

He stiffened. His shame deepened. I had succeeded in putting him on the spot. My appearance here, and my dedication to my own mission, nailed him down. Would he come with me, or stay with Perren?

"Where he stands doesn't matter anymore," came a harsh voice from a corner behind Scanner.

Sarda and I turned abruptly. Scanner slid off the table and whirled around. Several guards stood there, sighting down their phaser rifles at us. They flanked a stout woman with sharp, flashing eyes framed by a bowl of dark gray hair. Her mouth was curled into a forbidding grin, a sign of victory, as she took a few steps toward us. Comfortably flanked by her guards, Ursula Mornay had us at a stunning disadvantage.

She had aged considerably since the photo we'd seen aboard Rex. Now her hair was peppery with the years, her features harder, her small blue eyes creased with lines and time. Her shoulders were slightly stooped, but her youth had not been entirely sacrificed. She still appeared strong and steady as she held a phaser on us, evidently not satisfied to put her trust completely in her hired guards.

"You've done good work, Sarda," she said, still grinning. "Plenty well enough that we can take over. Now it's only a matter of time before I have all I need."

"What is it you need?" I asked.

Her quick eyes flashed at me. "You'd love to know, certainly. So you're Sarda's bold rescuers. Well enough. I don't need him anymore."

Sarda's brow creased and he stepped forward, putting himself between Mornay and us. "You dare not activate the flux device without my safety systems," he said with a startling emphasis.

"I have your systems, don't I? I don't need you."

"Professor, you cannot—"

"I'm putting you away for safekeeping. If I need you again, I'll have you. But under control."

"And my friends?"

"Your friends' lives will guarantee your cooperation. The logic of it is simple enough even for a Vulcan, isn't it?"

I thought of what Spock had told us about her, about

153

her tunnelbound view of politics and her hunger for power. Spock had postulated that Professor Mornay didn't understand the true consequences of her actions. With a little luck, I could manipulate that. Deep breath . . . and dive.

"Professor," I began, "you're in great danger here. You're too far out and too close to contested space for the Federation to protect you. If you throw the transwarp technology up for bid way out here, there's going to be—"

"I know what there's going to be," she said. The grin widened.

"And you don't care?"

"I have everything under control, don't I?" she said. Quite plainly, she agreed with herself, and that was the only person she cared to consult.

I took a step. "And where does Perren fit in? Does he understand the repercussions of your plan?"

She shrugged, her little mouth twisting. "Perren's ideas are quaint. He has no real perception of the scope of possibilities within my grasp, now does he? Why should he? He only cares about his work, and I let him do his work. I'm the only one who lets him. I do the thinking and he does the building. He doesn't argue with me. It's a good working relationship."

"For you," I said.

"Where else can he go?" She paced to our right, keeping the phaser leveled. "He wanted to force the Federation to look at our device, to realize the potential. I want the same thing. Except that I want the whole galaxy to realize the potential. Scope, you see. I said that before. Scope." Her tiny eyes narrowed with excitement at the idea and for a few moments she was seeing her vision of the future instead of us.

In a bold gamble, I decided to test the vision. I moved toward her.

And stopped short—her phaser twitched and her

eyes cleared. Behind her, the guards' phaser rifles snapped up. My reflection wavered in a half-dozen cross-hair sights.

So much for that theory.

"Oh, Piper, you're not that silly, are you?" Mornay taunted. "You're too military, aren't you? You think dreamers can't be sensible, can't see the whole picture. Well, you're wrong!" Her tone became a bark, her eyes sharp as fangs. "Scope! Once my device is tested, I'll be a major bargaining force in the new Federation."

"You sound like Rittenhouse," I accused.

"He had his plans. He failed. Now the turn is mine. The starship will be here soon, and I will demand that Captain Kirk act as the Federation's emissary. When we meet, it will be on equal ground." Her tone was casual, but her manner had a cruciality about it. Not the kind that could be argued with. Even Rittenhouse appreciated the capabilities of his enemies. It seemed Mornay didn't. That trait made her wilder, more dangerous. I closed my mouth and stiffened my jaw, determined not to argue with her. It was plainly a waste of time. Kirk was right to save her for himself to deal with. She didn't take me seriously.

Not *yet*.

She turned slightly when Perren walked in behind her, threading his way through as the guards parted for him, but her attention stayed with us.

Immediately I changed my course and raised a hand to him. My own impotence struck me when I saw my hand trembling. I had to force myself to speak. "Perren, are you sure you understand what you've gotten yourself into? Do you know that Professor Mornay intends to ransom transwarp to the highest bidder? Have you thought about the lives that would be lost in a cosmic scramble?"

Mornay laughed out loud at my prattle of questions.

155

Perren merely inclined his head. "I have thought it out," he said simply. "The resulting advantages are worth the risks."

"But there is a moral imperative even more important," I told him. "Would you have transwarp and the trilithium technology fall into Tholian hands? Or Romulan hands? Or Klingon hands?"

His angular eyes swept toward Mornay, though he didn't turn.

"Give it up," I implored, "before it gets too big to control. Transwarp can do great good under the right control. Don't make it a volleyball. She can't do anything without you and she knows it. Don't cooperate with her."

For an instant, a fleeting and definite doubt crossed Perren's emotionless face. His brows came together just that fraction of an inch, enough to tell me my words struck a disharmonic chord he recognized and feared. His chin lowered a fraction, cementing the flicker of uncertainty in our minds. Even Mornay saw it.

"I have . . . had to wrestle with my motivations," Perren admitted. "There is not always a right and wrong to choose between. Some circumstances require a choice between a wrong and a wrong. I have struggled with myself, but a commitment requires decision, which I made long ago."

"Then decide again," I prodded. "Isn't there honor in altering logic when the patterns of facts change?"

Mornay laughed at me again, a sound that could have been pleasant in other circumstances. She nodded at Perren.

"You'll cooperate," she told him. "You've put fifteen years of your life into this project. The risks aren't so great that you'll abandon it and give up the chance to bring total peace to the galaxy, are they?" She turned to us again and deflated Perren's importance by talking about him as though he wasn't here.

"How would he go back to Vulcan and explain to his family and his sponsors that he sacrificed galactic unity to a theoretical risk? The humiliation would be too great."

Affected by the stalled logic and the danger of losing Perren to Mornay's cooing, Sarda stepped forward to address his mentor directly. "You must reconsider, Perren," he said. "There are acceptable moral reasons—"

Mornay opened fire on him. Phaser-stun hit him full in the chest, catapulting him backward over a table. His arms and legs convulsed as he struck a wall. Scanner plunged in to catch him, barely keeping him from slamming to the floor. When I flinched toward them Mornay moved between into my path. I could do nothing but look on, quaking in the realization that the Vulcan friend I'd come here to rescue was now a tangled, tingling, limp symbol of Mornay's violent nature.

For a horrid instant as the phaser bolt struck Sarda, I thought the weapon was set to kill. I hadn't come here to get Sarda killed. The stun setting at least proved that Mornay was sincere about using Sarda's abilities again if she needed them. She wasn't ready to kill him. Or perhaps that was for Perren's benefit. If he hadn't been here, might she indeed have killed?

Her zeal to use that phaser kept the threat alive.

"You see?" she said. "I do not play." She warned me off with a wave of the phaser. She must have seen something, some active fury, in my eyes that even I wasn't aware of. When she once again had control, she eyed Perren. "Our goals will be realized. Things will settle our way."

Sensing the end of this dubious conversation, I opened my mouth to say something, anything, that would keep Mornay here and buy time for Captain Kirk to act. My lips parted, and imagine my surprise when I chirped like a communicator.

Every muscle in my body locked up.

Mornay blinked. "Of course!" she said. "Help from outside! I should have expected that, shouldn't I?" She turned to bark at one of the guards. "Find the communicator and bring it to me."

Easily done. A moment later, Mornay possessed both my communicator and Scanner's tricorder. She held the communicator and waited, and sure enough it chirped again. Kirk's signal! The check-in!

Scanner, still holding Sarda against his shoulder, tried to contain the bugging of his eyes and deliberately bit his lip.

I pressed my knuckles into my thighs. Now what?

Mornay came to me and held up the communicator. "Answer them. I'm sure you know what *not* to say." There was hunger and victory in her tone. She was about to find out who we were working with, how powerful we were.

Sweat trickled down my neck. The captain would give himself away when I answered that signal. I pressed my lips tight. My eyes stung.

Mornay caught the whiff of defiance. Without a pause, she made dramatic affair of switching her phaser to the "disrupt/kill" setting and turned it on Scanner and Sarda. Her expression said the rest.

I took the communicator from her.

Scanner tightened his grip on Sarda. "Piper . . ."

His message was clear enough. *Find another way, and fast.*

There was no other way. Think fast—that's what heroes do in these kinds of situations. So why was I still clicking along at sublight? With a shallow breath, I put my trust in the captain and flipped the antenna shield up. "Piper here. Is that you, Merete?"

The name shot from my lips a little too sharply. I could only hope Mornay would attribute it to my nerves.

A faint shuffle from the receiving end accentuated the tension as we waited for response. Then—

"Yes, this is Merete. Where are you, Piper?"

I took a deeper breath, all primed for a sigh of relief, then remembered the sigh would tell Mornay something. I stood there like a balloon, letting my breath out so slowly that I started turning red. "We're in one of the lab buildings," I said, stalling.

There was a pause. In my mind, a softly etched face stood beside her and told her what to say.

"Have you isolated Sarda?" she asked carefully.

"He's . . . with us."

Mornay's phaser jerked toward my friends in warning. The hints would have to stop, or Scanner and Sarda were finished. I'd never learned to lie, to bluff. Why didn't the Academy have a class in bluffing?

"Can you get out?" Merete asked, her tone telling me things.

"Not right away," I said. "The compound is booby-trapped." I watched Mornay to see if I'd said too much, but she didn't move. "It'll take time."

Another pause. Kirk's image nodded in my head.

"I'll contact you again in thirty minutes," Merete said. "If you've found a way out, we'll beam up and vacate the system before *Enterprise* arrives. It's time to haul in tight."

She had difficulty with the nautical phrase. She didn't know where the emphasis should go. The words were too even, too careful. But the message was real: *he knows.*

My shoulders trembled. I squeezed them tight and brought the communicator closer to my lips. "I agree. They've already worked our windward."

Mornay was practically under my chin in an instant. Her phaser now hovered between my eyes, conveying a message entirely different from Merete's. *Sign off or die.*

159

Why bother talking out loud at all? These subliminal messages, coming at me from a dozen different directions, were grating enough.

"Piper out," I said quickly, and closed the communicator.

Mornay snatched the instrument from my grip, her fingernails raking the side of my hand. She backed away. "Code words," she said bitterly. "And not even subtle." Without a single consideration for the privacy between the two Vulcans among us, she turned to Perren and demanded, "Who is Merete?"

Perren, however, very much realized the unethical uglies behind her question. His face went verdant with bottled emotions as, with effort, he answered, "An associate. Merete AndrusTaurus. A Star Fleet physician. She was loosely involved with Piper and Sarda when they interfered with the dreadnought affair."

His humiliation was obvious, even through the Vulcan shields. He knew damned well he was betraying something sacred when he defiled the privacy of the training melds he had shared with Sarda. Was it habit? Had Mornay exerted subliminal control over him for so long that he had forgotten his responsibilities to anyone else?

Ursula Mornay thought about what he had told her, then nodded and put her needly glare on me again. "Your friends out there can be traced. You've kindly supplied me with the means to attract their attention." She awkwardly gathered the tricorder into the same hand that held the communicator and said, "They'll be sure to answer a distress call from one of their own signals." She handed the two instruments to a guard and reset her phaser, then looked up at Perren. "See that they are locked up in the storage room. I promise you they won't be hurt unless they themselves force me to act. Such things are sometimes necessary, aren't they? For the ultimate kindness, we must fortify our-

160

selves. Take them immediately. The guards will go with you. Then meet me in the main lab."

Mornay knew Perren's weaknesses very well after all their years together. My heart sank to see it working.

Once again I locked my lips, redirecting my frustration long enough to help Scanner lift Sarda. Consciousness was seeping back as the phaser stun dissipated, but he needed help to walk. A short, cold walk to a small, cold room.

When we got inside, I let Scanner take Sarda to a crate where he could sit down. I turned instead to Perren. The mercenaries remained outside, and with my voice low, only Perren could hear me.

"Can you really think of selling transwarp to hostile powers?" I asked, my tone one of unexpected intimacy.

He tossed his head in a motion of frustration and said, "I assure you, Commander, I will destroy transwarp and myself if necessary, before I allow the flux technology to leave Federation hands."

That took me by surprise. For a moment I just gawked at him in confusion, then blurted, "So it's all a bluff."

"No," he said. "Not a bluff. Ursula will do what she threatens to do. She has her purposes and I have mine. For the moment, they are parallel. When the time of divergence comes, I will be able to control her."

"How can you be sure?"

"Question me no more, Commander!" he snapped. "You begin to irritate." That was obvious enough, judging from the way his lips curled in when he said it. With a fan of dark hair, he spun and left. The door clanged shut. We heard the grinding of a mechanical lock.

"Huh," Scanner grunted. "Vulcan is skin-deep." He glared at the door for a count, then turned back to

Sarda. The contempt he felt earlier for Sarda had apparently found new targets. There was none left here. He began busily rubbing sensation back into Sarda's arms and knees, ignoring those tiresome protocols about not touching Vulcans. Scanner never did pay much attention to them, and this wasn't the occasion to change him. "Come on, Points, you're okay. Here, lean on this. Atta boy. Got any feet down there yet?" He paused, then asked, "How are you?"

Sarda blinked to focus his vision and slowly said, "Unwell."

I flinched at the weakness of his voice and the effort he put behind it. I lowered myself onto the next crate, facing him. "Do you feel horrible?"

Only then did the whole impact of his regret surface and only for an instant. A sadness touched his downturned face. "I feel foolish," he murmured. The intense honesty startled us.

Scanner stared in amazed empathy and started to say something. I cut him off with a quick shake of my head.

Carefully rephrasing, I asked, "Do you think you're hurt?"

Sarda made a laudable effort to straighten himself, though his arms and thighs shook. Without thinking, Scanner and I each caught an elbow. "Nothing permanent," Sarda uttered weakly. "She has always . . . resented my association with Perren."

The effort drained him and he fought a bone-deep shudder, but the gloss was returning to his eyes now and his complexion was regaining its luster.

"We've got to talk," I said. "Come up with a plan of action."

"What action?" Scanner howled. "She's got us hemstitched!"

"Never stopped us before," I muttered back. "The captain's out there somewhere, expecting us to be ready for him."

Sarda blinked hard and straightened a little more. "Captain Kirk? Here?"

"Yes, with Spock, McCoy, and Merete."

Scanner added, "Yeah, and now they know we're in trouble."

I nodded, my nose wrinkling at the reminder. "And thanks to my bad acting, Mornay's ready for them. They'll walk into a trap."

"Maybe," Scanner agreed, "but she still doesn't know it's the captain, and that's gonna make her underestimate."

Nervous now, I slid off the crate and paced to the room's only opening, a newly mounted metal door with a wide, tinted duraglass window. I pressed my shoulder against the glass and peered into the stone corridor, where four mercenaries were eerily lit by those inexpensive little diogen torches. Those guards looked too casual about their job, casual in a dangerous way. Casual as though they did this for a living. Casual as though the phaser rifles were extensions of their own arms. My nervousness doubled. "We've got to buy Captain Kirk time. Mornay thinks he's on board *Enterprise*. The starship should be here soon."

"When?" Sarda asked.

I threw my hands up, only to have them clap down onto my thighs. "How do I know? Kirk never tells me anything! All I know is that Mr. Scott and Dr. Boma are bringing the ship in while Kirk lurks around here. We were supposed to break you out, and here we are locked up like penned ducks! We've got to get out of here and get on with our mission."

"Uh-uh," Scanner complained. He took that as a cue to lean back against the wall next to Sarda and put his hands behind his head. "Our mission was to separate Sarda from the witch and the warlock. We done that. He's separated."

I ignored him. It was that or whack him one, and I figured I'd save my strength. A few strands of thick hair fell around my face as I stared at the floor, cloaking me from their eyes. I'd have liked to think of my hair as golden, but somehow it never got past pyrite. The worse the situation got, the browner my hair felt. Even after all those weeks under Earth's gaudy sun. . . .

How did my hair get into this? I widened my eyes and shook my head to clear it. A deep breath helped me cope. "There's something weird about this," I grumbled, my brow knitting until it gave me a headache. "Something about Mornay isn't fitting with what we were told. I don't think she's as unenlightened as Spock thought. She was careful not to say things to us, as though she . . ."

I faltered, staring into a convenient wall.

"As though she what?" Scanner prodded.

My eyes narrowed as I thought harder, forcing myself to add up things that were abstract at best. "Perren doesn't know much about humans, does he?"

Sarda frowned. "Why do you ask?"

"He can't see through her. She's stringing him along. Saying the things he wants to hear. Like I said, she's not so ignorant. I don't think we should underestimate her. She knows better than to try to ransom the technology by itself. She knew enough to build the device. Is that going to be enough for her? You heard her talk about testing transwarp. It's the next logical step. She intends to take her leverage as far as it'll go!"

"Piper," Sarda said calmly, "your logic is acceptable, but Mornay has no support for such a project. Beyond ransoming the technology, she has no leverage. The dreadnought was supposed to be the test for transwarp, but it's not an option any longer." He paused then, fatigued by the long talk, and closed his eyes. Soon they opened again, slightly dulled from the strain. He was recovering, but I knew what full phaser stun felt like, and I frowned sympathetically.

"She might have more support than we realize," I went on, pacing now. "Rittenhouse had plenty of support. Star Fleet is only scratching the surface of the corruption. Who knows how deep it runs? Mornay probably knows exactly who to contact when she needs something."

"Even so," Sarda argued, "she will need specialized scientific help to mount transwarp on a ship, and that is assuming she can call upon people who know how to select an appropriate vessel. That takes specialized knowledge. She cannot simply call upon new scientists. Herself, Perren, and I are all who remain of Rittenhouse's science team."

I stopped pacing. Scanner and Sarda both gazed up at me, and I down at them, and I think we all stopped breathing. "No," I said. "You're not. You're not at all!"

The little stone room echoed.

"Boma," Scanner murmured.

"And he's already on board *Enterprise*," I finished.

Sarda's eyes widened as he stared at me. We had the same thought at the same time. We said it together.

"The test ship!"

Chapter Nine

"I suppose most of us overlook the fact that even Vulcans aren't indestructible."

—Amok Time

"IN HIGHER PHYSICS, concepts are not expressed as laws and certainties, but as probabilities. There is only a 62 percent chance that transwarp will work. The danger is not that it will fail, but that the test ship would fail to return from interdimensional warp travel. Professor Mornay and Vice Admiral Rittenhouse were willing to take that chance. Perren does not realize that Mornay still intends to."

Sarda struggled to hide the vestigial weakness left by Mornay's phaser attack. He knew we didn't quite understand the science he was talking about, but it didn't matter. We understood the danger. If from nothing other than the careful lack of inflection, Sarda made us understand the nightmare of being forever caught between dimensions.

"Seems there's a lot about Mornay that Perren doesn't realize," Scanner commented. "She said she's got no more use for you," he told Sarda. "How long before she doesn't need Perren anymore?"

By this time I had been standing silent for many minutes. All the parts of this puzzle were wild. A deviant professor whose theories, when twisted into reality, became a galactic threat; a renegade Vulcan, no less, whose thought patterns could barely be predicted by another Vulcan, much less a loopy pack of humans who'd come into this wholly unprepared; a starship about to become a sitting duck, no doubt sabotaged from inside by Boma—but how? Could one man shut down a whole starship crew? Even if he was a leading astrophysicist, even if he had built some of the finest war machines of the past decade, even if he did resent *Enterprise* officers for a court-martial that ruined his military career—then again, maybe he *could* do it.

More than anything I hated being trapped. If I had to fail, why did it have to be this way? If determination was a factor for Boma, then it would have to become one for me. I was on the inside, the captain was on the outside. I should be the one getting him in, not him getting me out.

I began to stalk the doorway. The guards knew they were being watched. They glared at me and shifted, lips twisting. Sometimes they rearranged the phaser rifles in their arms. They looked dirty. They looked ready. Exactly the kind of people Mornay would hire. Not an ethic to share between them.

I stared at them. Moved to the opposite wall. Stared some more.

One of the guards kicked the bottom of the door and swore at me, his lips curled back in silent rage.

My eyes narrowed. I kept staring. This was a delicate art. I had to hate them.

"Piper," Scanner warned quietly, "those blizzard brains are gonna come in here and gently reprimand you if you don't cut that out."

The wall was gritty against my shoulder, its stone cold and forbidding. It fortified my burgeoning resentment. I continued to irritate the guards with my eyes. "You can feel it," I murmured. Then, more strongly, I said, "There's a rift between Mornay and Perren. I mean to widen it."

"Yes. We must," Sarda agreed. "If Perren supports Ursula now, he will be immoral. He is in a dangerous dilemma for a Vulcan to face."

I spun around. "And we can use that. Perren's already vacillating. I saw it in his eyes."

His doubt surfaced immediately. "Piper . . ."

"Don't tell me I didn't," I snapped immediately. Under the sharp wave of my hand he fell silent. "The lives of the test ship crew—that's the angle to take with him. Either Mornay hasn't told him about using *Enterprise* as a test ship, or she's somehow convinced him it's safe enough to risk. But what are they going to do with over 400 crewpeople? It doesn't seem possible that two scientists could take over a whole starship full of military personnel."

"The logical assumption is that they will incapacitate the crew in some way," Sarda said.

"Or trick them into beaming down," Scanner added.

"Or blackmail them into beaming down." Once again the stone floor rolled beneath my feet. Back and forth, back and forth, pause for a heavy stare at the guards, back and forth again. "This is getting us nowhere. We could guess all night and still be wrong. We've got to get out of here and deactivate that sensor screen or tie up the guards or something, *anything* to help Captain Kirk get in here and do what he wanted to do in the first place. He's got to be informed about Boma and *Enterprise*."

Scanner stretched and arched his back. "I've heard of pipe dreams before, but not Piper dreams."

I returned to the window. My reflection was caught in the blue caste of the duraglass. Did I really look so tired? I felt old, but not experienced. Years had passed in minutes, all laden with this terrible impotence. Outside somewhere—my mind went out to the Argelian hills with their red and blue foliage, bathed in the light of the banded moons—there, somewhere, Kirk was waiting for me to take action. Had he understood my message? Did he know he was on his own?

The mercenaries in the hall started moving around, casting rude glances at me. The more I stared, the more they twitched. I couldn't get out, but they could get in. Their anger would bring them in. It was only a matter of degrees.

A fierce man with missing teeth and a long grassy moustache was the first to lash out. He struck the duraglass window with the butt of his phaser rifle. It bounced off. The glass hummed.

I refused even to flinch. My stare became a leer. I mocked him with my steadiness. Never mind being frozen with fear, of course. This seamy type of planet-trotter would have no trouble killing all of us with nothing but a shrug as explanation. In the reflection I saw Scanner tensely reach for the lid of a crate. Not much of a weapon, but if I had him scared, imagine what I was doing for the guards.

I didn't have to imagine. Vexation colored the faces outside the blue duraglass.

"Piper," Scanner began, a tremor giving him away, "people are morons until proven otherwise. You're courtin' live examples."

Several responses popped into my mind, but to answer him would be also to destroy the string of rage building outside the door. By now I had pressed up to the blue window tight enough to see both ends of the short corridor and keep all four guards itchy. They mumbled at each other, but they couldn't speak out loud. They didn't like my intense interest. Grass Moustache could barely stand to blink his eyes any-more, because he knew I would still be there when they opened. His three compatriots had better control, but were slowly losing it.

But I had singled out my target.

I focused on the pair of large coffee-brown eyes above that moustache. Eyes that loathed me. Ah, but

169

there is no peace in the land of pensionaries. You hire yourself out for a questionable living, you take what you get. Sometimes you get stared at.

This was more than being stared at. As the moments ticked by, I *owned* him.

His lips peeled back again as the rage boiled upward. His shoulder blades hammered against the opposite wall as he pushed himself off and brought the phaser rifle up. One coal-hard eye snapped shut, the other lining me up instantly in his sights. If only it had been courage holding me there, I would have had a better story to take home.

My legs turned to jelly. I was held in place only by sheer astonishment that my ploy had worked—too well.

"Piper, get down!" Sarda shouted. He slid off the crate, but not soon enough.

Grass Moustache fired his phaser rifle. A single lance of bright orange light decorated the gray corridor and made the diogen touches glow. I dropped to a crouch, covering my head. Above me came the sickening sizzle of cooked metal and melting duraglass. As the window disintegrated, I also heard Grass Moustache's fierce growl. Then shuffling, and another voice.

"Idiot! Cease firing. We haven't got any place else to keep them!"

"We'll keep them in an old shoe!"

"Get hold of yourself! Don't lose your pay over nothing."

Cautiously I looked up when the sizzling began to fade. The upper corner of the door was dissolved, along with a ragged portion of duraglass. Along the edge of the glass, a phosphorescent red glow was darkening as it cooled. Not enough. Not big enough. My hope sank.

I pressed my hands on the floor, wondering if I

dared stand up and show myself again through what remained of that window.

The chance never came. An explosion rocked the lab, a great boom that threw us all to the floor and vibrated in our bones. It was very close—maybe even this building. The ceiling crumbled and dropped chunks of plaster and stone in dusty clouds.

"Take cover!" I shouted across the room. I was gratified to see the two of them huddled beside a huge cooling cabinet as part of the side wall expanded into a barrier of loosened bricks. Unfortunately, it didn't collapse. On the other hand, if it did, would it take the whole ceiling—and us—with it?

From across the compound came another explosion, much more distant this time, but much more powerful. It set off a string of popping noises, as though pressurized containers were being exposed to too much heat.

Commotion broke out in the corridor. From the floor, I listened.

"What's happening?"

"Hellfire, that's what! Come on!"

"We're assigned here, not out there."

"Move, I said!"

Then, new voices from down the corridor:

"Where's Lugrode?"

"I don't know. I can't find anybody from the city side."

"What do you mean, you can't find 'em?"

"They're gone, that's what I slavin' mean!"

"Two of you come with me."

"Ain't movin'."

There was a distinct thud and a groan as authority was rudely reestablished.

"You! Stay on that door."

I got warily to my feet, still hunched down, but now able to peek through the bottom of the duraglass at the scampering mercenaries. The voices were a cacophony now, impossible to separate. Only when a man skidded in from the south side with a startling announcement did I begin to feel the revitalization of hope.

"The security signal on the weapons locker is jammed!" the man howled, as though somehow it was pinching him to be cut off from his weapons supply.

I spun toward Scanner and Sarda, fanning my way through settling stone dust. "They're cut off! And people are missing! He's in!"

"Huh?" Scanner blustered. "Who's in?"

"Captain Kirk! I don't know how, but he's inside!"

He slumped and rolled his eyes. "Aw, Piper, I wish yawl'd get off that nag and ride a real horse for a change." He sat down wearily.

I dragged him to his feet. "Get up," I growled. "We're getting out of here."

He stiffened, but the doubt lingered. "How?"

I had been gazing at the mutilated bricks of the wall, but now I spun on him. "Stop asking that and start thinking it! You heard. They're down to two guards on us and they're stuck with the weapons they have in hand."

"Sure," he complained. "Those puny little phaser rifles you could shoot a moon down with!"

"Get used to it, mister, we're getting out. Now."

Scanner raked both hands through his hair. "Dang! You're even starting to sound like him!"

His statement caught me by surprise. And an even bigger surprise—I didn't like it. My own silence sat on me like a rock. My lips clamped shut, my face aching. The smoke hurt my eyes.

Sounds of demolition continued to filter through the outside walls, punctuated by electrical crackling. Sarda was already palming the damaged wall. If he carried any of Scanner's doubts, he never let me see them. He may or may not have believed we could

break through that wall somehow, but he knew none-
theless that I would never be satisfied unless we tried.
What he didn't realize yet was that I would never be
satisfied until we succeeded. I'd die in this place
before I would force Captain Kirk to have to rescue
me. Somehow he had already managed to get inside,
confound the guards, put several of them out of commission, cut off their weapons supply, and set off a
chain of explosions to cripple Mornay and Perren. He
was a tough act to follow. I would never be satisfied to
merely applaud. If I went down on Argelius, this stage
would have the marks of my fingernails in it.

Scanner's words, fraught with annoyance and the
truth of fatigue, haunted me. I began to question my
driving force even as we picked at the bucking stone
wall and tried to wedge leftover computer parts between the large bricks. No more bursts of courage
came to mask my fear; now I had to deal with it all.
With the silence came an overwhelming need to get
back into space, into space vehicles, to systems I
knew and weapons I understood, to the place where I
had experienced one great triumph before. I began to
focus on that. If only I could get back into space . . .

*Before you can outguess an enemy in three dimen-
sions, you've got to be able to maneuver in two.*

"Fine," I spat under my breath.

This drew unwanted attention. Sarda hesitated. "I
beg your pardon?"

"Both of you get back." I moved in on the wall, not
really knowing what I would do when I felt the cool,
broad bricks beneath my palms. The bricks had shifted
against each other, leaving uneven gaps where moments ago there had been only creases. There had to
be a weak spot somewhere. "All right," I said through
gritted teeth, agreeing with yet another unheard urge
from you-know-who in my memory, "when in doubt,
do it the hard way."

"I'm afraid t'ask," Scanner muttered.

"Where's something we can throw at it? What's in those crates?"

I moved toward the heavy metallic storage crates, ignoring the shuffle behind me and the errant conversation.

Sarda's voice was lowered. ". . . useless to attempt to talk her out of it."

Then Scanner, more like a hiss. "Talk her out of it? Hell, I'm not even going near her!"

"Keep an eye on those guards at the door. Make sure they're not watching," I said as I shoved one of the crates toward the weakened wall, then doubled back for a second crate. "Help me lift this."

Insanity must be contagious, because I didn't get any arguments. Scanner heaved a doubtful sigh but made no comments as the three of us wrestled the second crate onto the top of the first. Sarda's Vulcan strength allowed him to serve as anchorman while Scanner and I lifted and steered the crate into place, wincing at the screech of metal against metal.

"Okay," I said. "One more."

"One more?" Scanner howled. "We jus' barely got that one up there!"

"That one in the corner should do."

"But that one's empty!"

"I know it's empty. How else could we lift it that high?"

"Piper, I think yawl need shore leave."

"No thanks. I just had all I need of Captain Kirk's idea of shore leave. Come on. We haven't got all day."

The empty crate was soon in place easily enough, high atop the other two crates, looming just under the plaster ceiling.

"Now what?" Scanner asked. The same question, silent now, hovered in Sarda's expression.

I wiped my palms on my thighs. "Help me get up there."

"What?"

"We'll never find enough junk in here to add up to the weight of a person, so I'll provide the weight to break the wall. It's simple."

"It's nuts! You'll kill yourself."

"Beats staying in here. Come on, help me."

I didn't want to have to make it an order, yet they both sensed the nearness of that extreme. I wasn't yet comfortable with command status, but if I had a phaser I would use it, and rank was a kind of weapon. Beside me, Sarda stood silent, hardly blinking. I looked at him.

Softly, perhaps seeking approval, I told him, "It has to be done. There isn't time for alternatives."

His hands disappeared behind his back. Slowly he nodded. "I would prefer to take the risk myself," he said.

"I know." My voice hovered between us. "But it's my responsibility."

Chivalry wasn't dead; they helped me climb into the highest crate. The metal was cold against my thighs and shoulders as I huddled inside and shut the crate, then braced myself as well as possible. A shiver wracked my arms and legs. Seconds passed as I fought to control it. I had to be ready, body and mind. My weight had to be used correctly.

"Ready," I said. Lying, of course. "On three."

Three came a lot sooner than I expected. I rocked the top of the tower while Scanner ticked off, "One . . . two . . . *three!*"

Into my small, dark world came the sickening sensation of the ground dropping out from under me. The planet tipped. My head struck the crate's metal wall. My own weight crushed down onto the back of my neck, forcing me into a ball. Then came an abrupt jolt as the crate struck stone. Within the crate, noise doubled on itself and pummeled my eardrums. I was falling again, turning again.

Another jolt. This one bent the crate into a weird geometric form, and me with it.

The crate struck the floor and continued to tumble at least one whole turn. The door was ajar now, bathing my confused eyes with raw yellow light. Diogen! The corridor!

Twisting painfully around, I kicked the door outward and rolled out of the crate onto a pile of destroyed bricks in time to see Scanner and Sarda stumble through a ragged opening in the wall. At the same moment, the two remaining guards, eyes bugged with astonishment, skidded around the corner to gawk at us, too stunned even to raise their phaser rifles.

It was Scanner who bolted to action first. He swept up a chunk of brick and pitched it hard. It flew down the corridor and struck one guard where his hand was gripping the phaser rifle. He choked and dropped the weapon between his knees.

Sarda was ready. He moved in quickly, wrestling the guard down, bracing the phaser rifle between them. Without thinking, I grasped a brick and gave it a two-handed heave at the second guard. He saw it coming, but never had a chance to dodge. The square of gray brick slammed into his chest and drove him against a door. He collapsed, gasping. Only then did Sarda succeed in pinching his own opponent unconscious.

He swirled around, his eyes afire, his arms flexed and ready.

For a head-clearing moment I remained on one knee among the rocks, gathering eye contact with my crew before plunging onward into the storm. We needed it.

I shoved myself to my feet, quaking with conviction. "Let's get out of this squirrel cage."

The outside of the lab building was even in more disarray than the inside. Once we escaped into the dark openness, my sense of immediacy was prickled

176

with a sense of vulnerability. Caution returned where moments ago it would only have been a burden. Sarda and Scanner followed me as we twined our way across a compound, hiding from running mercenaries who were scattered about, desperately looking for something to shoot at. Us.

I pressed my shoulders back against a wall as I peeked around its corner, motioning for Scanner and Sarda to close up tight behind me. My fingers made the shape of a phaser.

Keeping his voice low, Sarda asked, "What are you planning?"

"Find the captain," I said. My skin tightened as three mercenaries trotted past our hiding place, heading for the main lab. Surely by now they knew we were free. Well, we were *out;* free was something else.

"How we gonna find them without communications?" Scanner asked. "They could be anywhere in a kilometer radius."

"They're inside this compound, Scanner," I insisted. "The explosions we've been hearing have got to be Mornay's booby traps. Somehow Kirk and Spock are setting them off. It's just a fabulous tactic, that's all, letting the enemy provide the firepower behind the confusion. I should've thought of it the minute Perren mentioned the security system. Kirk should've been an urban guerrilla."

"With his track record," Scanner pointed out, "he prob'ly was. I dunno if we should try horning in on his business."

I relaxed for a moment and peered at him. "You never want to try anything. You're always afraid to take a risk. Why'd you ever join Star Fleet? Why didn't you stay in Tennessee and raise pigs?"

"I'm 'fraida pigs."

Simple question, simple answer. He ducked a swat from me, and I shook my head, unable to hide the grin that pushed its way up.

"If Mornay's going up to *Enterprise*," I thought aloud, "we've got to get back to Rex."

"Like I said," Scanner pointed out, "we need a communicator to key into the automatic transporter link."

"Ursula may not reach the starship," Sarda said then. His voice was a sudden, steadying buffet against the frantic compound noise and Scanner's Tennessee twang. "Captain Kirk may be able to prevent her from doing so."

"I can't make that assumption," I said, more sharply than I intended. "I won't let him down again."

The determination in my voice caused silence behind me. It swelled up like a cloak and covered my shoulders. Whatever happened, I had to make it true. *He* was counting on me.

As I stood there against the cold stone, every muscle in my body knotted, knowing that lives depended on my next decision, I realized the essence of the schooner *Edith Keeler*. Whoever the woman was, whatever she had been to James Kirk, she was now personified in square yardage of sailcloth, gleaming brightwork, brass, and bowsprit—she was what saved him from the horror of these hard moments in the life of a starship officer. It didn't get easier, as I had once hoped. I understood that now. I would never get used to these moments. I could only save myself from them, find some ship to sail away on, to become sane again and gather up what I needed to go back to space, just as he had learned to do. Even with cold ground beneath my feet, I felt once again the surging of the deck under me, with the deadly and beautiful ocean an arm's length away, nicely mastered. I heard once again the wind whistle inside the main, and I almost looked upward. If I could learn to pull those halyards and sheets at the right moments, maybe . . . just maybe . . . I could pull the right ropes here and get us out of this alive.

Key word: maybe.

No—I didn't want to hear that. Shut up, Piper, and get to work.

"Come on," I said before I'd even planned where to go from here.

We made it safely across to the next building, a shed of some sort with a maze of wooden fences in pathetic disrepair, but terrific material to hide behind. Unless they spotted our actual movements, they'd never be able to pick out our forms in this mess.

"Sarda," I began, "they must have some kind of communications board around here."

He moved close, keeping himself balanced in an awkward position by holding onto the cross beam of a crooked fence. "Indeed. In Ursula's main lab. She had to be able to contact supply ships, and her guards, of course."

"Just point in the right direction, will you?"

He ignored my irascibility and quite simply pointed. We skulked across the paddock area, skirting fences upon fences, halfway around the farm until only a short expanse of open area lay between us and the main lab.

"I'll go alone," I said.

Both arms. Not even a chance to get up. I looked to one side—a stern Vulcan truth. And the other side—Tennessee smoke.

I let my head drop for a moment and took a deep breath. "Listen, both of you. If I fail, then you'll still be free to try again. You heard what Captain Kirk said. This mission is more important than any one of us. Maybe more than all of us."

Sarda's expression never flickered. He had no intention of arguing, any more than he intended to let me go in there alone.

It was Scanner who spoke. "If we let you go, how're we gonna know what crazy thing to try next? Face it, Piper. Nobody thinks like you."

"Oh, thanks, Scanner, thanks a lot. And here I was, waiting for an oath of loyalty."

"Oughta know better by now."

I stole a glance at Sarda and was relieved to see that his mouth was drawn upward on one side and he was deliberately not looking at Scanner.

"All right," I conceded. "I've got enough to fight. I don't need to be fighting you too. But stay in close formation. Sarda, you know the way in."

"Roughly. I was not permitted to roam freely."

"You lead then. Scanner, right behind him."

Scanner moved into position. "Bet you wish you had a phaser," he teased as he shifted past me."

"Hell, I wish I had a slingshot," I admitted. Only then did it occur to me that I probably could have made one out of available materials if I'd had my training screwed on straight. Luckily, neither of them thought of that, and I got away with it. "Go," I said quickly, taking advantage.

My nerves electrified as we hurried across the open area, dodging searchlights as the beams swabbed the ground in search of us. Mornay must have been planning the theft of transwarp for some time—at least since the failure of Vice Admiral Rittenhouse's scheme with the dreadnought. She must have had this compound set up immediately afterward, and had the security system already activated when she, Perren, and Sarda arrived, though I now believed Mornay and Perren had planned this from the moment Vice Admiral Rittenhouse died. Even now, sporadic explosions and crackling voltage told us the chain reaction of sabotage was still running. Kirk must have found some way to trigger those booby traps. It was the only explanation that made sense—and I really needed things to make sense right now.

Except the part about Dr. Boma. My heart withered as I remembered that element. I deeply wished it hadn't made such sense. I had a sudden, absurd, overwhelming desire to stand up straight and yell at the top of my lungs, "CAPTAIN KIRK, YOUR SHIP IS IN DEEP TROUBLE! WHERE ARE YOOOOOOOOO?" Luckily, I managed to keep it to myself for the moment. Somehow, I'd find him. Together we'd make our way back to that distant schooner with the mysterious name.

Even as the reassuring thought filled me with strength, we slipped into an alcove and were met with a sight that siphoned the strength out again.

A few meters away, between the main lab and a carefully arranged pile of file crates, stood Ursula Mornay and four mercenary guards. They held their phaser rifles sighted coldly upon Captain Kirk and Mr. Spock.

I crouched, almost by reflex alone, and pulled Sarda down beside me. Scanner saw our movements and dropped instantly. Our blood cooled as we watched and listened.

The captain and Spock stood side by side, unflinching before the phaser rifles, but definitely sobered. She had them. Somehow she had caught them. But what about McCoy and Merete?

"How'd she get them?" Scanner whispered.

"Shh. Listen."

". . . really think you can pilot a starship with a handful of hired guns?" Kirk was putting to Mornay.

"I have crewpeople, Captain," Mornay said as she opened and tuned a hand communicator. "All I have to do is pick them up. And you'll help me do that, or your crew will remain in their semicoma until they die. I have a knife at your throat, Captain Kirk. I promise, I will cut you."

Scanner's voice buzzed faintly at my ear. "What's she tawkin' about? She got 'em strapped down in front of old movies, or what?"

"Obviously she has the crew hostage somehow," Sarda whispered back, even more faintly.

181

"A whole starship?"

I shushed them with a swipe of my hand, and myself was stilled by the expressive glance Kirk exchanged with Spock. I ached to read his mind the way Spock could. I saw a thousand thoughts in that one glance, truly a trade of minds, perhaps of plans. So close . . .

I pressed my hands on the jut of wood that partially hid us in our alcove shadow, pressed until the wood cut hard into my palms and forced me to accept the damning reality that Captain Kirk was out of reach, at least for the moment. My drumming message would have to stay inside my head even longer.

Mornay brought the communicator to her lips. "Samuel? Have the guards beamed aboard?"

From the instrument in her hand came a dull buzzing voice. *"All who checked in are aboard now. Some are still missing and we can't seem to find them."*

Mornay paced a few steps and eyed Captain Kirk, who remained carefully impassive. "I'm not surprised," she said. "As soon as you're ready, beam up the captain and Commander Spock. I'm sure they'll be cooperative, but have the guards ready just in case."

"They're ready, believe me. We've dealt with those gentlemen before."

The voice was distorted by the distance between us and the communicator itself, but there was no mistaking that arrogant cadence. Boma.

My message to Kirk fizzled within me. He already knew. And Boma had already won. The *Enterprise* was in orbit, and Boma was in control. It seemed unfathomable that one man could incapacitate 400-plus people who were supposedly Star Fleet's best, but then again, I was supposedly Star Fleet's best too.

I drew my shoulders inward, fighting a terrible shiver. Luck does run out, even for Star Fleet's best. Perhaps my luck had been spent on the dreadnought affair. Maybe that was the best I'd ever do. Maybe I couldn't beat that act. It was hard enough trying to get used to being called Lieutenant Commander when I hadn't even completely gotten used to being called Lieutenant. Everything I did seemed to be running about ten minutes tardy.

Incapacitate a whole starship crew? Damn her, that wasn't fair! I gritted my teeth and forced my insecurity to become anger. Anger was workable stuff, and she could only kill me once.

I dug what was left of my fingernails into the slat of wood and listened harder.

Mornay was fiddling with the communicator. "Perren, are you there?"

Static from the damaged electrical system caused the frequencies to jump, but soon the cool voice came through. *"I am making final installments in the portable memory."*

"Hurry up. We're ready to go."

"What about the guards?"

"They're already aboard the starship. We'll prepare to leave the solar system as soon as you beam up. We're going now."

"I shall be there momentarily."

Without the courteous, if mechanical, sign-offs usually used over communications channels, Mornay flatly readjusted her instrument and hailed the ship again. I kept my eyes on Kirk. He was absolutely unmoved, as relaxed as he had been during those long, quiet hours of ocean crossing when there was nothing to do but watch the sea roll. He wasn't tensed, ready to attack, waiting for that minute flinch that would give him his cue. Spock also stood calmly. Only when the eerie whine of a transporter beam caused my skin to tingle did I realize why the two officers made no effort to free themselves; they *wanted* to get back on board the starship. If there were fights to be fought, at least *Enterprise* would know its guardians were where they belonged, doing what she needed them to do.

As we watched, the clutch of oddly matched personalities dissolved into elongated prisms, and dissappeared.

Without a pause, I redirected my thoughts. "Let's go. The main lab, Sarda."

"This way."

We got about three steps before Scanner grabbed my arm and said, "Hold it. Yawl aren't gonna believe this. Look what I see."

What he saw was two familiar figures clumsily skulking their way across the compound, heading in the opposite direction from where we were going. Before I could stop him, Scanner had stuck his fingers in his mouth and let fly a shrill whistle. Seconds later, McCoy and Merete were gathered into our little nest.

"Where've you been?" McCoy hissed, eyes wide.

"Where've *you* been?" Scanner retorted.

"Looking for you."

"I can top that," Scanner crowed. "We bin lookin' for *everybody*."

I squirmed between them. "Scanner, shut up or I'll cork your face. Doctor, what do you know?"

"Didn't you hear that conversation?" Dr. McCoy flipped a hand back at the now-empty compound.

"Only the end of it."

"Oh." His eyebrows worked as he steadied himself to tell us what he had hoped we already knew. In one way he hated having to repeat it. In another, he was quaking to get it out. The conflict within him showed on his face, at once anguished and enraged. "Boma waited until the ship was in orbital status, then he gassed the whole ship with a hypnogenetic compound."

"A who?" Scanner blurted.

"A narcotic. Sleep-inducing gas. Deep and dangerous sleep. It causes severe reduction of metabolic rate." He inched closer, as though to intensify his words and used one hand to illustrate the terrible, intangible truth. "Anyone who ingests it can literally sleep himself to death unless an antidote is provided soon enough."

"The knife at Kirk's throat," I murmured.

"It's more than that," Merete said, glancing at Dr. McCoy as though she knew what he was thinking, what he was feeling. "It's a progressive coma. The time element makes a difference. Mornay didn't tell the captain that. Maybe she doesn't even know it."

"That class of drug is an idiot's playground," McCoy insisted, his fist now clenched. Suddenly I saw something in him that I hadn't before. He'd always seemed amusing to me in his moments of exasperation, but now he moved beyond exasperation to downright bitterness. He seemed to feel about the *Enterprise* crew the way Mr. Scott felt about the ship itself. The crew was *his*. His children. His expression grew stony with violence as he thought of what Mornay had done to them. "Many drugs in that category don't have antidotes at all," he said, nearly growling. "She might not know that or even care. She might just as easily be lying to Jim by telling him that she can undo what Boma's done. The crew might already be dead."

His fatherly wrath, and the accompanying sense of helplessness, spurred me to convictions even beyond my own. I leaned toward him and promised, "You'll get your chance to turn the tables, sir. We'll get there somehow."

"Yes, we must," Sarda interrupted. "Perren cannot possibly know about this aspect. He would never participate. I'll take you to the lab." He started away. The quickness, the suddenness of his movements triggered a foreboding deep inside me. He was hurrying now, but his motivations had shifted. Some hidden imperative in his movements told me that, and the echo on his heels was *Perren, Perren, Perren*. Was there enough logic in the galaxy to turn Perren now? Sarda disappeared into a narrow doorway, leaving only the question behind.

I motioned Dr. McCoy and Merete after him, meaning to bring up the rear guard.

Scanner stepped past me. "Don't worry. It's just hero worship."

Sharply I answered, "I can't count on that."

Unease set in on top of the fear. I set my determination on kill and pushed my motley group onward into the lab building after Sarda. My memory kept scouring the vision of Kirk's face, his glance at Spock, Spock's silent response, for some hint of their plans, or at least their opinions. No answers yet, though. I was still on my own. Rats! Things were really getting bad when I couldn't even pretend that Captain Kirk had all the solutions in his pocket.

Sarda paused at the end of one hallway, confused by the dimness and trying to remember which corridor held the main lab. The passages were narrow and moist, the stone walls considerably older than those of the building we'd been held in. We had no idea how long the farm had been abandoned, but a faint animal scent still clung to the mossy walls. The corridor was a dead end, with only one doorway at the left.

"Sarda," I called quietly before he reached the door.

He stopped, halting the whole line of us, and I squirmed past the others into the lead.

"Stay behind me," I told him. Leading with my shoulder and a good dose of nerve, I peeked into the lab. Nearly stripped bare, the lab held only a few engineering consoles, a computer outlet, and a few empty metal crates. There weren't even any chairs left, if there had ever been any in the first place. I motioned the others inside. Scanner nudged the door shut.

There was only a little more lighting in here than in the corridor, though these lights were electrical rather than the diogen filament torches that ran through the hallways for function rather than for close work. Evidently Captain Kirk's handiwork with the electrical system had depleted the power leading to the labs. But that didn't matter any more. There wasn't anyone left but ourselves. The work done in these labs was ominously complete.

Sarda appeared beside me. "The communications board should be near the mainframe outlet. They would have no reason to take it with them." As he spoke, he hunted through the piles of discarded equipment and storage crates. "Yes, here it is. Partially dismantled."

The two of us lifted the portable console up onto a nearby cabinet. It looked like a computer board with a hangover.

"Can you fix it?" I asked, grimacing in empathy with the mangled board.

"They likely did not intentionally dismantle it," Sarda said, "but merely cannibalized some parts. We may be able to bypass those and create enough signal to trigger your ship's transporter."

"Scanner, what do you think?"

He moved in between us and thoughtfully twisted his mouth. "Doesn't look too bad. You want me to try?"

My shoulders drooped. I gave him a deadly glare.

"Okay, I'll try," he said, and put his hands on the console.

The doctors and I spent several minutes gathering the bits and pieces that fit Scanner and Sarda's descriptions of what they needed, and the communications console quickly began looking more like its own kind. Scanner pulled up a crate and sat down before the tilted mechanism, and began attempting to contact the automatic pilot aboard Rex. "He's up there, I know he is," he muttered self-consciously.

"Can you boost your gain?" I asked.

"Rex'll answer, don't worry."

I couldn't help it. I still had trouble trusting a ship

that looked like the remains of a brewery explosion. I leaned over his shoulder, trying to make sense of the red blips on the tiny screen as they ran through white cross hairs, seeking matched waves. "Maybe you need more power. There's got to be a—"

Nonregulation bulldozers hit us from behind. We never even heard them coming. Only their vicious warning growls preceded the impact, and only by a fraction of a second. I was struck hard in the middle of my back with just enough balance of force and restraint that I was momentarily stunned but still quite conscious. The room spun, a whirl of pain and faces. My legs withered under me as the pain in my back took hold and my nervous system responded. Something gripped my arms and pulled me up and around, then crushed me back against a pile of crates, and a gnarly hand cupped my throat. For an instant I almost tried to strike back. Mercenaries were only human, after all—

But these weren't Mornay's hired guards. These faces hated us well beyond the value of a credit payment.

A Klingon disruptor brushed my cheek. Stale breath wreathed my face.

His head at a menacing tilt, Gelt snarled his satisfaction. "Dance with me."

With great effort I pulled my eyes from his and confirmed the nightmare: four Klingons at attack stance held disruptors cleanly on Sarda and the others.

"Where is it?" Gelt demanded. "The science you're making here."

"We're not the scientists," I choked past his grip. I tried to keep the pain out of my voice for the sakes of my friends. "As you can see, they took their equipment and left. We're not even sure what they were doing."

Nary a flicker of belief damaged his anathema.

"Transwarp," he whispered. Well, so much for that bluff. "Where is it?"

All right, if he wanted answers, I'd give him answers. "About 35,000 kilometers away from here by now, I'd say."

His grip at my throat tightened, clawing inward under my ear. My carotid artery pounded, and I had to drag in what little breath he let me have. Starved for oxygen, my lungs began to ache and the pain in my back throbbed enough to make me dizzy.

"Straight up, I'll wager," Gelt said.

His smugness enraged me, as it had once before. I bumped my arms against his hard chestplate just to show him how I felt, and forced my voice to rasp past his grip. "That's right, fossil face, and there's *nothing* you can do against a starship."

There was something intensely satisfying about being despised by a Klingon. Not particularly pleasant, but satisfying anyway. If my mouth hadn't been rock dry, I'd have spat at him. Past his ugly face, McCoy and Scanner were refining the art of astonishment.

Gelt's lips peeled back in hatred as he fanned his gun arm outward and barked at his nearest fellow tarantula, *"HIch Qorch! Toogh!"*

As soon as his hand was free, Gelt ripped open his belt guard and pulled out the kind of dagger that's so mean looking it draws blood with appearance alone. And it was still in a sheath! Gelt wanted to see the blade, though. With a snapping motion, the sheath struck the floor and bright silver glinted between his face and mine. "Your friends are corpses," he said. "But you . . . you are what we call *bortas choQ*. Do you know the words?" His hand pressed tighter on my throat. His teeth were gritted, his whisper one of hunger. Only his lips moved. "Revenge meat."

The blade rasped wide. Now there were claws on it. Never let it be said that Klingons had no sense of drama.

I tensed, waiting for the impact. Die with a Klingon blade between my ribs?

The room erupted into flaming lances. From a hidden alcove came a burst of phaser fire. First one Klingon, then another were blasted across the room into heaps. Not really understanding, I reacted first and thought about it later. I jammed my knuckles hard into Gelt's right eye as he turned to look. He howled, and lost his grip on my throat.

Two more Klingons were sighting down at that alcove, exchanging disruptor fire for phaser bolts while trying to take cover behind a table and a lighting stand. Sarda dropped back onto a counter and brought his legs up, and nailed one of the Klingons in the side of the head with both heels. The Klingon went down, but rolled over and staggered up again, to be caught by a phaser shot. He skidded into Gelt's legs, and both went down.

Free now, I fought to stay up on thready legs. Gelt was trying to get up from an awkward position, tangled with his unconscious cohort, and I knew I had only seconds. I reached upward, grasped a heavy airconditioning unit from a newly carved wall outlet, braced my feet on the wall, and heaved. It stuck. With an inelegant shift of my weight, the unit jolted loose and I pulled it down on Gelt's head, adding what strength I had left to the already weighty object. Gelt convulsed once, and went limp.

I slumped against the wall, gasping. My vision dissolved into a black tunnel before I could assimilate what was happening with the last Klingon. My ears roared, then whined, then began to accept the gift of blood and air again. I hung a hand on the open collar of my flight suit, glad it wasn't a turtleneck.

I hadn't realized I was slipping down the wall until Dr. McCoy's voice beside me was accompanied by firm support from both sides. "Are you all right?"

Scanner was there too. "Did he cut you, Piper?"

I shook my head and blinked down at the fuzzy shape of a Klingon disruptor, still clenched in its owner's hand. "How come," I rasped, "we're the only ones obeying . . . Argelian law?"

A sigh of relief fell from Scanner. He looked first at the inert form of Gelt, then at me. He shook his head, struck by my raw invertebrate-level hatred of Klingons. "You know, I think you must have some tribble in you," he observed.

My vision was starting to return now that I could breathe. I coughed once, mostly to make sure I wouldn't make a fool of myself when I answered them. With an indelicate shove, I straightened up. "Scanner, get back to work."

"You all right, though?"

"Sure . . . go on." I pushed him back toward the communications console. Not very convincing; I was still leaning on Dr. McCoy, surprised at the strength in his slender form.

What had happened? Had I been imagining it when I saw Captain Kirk and Mr. Spock being beamed away? Were they here? Had the cavalry come in again?

I blinked and took deep breaths, willing my vision to clear.

But the form in the alcove was neither Kirk nor Spock.

Perren moved somberly from the archway. The phaser was still held upward, but he was looking down at the last of the Klingons, now a quivering lump at his feet. He was carrying a nondescript metal case by the handle, which left his right hand free for the phaser. Now he looked up and made a fleeting eye contact first with Sarda, then me. Clutching the metal case tightly, he moved out of the alcove, keeping his back to the wall and the phaser firmly raised.

I moved away from McCoy. Walking was an effort. My back throbbed where Gelt had bludgeoned it. I didn't stop until my own crew were all behind me.

191

Sarda came up at my side, though, and I knew there was nothing that would wave him back.

"Thank you," I said.

Perren nodded a single, simple nod. "You're quite welcome."

Disturbing moments shuttled past as we wondered if we were captive again. Five of us against one Vulcan and a phaser . . . incalculable odds indeed.

Perren, perhaps sensing that, provided the answer. "I have no intent of challenging you," he said, not quite able to mitigate the edge of warning in his tone. He moved sideways, toward the door, the rich green quilt of his tunic making a shock of color against the gray stone. "I am sorry our goals cannot harmonize."

"Neither do yours and Professor Mornay's," I told him, also moving slowly toward the door, hoping he wouldn't feel threatened yet. "Mornay intends to use *Enterprise* as a test ship for transwarp. She doesn't care about the safety systems or the lives of the crew."

"The crew will be beamed down when we reach our destination," Perren said. "They will live."

"They may already be dead," Dr. McCoy spoke up forcefully, a distinct blade of professional experience giving credence to his statement. "Mornay's either lying or fooling herself about how easy it is to provide an antidote. Narcotic gases shouldn't be played with, and to her it's all a game." He nailed the words to Perren's chest with a hammering truthfulness.

"She's finished with safety, Perren," I carried on. "If transwarp fails, she'll take over 500 people with her into interdimensional hell, and if it doesn't fail, the crew of *Enterprise* is already forfeited. She's fooling you. Don't let her."

Doubt flickered on his fine Vulcan features, but only a flicker, and soon controlled. He swallowed stiffly. "Ursula has planned carefully. The narcotic is not lethal."

"She's a theorist," Merete interrupted in the toughest tone I'd ever heard from her. "She's not a medical specialist. No one can learn how to handle hypnogeneticides overnight. It takes months just to isolate correct dosages. Are you going to believe her or Dr. McCoy?"

Perren wrapped his arm around the metal case, and I was stricken with the undeniable image of a child clutching a stuffed toy. For many seconds he never moved, nor even blinked. The inner battle slimmed his eyes and drew his blade-sharp brows together. Beside me, Sarda tensed with a kind of empathy only Vulcans could understand, a remote kind of blending in which the integrity of personal privacy was constantly at risk.

The wild, impossible victory against a sister ship recurred in my mind, and Captain Kirk fed me one of his favorite tactics from the reaches of my memory. *Push, push, push till it explodes in your face.*

"You're being used," I insisted. "She'll turn on you. Hundreds of lives will be the cost."

"Piper is right, Perren," Sarda said. "I entreat you, believe her."

He hadn't used the word "correct." He had said "right." A subtle difference; a moral difference.

Perren stepped over one of the unconscious Klingons and reached the doorway, then hesitated. He seemed unwilling to leave us until he had made his conclusions and then explained them to us. That alone showed me his unsureness. His need to explain proved to me that we were breaking through.

"I must tread a center course," he said finally, and not without some diffidence. "I must stand by my calculations and my hardware. I am willing to do so for the sake of my goals. This—" He waved his phaser once over the fallen Klingons. "—is the sort of event I am trying to stop." The twitching bodies of our ene-

193

mies, still caressing their weapons, illustrated his point neatly. "Ursula underestimates Vulcans. It is a perfect cloak for me to wear."

Sarda stepped toward him, now standing slightly to one side between me and Perren. "It is illogical to sacrifice the lives of an entire starship crew," he said, reverting to simple didactics.

"It is illogical to sacrifice all I have worked toward on the basis of a danger that is only theoretical." Perren's voice jumped a shade toward that irritation I'd heard before. "If the starship crew is already dead, then they are no longer a factor. You are free now. I shall neither help nor hinder you. There is nothing your ship can do against a starship." He looked from me to Sarda, the change evidenced by only the barest tightening of his mouth. "I regret that we must part."

Sarda remained absolutely still. Only I, standing so near to him, perceived the advance of his tension and his efforts to hold himself back. "We need not part," he said.

Older and fully trained in his Vulcan controls, Perren had less trouble subjugating his regret. Having been caught up in the rare experience of human-Vulcan friendship, I'd wondered for a long time now what friendship would be like between two Vulcans, if indeed this was friendship and not merely that strange training bond necessary between mentor and pupil. As Spock had pointed out to me, Perren and Sarda had much in common from the beginning—mostly the fact that each had had trouble fitting in to current Vulcan conformity. It must have been comforting for Sarda to find another Vulcan who understood his awkward place, someone of his own race that he wasn't obligated to explain himself to. I wished I had thought of these things earlier. I'd have been more prepared for what was coming.

Perren nodded, but not in agreement. It was something different entirely. "Then I regret that we part before our objectives can be shared. It remains only for me to wish that you live long and prosper." He spoke slowly now, without the edgy tone of underlying rebellion that had always been there before. Backing out into the corridor, maintaining his expression, he vanished.

My hand reached out for Sarda, who was already moving.

"Sarda, wait!" I gasped.

He paused at the door, cast a glance back at me, and fitfully gripped the stone for an instant as though hoping to find something to say that would explain. He was torn in half. Even a Vulcan couldn't hide that much torment.

He pushed himself off the door frame. We heard his boots on the hard floor of the passageway.

"Sarda!" I started for the door.

Scanner's voice caught me back for an instant. "Piper, I got it!"

I drew an invisible circle around him and the doctors with my finger as I skidded to a stop at the doorway. "Beam up! I'll contact you!"

Deep Argelian night had thoroughly penetrated the stone building now that most of the electricity had been strangled. I was tired of feeling cold. I'd only felt warm once since leaving Earth, and that was because of a Klingon growling at my throat. Even running through the building failed to heat my blood. The injured muscles in my back screamed with each stride, and my head pounded now whenever I took a breath. At every turn I caught a glimpse of Sarda. He was healthy and fast; keeping up with him was terrible work. At the turn of the last corridor, I gave in to a useless urge and called once again, "Sarda, wait—"

To my utter amazement, he whirled around and stopped. Was he surprised that I followed? Had he forgotten so much?

195

He turned again, in time to see Perren's distant form retreat into a smaller building.

I jogged to a halt a few feet from Sarda and steadied myself with a hand on the wall. He turned once again to me, hesitantly at best.

"He's probably getting the last of his equipment," I said, drawing a deep breath, "before he signals Mornay to beam him up."

Sarda gazed once again through the night at the other building, now still and darkened. When he turned back to me, the quandary in his eyes was frightening. His fists balled up. I doubt he was even aware of it.

"I cannot leave Perren in this situation," he said.

I closed the space between us by another step. "You're not leaving him. He's leaving you."

With a step of his own, he widened the gap. "Piper, you do not comprehend Vulcan complexities. I have no time to explain them to you."

With a nod I showed him that he was right. Slowly I asked, "Do you really think Perren doesn't understand what he's involved in?"

Inner struggle tightened his mouth. "That is no excuse to abandon him."

My shoulders sagged as I tried to think of logical arguments. But even a partially trained Vulcan knows his own thoughts. If he had made up his mind to forfeit the past for the future, even a hazy future, I knew no power in the universe could pull him back.

When arguments were not enough, when logic could only fail, it was time to go beyond them. My shoulders squared as I backed away a pace, showing him that I was ready to accept his decision.

"Then you'll have to choose."

Sarda no longer glanced indecisively at the building that had swallowed Perren only moments ago. His eyes lost their focus as he gazed at me, and I felt utterly unseen. Perhaps he was searching for a way to explain the inexplicable. With my silence I hoped to show him that no explanation was necessary. As for my own message, my presence on this planet would have to speak for itself.

Sarda privately navigated his sea of uncharted emotions without help from me, for I could no longer help him, no matter how much I wanted to.

He raised his chin a fraction. "There is only one choice," he said, his voice solemn and low.

I willed myself not to nod, to flinch, or even to breathe. I wouldn't show the tiniest hint of feeling betrayed. I hadn't been betrayed, after all; he had simply made the best decision for himself. That was all I had any right to ask of him.

Searching for the final words, the words that would get me smoothly out of this terrible last encounter, gave Sarda an extra few moments.

His arms relaxed at his sides. "I go with you."

Chapter Ten

"The trigger has been pulled. We've got to get there before the hammer falls."

—Errand of Mercy

WHEN WE GOT back to the ship, it was unfortunately in the same shape as when we left. I finally had to admit Rex wasn't just an industrial nightmare but the ship I was stuck with. It felt pathetic and small as we gazed out the viewing portals at the pure beauty of *Enterprise,* her design still striking me as elemental. I would probably always get this shock of awe at a glimpse of a starship, and I would probably never get used to it or take it for granted. Engineers and space technologists may have designed her, but they shared the heart of an artist.

"Are we in one piece, Scanner?" I asked, leaning over his shoulder, still peering at the starship in orbit several degrees farther out.

"Functional," he answered with a shrug. Even so, he tapped several linkages just to check.

"How long will it take them to install transwarp?"

From behind me came a mellow voice finally free of its stress. "Perren has become most efficient in his engineering," Sarda said. "He and Boma can install the complex into a starship's warp system in roughly eighteen hours. Likely they will not do it right away, but retreat to a safe haven where they have access to other people who are also followers of Rittenhouse."

I nodded my thanks to him. His presence still surprised me, but I was finally warm. In our crisis aboard the dreadnought those few weeks ago, he had been forced to stay at my side because of circumstances. Today the decision was his own. For the first time in a long time, I stopped worrying about what Captain Kirk thought of me. Sarda's testimonial was all I needed. Even now I felt the warm buzz of telepathic support from him, a subtle echo behind my thoughts that gave me that extra supporting nudge. I still couldn't interpret that buzz—whether it was intentional or not, whether it was normal for Vulcans or not—but it was welcome, deeply so.

"We have to act immediately," I said, sliding into the command chair. The new leather breathed under me and cradled my legs and back as though it knew I was still fiercely aching from Gelt's assault. As if to remind me, the Klingon disruptor I'd taken from one of the unconscious swine dug into my rib. I pulled it from my belt and handed it to Merete; Sarda did the same with his. Scanner wisely vacated the seat beside me and moved to the navigation/sensor station farther to the right, allowing Sarda to take the place beside me.

"What do you have in mind?" Dr. McCoy asked with a controlled touch of incredulity. He was leaning forward in one of the passenger chairs, watching his home ship and no doubt wishing he was there to do his part.

I empathized with his frustration, and it kindled my sense of purpose. "We've got to keep them from warping out of orbit."

Every eye in the ship struck me. Scanner straightened up like a long skinny balloon and yelped, "Oh, yeah? While we're at it, let's rearrange the solar system so the planets all line up in a row."

McCoy leaned even farther forward. "This ship against a starship?"

"Sure," Scanner mocked. "If you can get me within

199

fifty meters, I can cut 'em up with my little laser torch. If you can get me within ten, we got a claw. S'pose they'd notice?"

The doctor ignored him. "Wouldn't it make more sense just to get away and notify Star Fleet?"

"By the time Star Fleet could get out here," I said, "Mornay could have taken *Enterprise* anywhere in the known galaxy. They're not leaving this system if I can help it."

"Piper, we don't even have phasers big enough to carve a moustache on that ship's face," Scanner said, pointing descriptively.

An unexpected voice interrupted us. "Leave her alone."

Gazes shifted again, this time aft. Merete stood alone in the obscurity of the hatchway, one hand braced upon the ship's gnarly bulkhead as though to say she trusted it. Her face was eclipsed by a band of shadow. The hem of her robe made a purple wedge in a walklight, and at the shadow's top a crescent of pearl-blond hair shone in the glow of a tiny bulb near an electrical access. Beyond that, there was nothing of her to focus on but her intense presence of purpose.

"Piper is our commanding officer," she said. "We're going to do what she says and we're not going to argue anymore. If we die," she added softly, "then we die well."

Merete was so quiet and unobtrusive that I often forgot how much I told her, how much of my past and my present thoughts she kept diligently stored for me, things I'd said both intentionally and unintentionally. Only when one of those things surfaced at exactly the right moment, thanks to her sensitive timing, did I remember to appreciate her. I wouldn't forget again for a long, long time.

True to the drama of the moment, she never moved. She let her words sink deep into the fabric of what was to come, and drew no more attention to herself. She

200

wanted me to have the attention, we all knew. Even Dr. McCoy settled back as though he too somehow felt better about all this.

Sarda moved slightly, switching from helm tracking to the computer readout screen before him. It cast a fine blue glow on his pale alien features. "The *Enterprise* is moving out of orbit on impulse power. Taking a heading of point three-seven."

"Heading out of the solar system," I uttered. "When they get clear of the planets, they'll go to warp. Follow them. Just don't get so close that they'll want to fire on us. They'll know we're coming."

"I can already hear 'em laughing," Scanner said.

"Let's hope they are, Scanner," I countered immediately. "It's an advantage not to be taken as a threat too soon."

"They won't fire on you," Dr. McCoy pointed out. "It's a waste of energy. They know they can outrun us at warp."

I looked at Sarda, and he silently confirmed the logic. Obviously Leonard McCoy hadn't spent all those years aboard a starship without learning a thing or two about military logistics.

"Thank you, sir," I said to him, then hunched forward on my command console as we eased out of orbit and slipped into the path of the distant starship.

Rex's old impulse engines grumbled, but soon pushed us up to the speed of *Enterprise* and even a little beyond. We gained on her slowly, while three of the system's planets rolled by. Four other planets were well out of our trajectory and only one remained for us to pass before we cleared the solar system.

"Scanner, how do these terrific tractor beams of yours work?" I asked.

His boyish face screwed up. "Huh?"

"How do you haul something that's heavier than your engine thrust capacity?"

"For short range, you anchor on the nearest planet or moon and use it for traction."

"Can we brace on a planet and hold *Enterprise?*"

"Hold *Enterprise?* Well, I guess so, long as she's in orbit or somethin', but—"

"No buts."

"You gotta have some buts, Piper." He spun his chair around to face me. "We can't hold a ship the size of *Enterprise* against her own thrust, not even if we hang onto a whole sun. We could tow her, but only if she was adrift." The acrid tone was gone from his voice, likely driven out by Merete's blanketing promise. I particularly noticed it.

"How closely can you pinpoint the tractor beams?"

"Hell, I could pull the yoke out of an egg at 20,000 kilometers."

"Good," I murmured. "That's good."

"I give. Why's it good?"

My right shoulder went up and down once. "You said this ship is a *Fesarius.* Let's see what it can really do."

Scanner puffed up at that comment. He had no idea what I had in mind, but he was suddenly anxious to prove the truth of his own promise. Even if it killed us. If it didn't work, none of us would be around to flay him with an I-told-you-so.

"Sarda," I began, "pinpoint the joist where the port warp nacelle is attached to its strut and feed the coordinates into Scanner's tractor beam. That's what I want, Scanner. Put a lariat of traction right around that joist."

It was so wild he couldn't even think of anything to say. He blinked hard and took a deep breath, then glared accusingly at his equipment as though to get a mental running start on it.

"Make the beam as tight as possible," I instructed. I punched the nearest computer access switch. "Computer."

"Working," the pleasant voice answered.

"Release all safety monitors, overload capacitors, and limiters for the tractor system to manual control at the helm station."

"Acknowledged."

Good. No arguments from underneath either. I needed that.

Scanner shook his head, unable to resist a 50 percent grin. "That's the first time I ever heard anybody ask a ship's permission to rip its guts out." He squinted and peered at me over his shoulder. "You sure you got enough authority to do this?"

I gripped the arms of my chair. "Power up the warp engines. Zero thrust. Power only. Sarda, feed the energy through to that tractor beam. We've got a lot of starship to pull on."

"Powering up. Maximum in twenty-point-seven seconds." Even as he spoke, *Banana Republic* began humming with bottled warp power.

"Hold at maximum," I said. "Go to two-thirds sublight, heading sixty degrees subport."

"At that rate," Sarda read out slowly, "we will be within tractor range of *Enterprise* in . . . one minute, eighteen seconds."

"When will we be in tractor range of that last planet?"

"We are nearly there now."

"Scanner, get ready to grab onto the planet. I think you know what I want to do."

Perhaps it was fortuitous that he only nodded. He bent close to his sensor console, coordinating the impossible.

I put my glare unflinchingly upon the ivory essence of *Enterprise*. In my mind the starship had sails. She surged now through an ocean of splash and stars, but there were no steady hazel eyes gazing over her bow. She knew he wasn't on her bridge and she felt helpless, like a warship with no rudder, rampaging frantically through a blockade. She was calling out to me.

I had finally reached the point at which sacrifice is more than bravery's flag. Finally, my life meant less than my mission. Never before had I truly believed I would die, much less take these four fine lives with me. Fail, yes. Die . . . no.

But now, this time, I was ready.

"Piper, they're outrunning us," Sarda said, urgency spiking his words.

I clutched the command console. "Don't let them. If they warp out before we can engage—Merete!" I snapped. "Get to Scanner's station and keep your eyes on the matter/antimatter flux monitor for *Enterprise*. Tell me *exactly* when she's about to go to warp."

Her footsteps announced that she was crossing the limited deck space, and I resisted the glance that would have confirmed it.

"They're at point five . . ." she read out. "Point five-five . . . six . . ."

"Scanner—"

"I'm ready."

"Just the nacelle."

"Ready."

Tension crackled in the cabin.

Around us the sound of our engines drummed their effort.

My hands left sticky prints on the command board. "Sarda, get us up there . . ."

"Closing. One-hundred-fourteen kilometers now."

"Warp point-eight," came Merete's soft voice.

"Seventy-thousand kilometers."

"Point eight-five . . ."

"Forty thousand kilometers."

"Point nine . . ."

"Twenty-five-thousand kilometers."

The old ship thrummed. Its voice made a solemn backdrop for the voices of my crew as they ticked off the elements of chance. *In range, in range, in range . . . we've got to get in range . . .*

"Point nine-two, Piper," Merete read out, unable to control a quiver of warning. "Point nine-five . . . nine-eight . . . nine-nine . . . warp sp—"

"Now, Scanner!"

A massive jolt sent us all rolling. Neither human strength nor Vulcan could hold against the sudden force. *Banana Republic* used the planet for an anchor and set itself up as a pulley between natural stationary force and the science of propulsion. Every casing, baffle, strut, crosspiece, and joist on the old tug was abruptly put to the test of its lifetime. I was plastered to the port bulkhead, crushed between the emergency exit and the forward claw control, unable to turn or even move at all. *Banana Republic* went up on an invisible axis like a bead on a taut string, tilting in space between the planet and the starship, finding its own best angle against the killing forces that were tearing it inside out. Never before had it been asked to hold a piece of a starship against warp thrust.

The cabin lights dimmed and sagged out as their power was sapped, leaving us with only the off-angle light of the Argelian sun to see by. Even the tiny emergency bulbs flickered along the walkways. Staticy crackles splintered through the electronics. Around us the roar of our engines expanded to a deafening whine. The engines were coming forward for a visit, or at least a last meal. The grating noise of coilplate being stretched like muscle tissue was as sickening as it was terrifying.

Artificial gravity lost its grip. As it struggled to regain control, it pulled our bodies in a dozen directions at once, as though it meant to tear us apart limb from limb. I heard someone yell, but the words were indiscernible under the din of mechanical torsion. I ached to help, but all I could do was cling to the base of a nearby chair and wait for the hull to rupture and all

205

our precious atmosphere to hiss out into space before we exploded into a billion bits.

As suddenly as it had begun, it ended. The great yank was over. The tractor beams automatically compensated for the lack of thrust, luckily, or we'd have found ourselves buried in that planet's surface.

Moans filled the cabin. Behind them, the engines sputtered and groaned, slower and slower, grinding like old batteries. The power was gone, no matter how the backup circuits combed the system for more.

McCoy was pulling Sarda to his feet as we gathered ourselves on a pitched deck. The artificial gravity was off kilter, and not likely to improve.

I dragged myself back to the helm after doing a quick head count. They weren't in good shape, but they were all alive, which relegated them to my second concern. Scanner and I made it to the viewport at the same time. Sarda, limping noticeably now, was soon to follow.

The *Enterprise* was still there . . . sort of.

"Goddang!" Scanner gasped. "You twisted it!"

Sure enough, the starship's port nacelle was off kilter on its strut. Not broken off, but wrenched enough that the delicate balance needed for warp speed was quite impossible.

"Remarkable . . ." Sarda breathed.

Dr. McCoy peered between Sarda and me. His expression was easy enough to read. Very low, with a strange and solemn intimacy, he murmured, "The angel falls . . ."

I stared at him. The grimness of his message, sent across space to our captain, caught me by the heart.

Merete broke the sweaty silence with a prophetic truth. "So much for the test ship."

McCoy straightened his thin form and poked a thumb outward. "If I were you, I'd fix that before the captain sees it."

Several seconds lolled by while Rex—and I—panted for life. Beside me, Sarda was stiff and silent, his breathing also ragged as we shared an unbelieving glance.

"Status," I choked.

He pulled himself to his station. "Checking."

Scanner still gawked at the starship as *Enterprise* rotated slowly in space on a bizarre angle. The wrenched nacelle made her look like a child's broken toy. "How you gonna explain to Kirk that you twisted his ship?"

"They can't go to warp," I thought aloud. "When help arrives from the Federation, we'll all still be here."

"I dunno about you," he rasped, "but I left back when you started tawkin' about tractor lariats. I may never come back."

"Sarda, where's that status report?" I must have really wanted to know, since I asked twice.

Sarda bent tightly over the readout hood. "Warp power depleted . . . tractor capacity down 86 percent . . . impulse drive out . . . major structural damage to central bracings and all main couplings . . . stress damage in major underpinnings and the matter/anti-matter containment baffle . . . emergency leakage control is still in operation, but all other electrical maintenance systems are at tolerance." He fell silent for a moment, not to speak again until he straightened and directed his quiet words to me. "Piper . . . life support is completely down."

Beside me, McCoy stifled himself from repeating what he had just heard. Hearing it twice wouldn't make it less true or provide a solution. Merete, though, couldn't keep from struggling upward to Sarda's station and peeking into his readout hood.

I had to push my voice out. "How long, Sarda?"

"On remaining battery power, no more than eight minutes."

I pressed a hand to my pulsing forehead, took a deep breath, and shook myself. "Uh-huh . . . well . . . this is a good time to go see how the captain's doing."

"Are we within transporter range?"

"Barely," Sarda answered tonelessly.

I struck him with a look. "That's a yes."

"Yes."

Merete asked, "They'll pick up our transporter beams, won't they?"

"Undoubtedly," Sarda said.

McCoy pushed close. "I'm no engineer, but it's my business to know how the ventilation system on that ship works. They can flood any compartment with narcotic gas at the touch of a button. We won't last two minutes."

"No choice, sir," I told him. "We'll just have to hope they're in disarray right now and can't move that fast."

"You know better than that," he warned, and he was right.

I turned to Scanner. "Are there oxygen masks on board Rex?"

"You mean portable ones? Nope. Just the kind that have to stay tied into the wall units. Quit lookin' at me like that, Piper, I didn't design the damn things."

"We'll have to use the emergency masks aboard *Enterprise*."

"Beaming in one at a time? We'll never get the chance."

"We'll have to make the chance. Sarda—"

Without a pause Sarda answered, "Six minutes, twelve seconds left."

"There's our alternative." I led the way aft toward our tiny transporter alcove. "Sarda, how long to beam five people from one pad?"

Calculating on the run, he called, "A total of one

minute, thirty-three seconds if we beam consecutively, including recalibration time for each beaming, plus preset time for the operator."

"I'll operate it," Scanner volunteered. "I know this unit like the inside of my mouth."

"Get it ready. Merete—"

She was beside me in an instant, and we were both looking down at the Klingon disruptor she held. "It's basically the same as a phaser," she said. "This word indicates the force ray, the kill/disrupt setting. That doesn't leave a body. This is kill/intact/heat. It *does* leave a body. These are stun settings one, two, and three, one being the lightest strike. Three is the worst; it causes instant viral rotting of living tissue. It's technically a stun setting, but the victim isn't meant to live long. And this toggle gives you narrow beam, wide field, or microbeam."

"Got it." I slipped the disruptor into my belt again and handed Sarda his own, repressing a shudder of disgust at having to use weapons of such calculated cruelty. "Merete, Dr. McCoy," I addressed, turning in the narrow passage as Scanner set the coordinates, "you go first. Don't wait for us. As soon as you materialize, put on the nearest emergency masks. Then head for sickbay and get that antidote process going."

"You bet we will," McCoy said with a thorny nod. "Good luck."

"Good luck, Piper," Merete echoed solemnly as McCoy maneuvered her onto the pad first.

I scowled and nodded my best response, which wasn't much considering the circumstances. It was definitely a yeah-right-get-going acknowledgment, but I just had to hope she understood. Certainly she deserved better from me.

"Energize," I said, and Merete dissolved into a pale spectrum. "Hurry, sir," I told McCoy instantly, "you're next."

The transporter hummed once again, flushing us all with the faint nausea common to nearby dissolution, and McCoy was gone.

"Sarda," I said with a terse motion.

"I prefer—"

"No arguments. Go."

Logic, thankfully, told him I was right. He pressed his lips flat and moved into the cavity, where, a second later, he buzzed into nonexistence.

Scanner busily reset the mechanism, working with calm assurance.

"You go next," I said. "Captain's last off the ship and all."

His hair flopped over one eye as he shook his head. "Not this time."

"Scanner—"

"Nope." He nodded toward the chamber. Then he grinned. "No arguments."

I was relieved that I could still smile.

A touch of regret surged through me with the first sensations of dissolution, to be leaving my first command vessel behind and derelict. *Rex*'s rumpled inner hull blurred around me, disintegrated, and reassembled into the clean white bulkheads of *Enterprise*'s hangar deck.

"Good choice, Scanner," I mumbled as the last quivers of dissolution faded and reality became whole again. The hangar deck was the emptiest place on the ship, and the biggest single space, thus the hardest to fill with any kind of gas. Sarda stood a few feet away, plainly relieved to see me materialize. Per orders, the doctors were already gone.

I stepped immediately away from the beaming area; *Banana Republic*'s transporter was just about old enough not to have the safety devices that modern equipment had, and I had no particular desire to merge molecules with Scanner. Sure enough, he hummed into being only three seconds later, exactly where I'd been standing. True to his word, he was fast with that geriatric transporter.

"Masks?" I blurted.

"Yonder." Scanner led the run across the hangar deck to what he knew was the nearest emergency-provisions locker. Of the three of us, he had served longest on *Enterprise* in a true crewing capacity. For Sarda, the starship had been a science assignment, drawn only shortly before I too had found myself unexpectedly *Enterprise*-ing.

Scanner pulled himself to a halt on the locker's handle and yanked it open. There were small fire extinguishers, but the hooks for four oxygen masks were empty. "Dang! Mornay musta had her people go round and collect 'em in case the captain got away from her."

Sarda shifted as though he was about to explain the illogic of that, then changed his mind when he remembered that Ursula Mornay had plenty of illogic to go around.

"There've got to be others, Scanner!"

He glanced around the hangar bay, then made a decision. "Right. And I know where. Come on."

Since we were already on the starboard side, we dashed with him to the small hangars where the Arco attack-sleds were stored. Had we been closer to the port side of the hangar deck, the big Galileo and Columbus shuttlecraft would have provided perfect protection and plenty of masks, but this was much faster at a moment when time was crucial. Mornay undoubtedly knew we were on board by now, and would soon take action against us. We had to be ready.

Sarda got the hangar door open and Scanner squeezed through immediately, scrambling to the top of the nearest sled and forcing its hatch open. That was when a telltale hiss in the vents told us that Dr. McCoy had been completely right. Gas!

"Scanner, the gas!" I shouted.

His arm disappeared up to the shoulder and he grimaced with effort, but soon pulled out a mask. He straightened and tossed it to me, then buried himself deeper in the Arco's hatch, searching for another mask. Above him, ghostly pink fog shot from the ceiling vents.

"Scanner, put your own on!"

In a moment he resurfaced and glanced up at the pink gas, then called, "Sarda! Here!" A second mask flew.

"Scanner, hurry!" I called.

He was still digging deep into the attack sled when the gas started to spread around the sled. He finally came up with a third mask securely in hand, and struggled to balance himself on the slippery hatch bracings. Had he been at floor level, he might have had a chance. But there were ventilators directly over his head, spewing gas. It spread ungodly fast.

"Judd!" Sarda's voice was muffled by his mask.

Scanner wavered. He made a final effort to bring the mask to his face, but his muscles flagged and he collapsed onto the lid of the hatch as it drifted shut beside him. He slid onto the solar wing with a hollow bump and sagged into our arms. Though he was already unconscious as we eased him down, his hands clutched at our clothing. He was still fighting. His sheer determination affected us both, perhaps Sarda even more than me. He supported Scanner's head and gripped one limp hand, but there was nothing we could do.

Sarda's brows knitted in anguish as he put his hand on Scanner's chest, then looked at me. "He took a full dose. His heartbeat is too slow."

My fist struck the Arco's photon sling to vent a burst of rage. "We can't help him. I just hope the doctors made it to sickbay. It's up to them." In the next seconds, I made one of the hardest decisions of my life—and for someone who was only twenty-five years

212

old, I'd had too many of those. I stood up and said, "We have to leave him. Mornay'll be sending her guards down here. Let's be gone by then."

Sarda forced himself to agree, and we crossed the hangar deck at a run.

The corridor shocked us with the sight of a dozen crewpeople collapsed in midstride. They were pale and pasty, as though phasered down. Sarda quickly knelt among them, checking pulses. "These people are barely breathing," he said, unable to keep the heaviness of disgust out of his voice. "This midshipman's already dead."

One, and counting. I thought of Scanner. *Dead. What a word.*

The hiss of a turbolift door down the next corridor drove us quickly up the nearest deck-to-deck spiral crawlway. We barely made it, and I had to draw my feet up, out of sight, while several of Mornay's hired lizards ran past the opening toward the hangar deck.

I listened until there was nothing left to hear of their footsteps. Above me, Sarda climbed a few rungs, then stopped. I felt his concern.

"It's not likely that they will move him, Piper," he said, keeping his voice down.

Until he said it, I hadn't been sure of what I was thinking. I squinted upward into the brightness of the tube. "I guess you're right."

He pulled off the uncomfortable mask and attached it to the communicator belt under his uniform shirt. "Where are we going?"

Nice handy ladders . . . empty tube . . . big ship . . . I stripped off my own mask, hooked it to a belt loop, and shrugged. "Up."

And yet, a more specific destination kept turning in my mind, no matter how I tried to apply logic to the situation. Sarda had surmised that Mornay, Perren, and Boma wouldn't try to install the transwarp device until they reached a comfortable location where they were totally in charge. They wouldn't be in Engineering, then. No point in going there. The doctors didn't need my incompetence in medicine to help them find the antidote for the narcotic gas, so no point in going that way. Besides, Merete and McCoy weren't the people I needed to see right now. I had prevented any hope Mornay might have of taking the starship out of the solar system on warp power, and surely they knew by now that nothing but several weeks in spacedock would realign *Enterprise*'s delicate nacelle balance. They wouldn't bother trying to repair such wild damage. All that sounded perfectly logical, and I was ready in case Sarda asked, but my real motivation was nothing more than a subliminal echo deep in the least logical corners of my thoughts. It was an irresistible call. Rotating and growing ever stronger in my mind was a single word: *bridge.*

The *Enterprise* was as quiet as a floating coffin. Each entry into a new deck, a new corridor, chilled us with the sight of collapsed crewpeople dropped in their tracks by Mornay's ruthlessness, then mashed together on the starboard side because of our little trick with Rex. The starship was worse than empty. It was cataleptic.

And traveling through it, thanks to me, was like a maze of dead ends. Everywhere we turned, doors refused to work or were jammed partially shut, turbolifts scraped and rasped in their tubes, or refused to open for us at all because they were simply too damaged to allow passengers to trap themselves between decks. The ship's automated maintenance system was fully enabled, cutting off many access routes through the ship that were now dangerous.

Even worse—I couldn't feel the presence of Captain Kirk. Common sense told me he was here. I'd seen him and Spock beamed on board. But I couldn't *feel* him. Where was he? Had Mornay, in some fit of unpredictability, beamed him somewhere else to com-

plicate any bid he might have for freedom and the
welfare of his ship and crew? Might she have gassed
him and Spock along with their crew, in case she
needed to impress Star Fleet with the caliber of her
hostages?

As we wended our way through the innards of the
great ship, I kept trying to find Captain Kirk with my
intuitions. I clamped my mouth shut when the inclina-
tion arose to tell Sarda my feelings. Vulcans already
thought humans were a little short of a harvest, and I
didn't need to throw more fodder on that field.

Finally we were spared any more sights of the
crippled crew when we reached a direct turbolift to the
bridge. We stood side by side and looked at it as
though there was no lift inside and we'd just fall away
into eternity if we stepped in.

"Disruptors," I uttered, clueing us simultaneously
in to the missing element. As with a single motion, we
drew the weapons from our belts.

"Set for light stun?" Sarda asked.

"Heavy stun."

He looked up. "Not the third setting."

"No. Second."

I looked at my weapon after setting it, unable to pull
my eyes or thoughts away from the dial. I knew Sarda
wondered why I was hesitating, but I had no clear
answer yet. My fingers moved like separate beings on
the disruptor dial. An extra three clicks. And a lock.
Kill/disrupt.

"Kill?" he asked. Whether he was surprised or
disappointed, I couldn't yet tell. He hadn't been with
us when Captain Kirk made me believe in the urgency
of the situation—that any single life was expendable,
even my own. The time had come to act on that sour
truth.

Sarda left his own weapon on stun; I was glad he
did. It fit into my plan.

Even through the conviction, his question made me

215

think twice, forced me to make the awful decision a second time. "I have to be taken seriously," I told him. "It's imperative."

Neither of us liked it very much. Only that, the evenness of our regret for what we had to do, kept Sarda from controverting my decision. That, and other things between us that still defied definition.

With a sigh of commitment, I stood up. Fortified against my own decision, I led the way back to the bridge turbolift.

There were no words between Sarda and me as we rode to the bridge, flattened against the sides of the lift. Words had lost their value. And my mind was already on the bridge.

The doors hissed open. With a shout of warning, I burst out, followed by Sarda, led by my disruptor. Several faces snapped around in shock. Weapons came up.

I picked a target and fired. A scream filled the bridge as one of Mornay's mercenaries withered into gory lights and smoke. I turned my disruptor on Mornay, my readiness to kill confirmed by the leftover scent of incinerated flesh and bone.

The first voice was a distantly familiar one. I hadn't heard it in a long time, and then only briefly, but it hadn't been soon forgotten.

"You again!" Samuel Boma's face flushed beneath its deep brown complexion.

Professor Mornay, gripping the handrail on the upper walkway, glared at him. "I told you someone had invaded the compound to get Sarda out," she said roughly.

Boma drew in his brows and pointed. "You didn't tell me it was *her!* I could've warned you!"

"Why? Who's she in particular?"

Boma shook his head. "You don't want to know." It was hard to believe this was the man who had designed the dangerous dreadnought that was meant to put the

216

galaxy on the edge of war, who had kept his cool enough to fool Star Fleet into accepting his help, and who had somehow managed to take a prime commander like Montgomery Scott by surprise and gas down the entire crew. I forced myself to remember those things and not slacken my guard.

By now I'd assured myself there was no one on the bridge but who I saw: Mornay, Boma, and three remaining mercenaries who were manning helm, navigations, and command intelligence stations. There was no sign whatsoever of the bridge crew—Mr. Scott, Mr. Sulu, Uhura . . . the bridge looked raw without them.

"Sarda," I said, the order silently following.

He took careful aim, holding the disruptor in both hands, and one by one struck each guard with a stun bolt. Mornay and Boma had no choice but to watch and wait until the four of us squared off across the bridge from each other.

"Where's Perren?" I asked. "Did you leave Argelius without him after all, Professor?"

She gave me a smug nod. "Keep guessing, hot spur."

I battled against the quiver of my voice and demanded, "Where's the captain?"

"Held tightly hostage, that's where."

"Those aren't answers, Professor."

"I don't owe you answers. My guards are on their way up here. Do you think I'm foolish enough to let myself go unprotected? The instant you entered the bridge, my security forces were alerted. When the turbolift doors open, you're dead."

That word again. I ignored Sarda's glance. I wouldn't have known what to tell him anyway. I waggled the phaser at Mornay and Boma, who were standing near each other near the Engineering subsystems monitor. "Down there, please, both of you."

Boma hesitated, but Mornay merely widened her weird little grin. Now what? What could I do if she

217

wasn't even intimidated by a Klingon disruptor set on kill?

"Gladly," she said then. "Out of the line of fire." She led the way down to the command module, stepping over the crumpled body of one of the guards. Boma followed.

I hated the fact that she was right; putting them down there made it easier for her marauders to fire freely at us when they appeared. "Sarda, can you jam that turbolift?"

He moved immediately to the communications station and placed his disruptor down on the console to free both hands. What I asked of him was no easy task. The turbolifts were especially designed to countermand any artificial jamming, to avoid trapping passengers anywhere on the ship. Sarda would have to reroute its programming both through the computers and through the engineering of the ship. If he had time. If, if, if. Another word, like dead.

When he had done what he could at Engineering, he crossed by me to Communications and started tampering.

I snaked sideways along the handrail past Sarda and down the gangway, trying to put myself in a position where my single disruptor could protect Sarda from whatever came out of the turbolift while still keeping a wedge of threat over Mornay and Boma.

"Hurry, Sarda," I urged.

"Trying."

The communications station clicked and whirred under his hands, but I could see in the tension of his jawline that he wasn't succeeding against the automatic resistors of the turbolift system. That was confirmed when the turbolift doors puffed open.

Sarda rolled away from the station to give me clear aim. His disruptor, left on the Engineering console, was out of commission for us.

My finger flinched on the trigger, ready to kill again.

218

The phaser that came out of the lift to aim at me was also quite ready to commit murder.

"Nobody move!" a strong voice shouted. A single phaser. Human eyes behind it. A hero's eyes. A captain's eyes. They reflected his ship.

"Captain!" Like an idiot, I was still holding the disruptor on him.

He recovered sooner and redirected his weapon at Mornay, quickly assessing the situation, lumped-up guards and all. He was still wearing the brown tunic and beige trousers from Argelius, which told me he'd been too busy to slip back into a uniform. Either that, or the uniform had nothing to do with who he really was deep down.

I forgot to breathe. "You're here!"

He nodded. "Commander, would you mind?" He pointed at me, then down at Mornay and Boma.

The disruptor. Oh, damn. My hair bounced as I looked from him to Mornay, back to him, and back to Mornay. Finally comprehension sank in and the disruptor in my hands moved itself to the people it was supposed to be guarding. "Right . . . ," I murmured. "Sir, there are guards on the way up here," I said breathlessly.

"Yes, I know. They had a little trouble getting by Mr. Spock and me."

I readjusted my feet. "Oh." So much for the guards. "Where were you, sir?"

"Before or after we broke out of our cells?"

"Uh . . . after."

"We've notified Star Fleet Command," he said, "given Bones the specific name of the drug the crew is under, incapacitated most of the professor's guards, and put an isolation field around the transwarp mechanisms," he now looked at Mornay in prime connection, "so even the Professor and Dr. Boma won't be able to engage it."

The bridge fell silent.

I lowered the disruptor slightly. "Is that all?"

Numb, dreaming, drunk . . . I could've taken my pick.

"By the way, Piper," the captain began, circling the upper deck with his phaser still steady on Mornay and Boma.

"Sir?"

He raised a brow at me. "You wrinkled my starship."

A ball of compunction blocked my throat. "Aye, sir, I know that, sir. You should see what it did to *my* ship. I'm sorry. I didn't know what else to do."

"No apologies," he said. "I was considering the self-destruct sequence myself."

I blinked. "You're joking."

"It wouldn't be the first time." His strong words were directed every bit as much to the two on the lower deck as to me. He meant to have his message clearly given. "A starship commander must always be ready to use the last resort. You'd be surprised."

Darn right I would be. "Aye, sir," was all I said. Behind us somewhere, my first command ship drifted, derelict. I heard its noble moans in my mind.

Mornay and Boma exchanged an unreadable look.

I should've blown the doors off that damnable turbolift when I had the chance. The contemptible thing opened again behind Captain Kirk. Presuming it would be Mr. Spock, the captain didn't turn soon enough.

"Phasers down! Don't move, Captain." The form was Vulcan, but not Spock. Perren held his own phaser square at the captain's spine. He reached around and pulled Kirk's phaser away from him, put it on the floor, and kicked it down the gangway where nobody could reach it. "Now yours, Commander."

My glance connected briefly with the captain, but there was nothing I could do. Perren was unpredictable, I'd seen that for certain. The captain's face grew rosy with anger. He didn't like being caught off guard—another thing we had in common.

I lowered my weapon.

"Down here," Perren instructed.

Until I could think of something better, I did as he instructed. Soon, both weapons were lying down the gangway, out of reach.

"Now move over there, Captain Kirk."

The captain stiffly obeyed, but I noticed his true nature remained unsmudged—he made sure he was standing between that phaser and me.

"That's right," Mornay spoke now. Her voice seemed strange after all the fluxes of victory and defeat that had passed the bridge in the last few minutes. The weird grin was gone, though. Her transwarp mechanism was out of commission for quite a while. Isolation fields couldn't just be pulled down overnight. "My turn again, isn't it? I'm not giving up. I'll get away." She tapped her graying temple. "It's all up here. And you'll never interfere again, any of you. Perren," she said, her tone rising, "for the good of the galaxy . . . kill them."

Vulcan or not, he was quite liable to do it. He'd let us go once before, and we'd returned to haunt him. The horrifying thought arose that Mornay might indeed know him much better than Sarda did, and might have more control over him than we guessed.

No time for analyses.

Perren hesitated, but it wasn't the kind of hesitancy that gave me any confidence. He leveled the phaser on Captain Kirk.

Suddenly I said, "No." I stepped past the captain, and, in the boldest bet of my lifetime, walked straight into the line of fire. Perren's stare flickered at me. "You know I understand you," I said to him. "Maybe better than she does. And I think you know her

221

opinion of you. You can't keep retreating under her banner. You're going to have to make a new decision for yourself, right now. Because I'm going to take that phaser away from you."

If I died doing it, I would be the only one to die. Perren knew the captain and Sarda would be on him in an instant. He'd never have time to recover with me standing so close to him. And everything would grate to a halt once again, and for good.

Forced into confrontation with himself, Perren parted his lips as though silently trying to explain—to himself, probably.

I lifted a hand. Put it out. Touched the phaser.

He raised his chin, eyelids drifting down as he looked now at our hands, cupped on the same weapon. His fingers tightened, then relaxed.

With a tug, the phaser was mine.

Perren, his head lowered in deep contemplation, dazedly joined Mornay and Boma on the lower deck.

But the hatred was not over. It boiled now in the pitch black of Boma's eyes. Perhaps I had ruined his plans one time too many, and with too much finality. Even as Perren stepped down, Boma's rage stripped him of caution and propelled him across the bridge; his target: my throat. Not entirely a tactic of momentary insanity, his sudden action took me by surprise. Frozen, I never had a chance even to raise the phaser.

Taking advantage, Ursula Mornay hunched her shoulders and grabbed for the discarded weapons lying on the upper deck. The bridge burst into wild motion.

This time, though, I wasn't alone on the summit of Mount Danger. A flash of beige and boot—the captain braced on the bridge handrail and vaulted into Boma without so much as a pause for breath. He caught Boma cleanly in the chest just before the astrophysicist's hands would have torn me bodily from the upper deck. Boma went down hard against the helm, the wind gushing from his body, and he fell limp.

Mornay's eyes widened in astonishment, but she had the phaser by now and backed against the weapons console, trying to get a better grip on the handle. Before her, Captain Kirk appeared over the handrail and straightened, his eyes full of warning. He had no weapon, he had no advantage. Only his eyes. The blades of truth.

He lowered his chin slightly, almost as though scolding her. "It . . . is . . . over."

The bridge fell to silence.

Challenge rumbled between them. Then, like thunder in the distance, it ended. Ursula Mornay narrowed her small eyes, her face shriveling into a sneer, and she lowered her phaser. The captain relieved her of it.

With a sigh, he reached down and hauled Boma, staggering, to his feet and gave him a heave toward the upper deck. "Mr. Sarda."

The voice beside me was almost a whisper. "Aye, sir."

"Escort the professor and Dr. Boma to the brig. If they so much as flinch," he added with a stern look at both prisoners just for effect, "paralyze them."

"Aye, sir." Sarda glanced at me, and whether or not he meant to be asking me for it, I handed him Perren's phaser. He gestured Mornay to the turbolift, careful to keep the weapon keenly trained on the little woman we had learned not to trust. He glanced at Perren, who remained near the viewscreen, awaiting his own fate. Clearly Perren was no longer part of the threat. The captain said nothing, but silently waved Sarda on with his assignment, confirming that he intended to have Perren handled in some other way. Soon Sarda was gone with Mornay and Boma.

Captain Kirk came to my side of the bridge, still on the lower deck below me, instantly at ease. He leaned one hand on the deck rail and said, "I like your style."

A deep breath came out of me a bit more gustily than I would've liked. "You should," I said. "It's yours."

223

Chapter Eleven

"It should be hauled away AS garbage!"
—The Trouble With Tribbles

I WAS TRYING to absorb the end of the nightmare when Captain Kirk extended his hand to me. Why did he want to help me down from the gangway? Almost on the thought, the answer wrapped itself around my heart. The captain's handshake suffused me with honor, a thousand times more than any promotion ever had, or ever could.

As if sensing my need for a moment of not being the center of attention, Kirk moved to his command chair and thumbed a button. "Kirk to Engineering." When there was no response, he punched again. "Kirk to auxiliary control."

"Spock here."

Ahhh, that sonorous voice! How welcome it was!

"Mr. Spock, the bridge is secure," the captain informed him.

"That is satisfying news, sir. Congratulations. May I ask the condition of the prisoners?"

He wanted to know about Perren, I guessed. From opposite sides of the bridge, the renegade Vulcan and I exchanged a meaningful regard, but nothing more. This was the captain's moment.

"Professor Mornay and Dr. Boma are on their way to the brig. Perren is still here with us."

A brief pause gave weight to Spock's next question. "And Mr. Sarda?"

The captain peered at me from the corner of his eye. "He's in charge of the prisoners."

Relief went through me like a knife. I closed my eyes and breathed deep, then let myself stare at the floor as Kirk's support for us soaked in. Had he been in my place before? Did he know what it felt like?

"Ship's status, Spock?" he was asking.

Very poor, Captain, as you might guess. However, we do have maneuvering capabilities on impulse power. We should be able to ambulate back to Argelius, if we take care not to strain the systems. I am presently attempting to re-engage electrical support for the guidance systems.

"Keep me posted. Bridge out." Again the command chair clicked. "Kirk to sickbay. What's the antidote situation?"

McCoy's voice shot through the com system with a reassuring confidence. *"We've isolated the antidote, synthesized it, and introduced it into the circulation system, Captain. The crew should start waking up within about fifteen minutes, depending on the individual."*

"Will they be functional, Doctor?"

"The intoxicant was wicked stuff. They'll wake up, but for the next six hours or so we're going to have a mighty sick crew on our hands, Jim."

Kirk lowered his voice noticeably. "Any count on fatalities yet, Bones?"

"No way to tell yet." McCoy sounded edgy.

"Guess."

"We hope to hold it under a dozen. Doing our best, Jim. I promise."

I felt the presence of Merete when Dr. McCoy said "our best," and knew she had found her own way to contribute to the situation. She could easily have stayed behind on Earth and gotten safe transit back to Star Fleet Command to await her next orders. Her presence had seemed so natural that, until now, I

225

hadn't remembered to appreciate it. I sent her a tele-pathic good luck and, remembering how she always managed to get to the core of my tensions, flexed my shoulders in an attempt to relax the muscles in my neck. With that I also took a deep breath and caught traces of a sweet odor, heavy and lingering descending from the upper vents. Merete's silent response—the antidote.

The captain addressed me quietly. "Piper?"

I shook myself into focus. "Aye, sir?"

"Where did you moor *Keeler?*"

"She's docked, sir. At Man-o-War. I took the liberty of arranging to have her brightwork sanded and refin-ished as long as she's just sitting there. I left Ambassa-dor Shamirian in charge of her."

"I thought you would." Leaning that way, with one elbow on the command arm, clasping one wrist as casually as a tiger rolling onto its back in the sun, Captain Kirk became everything a human could be. His soft hazel eyes brushed me and hovered beneath feathery brows that minutes ago had defined his sense of purpose. The purpose relieved, his face returned to the portrait of wisdom I'd known on board that lovely schooner so far away. For that instant, he and I were everything and everyone in the universe, mentor and pupil, captain and mate, captain and captain.

The communication was real. It drew his lips out-ward into a restrained grin. "Good job," he added.

I smiled. "Thanks." Funny that I felt as gratified by his trusting me with his schooner as I was by his trusting me with this mission. Of course, after many weeks at sea with James Kirk, I knew what the schooner meant to him. The mission only meant risk-ing death. The schooner meant life itself. The schooner, the starship . . . a strange and provocative mirror image.

"That was quite a wrenching you gave us," he said

226

then, reinstating the paranoia. "I had no idea a construction tug could do that."

Several possible responses flooded my brain. "Neither did I."

His brows went up and down in a dismissing motion. "Well," he said, "I won't want to be around when you explain it to Mr. Scott."

The moment's elation sank out of me. I muttered, "Me neither." Maybe there was something to be said for narcotic gases after all.

The captain moved around the back of his command chair, caressing the leather. All the while he was looking at Perren, who stood on the far bridge, swallowed by his own thoughts, or perhaps by the emptiness of them. Abandoned by his scruples, Perren was caught between the gears of bad and good, for the moment quite content to surrender himself to the wisdom of others. A sudden and completely unexpected sorrow rose inside me, touched with pity for him. Was he so wrong to wish to free the countless conquered worlds in the neighboring hostile empires? He felt guilty for the privilege of having been born Vulcan, of being born into the Federation, where his abilities were able to flourish without leash. I had once thought of the Klingons' right to be what they were, had once armed weapons to defend that clause in the Articles of Federation that guaranteed the privilege of self-rule to any government that didn't wish to join the Federation as much as to those who did. Never before had I thought so sympathetically of those billions of beings who might never get the choice at all. Perren made me think. The sacrifices were his, and I had ruined them. I would do that again, of course, but would things always have to be this way? Was freedom of choice only a matter of proximity in the galaxy? Where your borders lay?

As I gazed at Perren now, these thoughts folded in

on me and I became confused. I tried to isolate my regret, but after all we'd been through I couldn't clear my head enough for simple rationalities, much less a complex moral question. When all this was over and there was time to read, time to ask, time to listen, I promised myself I would keep learning. Perren's face, all angles and soft shadows under the bridge lights, evoked from me a warrant of reevaluation.

Kirk shook me out of these half-thoughts. "Piper, take the communications station and put out a dispatch to Star Fleet. Advise that we need an interstellar tow to the nearest starbase, and that we'll meet them at Argelius."

Striding across the bridge, I spontaneously asked, "What about the *Banana Republic,* sir?" It was out before I had a chance to bite it back.

His straight brows went flat on his eyes as he turned slowly. "What about the *what?*"

I whirled around and froze again. *Well, tunnel-mouth, how do you get out of this one?* "Um . . . by the way, Captain, I never had a chance to thank you for arranging a command for me. So . . . thank you."

"You're welcome. *Banana Republic?*"

Hang him, he was going to annoy me into explaining. Strapped, I fabricated a graceful, diplomatic lie and served it on a silver shrug. "First thing that came to mind, sir . . ."

Okay, so it wasn't graceful or diplomatic. It got me off the hook.

His brows did a little dance again, but he let the subject die young and waved me onward to communications.

It felt good to sit down. The bridge chair groaned lazily as I relaxed into it, confirming the illusive idea that things were settling down. Only a fleeting glance at Perren, and his at me, kept us clinging to past actions. Captain Kirk probably intended to have me escort Perren to the brig, as Sarda had escorted Mornay and Boma. Perren was unpredictable and the idea of ushering him below brought on a clutter of possibilities. I would still have to be careful. I swiveled around, putting my back to him. He wasn't my problem any more. Feeling taken care of for the first time in too long, I quietly tapped out the dispatch to Star Fleet Command and put it on a priority band. After all, it wouldn't do to have a starship hanging around in the middle of nowhere any longer than absolutely necessary. When the message was intact, I committed it to the system and pressed the Subspace Send-Code. Then I leaned back, my wrist still resting on the rim of the console. The board hummed merrily, doing what it did best. Machines were easy to please. A small grin tugged at my lips. Poor old Rex. Quite a show.

Buzz buzz buzz buzz buzz buzz.

I sat bolt upright. The tamper alert light was going wild. Somewhere in the system, the dispatch was jammed. Raking a hand through my hair, I chided myself for still being on edge, flexed my shoulders, and bent over the board. I didn't know much about communications cross plays, but I hadn't given up without a fight yet.

"Clanky plumbing," I accused, realizing that, of course, *I* had done this to the starship myself. If things wouldn't work, it was because I had made damn sure they wouldn't.

I pecked away at the toggles and inputs, trying to clear the system before Kirk got the idea that I needed help. All the electrical routes seemed to be working, but—there was an intrusion of impulses. From outside!

"Captain, we're being jammed!" I shouted.

He was beside me in an instant. "From where?"

"Port astern. Transmitters are being impeded. I can't get the message out!"

In a single motion he flew from the upper deck to the helm control and rattled orders into the board. As we watched in growing awareness, Perren moved away from the main view screen and gave us clear sight of our port astern space. The screen solidified quickly, with only a waver of sensor shift before focusing on two hawk-shaped warships just coming out of cloak.

I vaulted from my chair and grasped the deck rail, staring. "They must've moved in while we were playing musical phasers!"

Kirk reached back and nailed the com link on his command chair. For all the good it would do to an unconscious crew, the captain's urgent words echoed through the corridors of the crippled starship. *"Battlestations! All available hands to battlestations. Mr. Spock, to the bridge."*

"Piper, take the helm."

The Red Alert klaxon howled. Bridge lights darkened and became the warning scarlet that told us we were in trouble. The helm was sluggish under my hands.

"Raise all shields," the captain said. Calmness had returned to his voice. Somehow he had gotten it back.

Even emptied of its human elements, the bridge came alive. The computer systems fought the damage and sucked energy into themselves to do their jobs. Diagnostic readouts of the ship in tiny skeletal duplication, all done in computer blues, greens, and reds, were constantly shifting across the upper display boards, giving visual reality to the damage I'd done. And on at least two dynoscanners loomed the configuration, distance, and approach data on a pair of Klingon warships. Bigger than birds of prey, these were of the older, sturdier design, engineered for firepower and engine thrust. My throat closed as I watched the actual ships growing nearer in the main viewer. Because of me, *Enterprise* was helpless.

I wiped a trickle of sweat from my chin and pecked

at the helm control board, trying to think my way through unfamiliarity with these controls. "Only half-screens available, sir," I told him.

"They certainly didn't waste any time finding us," Kirk said to no one in particular. That was me, that no one.

In a fit of self-deprecation, I grumbled, "Klingons are stupid, but they're not that stupid."

Still dressed in cape and tunic, Mr. Spock shot out of the turbolift, cast one glance at the main viewer, and rounded on his library computer station. It started spewing data at him the instant he touched it, like a child jumping up and down to tell a parent about its troubles. "Captain, we're being scanned," he said immediately.

"Jam their frequencies," Kirk ordered. His scowl told how much he resented the invasion. "Let them guess."

Able to tie into many divisions of the bridge from his board, Spock fed the order through and prevented the Klingons from knowing the details of our damage. Anything more complicated would have to be done from the home consoles in each division. "Their weapons are armed, Captain, but they're not coming within firing range. They are separating . . . coming about to flank us on either side."

As he spoke, the scenario took place on our viewer. The two ships peeled away from each other and disappeared out opposite corners of the screen. The captain circled his command chair, his eyes narrowed like a fox in a hunt. Prey or predator? Which role would he take, and why?

"Do we have phasers, Spock?"

"Nonoperational, sir." Spock was quiet and terminal about it. He knew perfectly well what he was saying and, Vulcan or not, made no attempt to hide the heaviness he felt. A basic hopelessness was evidenced by his lack of explanation. Phasers weren't working, and they weren't going to be working any time soon. Not soon enough.

Was there anything on this starship that we *hadn't* destroyed?

The captain prowled the bridge. He was trying to think like the Klingons, and I was trying to think like him. I caressed the helm's edge, feeling very, very small. This was my fault. If I hadn't jumped to conclusions, assumed Kirk couldn't handle Mornay—if I hadn't crippled the ship—

Spock turned to us, a communications hook in his ear. "Sir, the Klingon commander is hailing us."

Kirk acknowledged it with a wry look. I felt a snide comment coming, but he repressed it and said, "Visual, Mr. Spock."

Velvet space dissolved, replaced by craggy Klingon features. It wasn't Gelt, I noted with some relief, though there was little doubt about how Klingon Central had found out about us. Once again I cursed myself for my common altruism. I'd left Gelt and his crew alive when I had the chance to put them out of my misery. As I watched, aching inside, the Klingon captain spoke. *"Commander,* Enterprise, *this is your captor. Your ship is disabled. We will take her in tow and return to the Klingon annex on the opposite side of the Federation Neutral Zone. As soon as we touch Klingon space, you will be classified as salvage."*

Kirk grew rock still. "Captain, you draw this ship into Empire territory and it'll be the last thing you do. I'll detonate her the second we leave Federation space, and you with her."

His words chilled me to the marrow. I believed those words, that tone. He would. And I would help him. I no longer felt death lurking at my door. I'd kick the door open and go in style, along with the finest ship in the universe and her captain.

The screen wobbled and turned to space again. Kirk

looked over his shoulder; Spock frowned and shook his head. "They've cut us off," he said.

Kirk bent over his command console. "Kirk to sickbay."

"McCoy here."

"Bones, what condition is Scotty in?"

McCoy took his time answering. *"Still unconscious. But his metabolic rate is increasing and he's responsive. Why? Are we the only ship in the quadrant again?"*

Captain Kirk sliced through what sounded like a private joke. "I've got to have him on the job. You've got to bring him around."

McCoy's tone changed. *"Jim, I don't know if that's possible,"* he insisted. *"A direct dose of this stuff could kill him."*

"Can't you try—"

A crunch of energy shuddered through the ship.

Spock squinted into his graphic readout. "Tractors, Captain, from both sides."

"Can you feed back their energy?"

"Not without overloading our impulse field flux. In our present condition, the firing chambers would overflow into the magnatomic tubes."

"Heading?"

Spock straightened so abruptly that it hurt my back to see him do it. "The Neutral Zone. They're taking us home." His statement rang of the cryptic.

Behind Spock, framing his caped form, the string of graphic schematics and bar charts across the rim of the bridge was nothing less than beautiful, in spite of their data. The Red Alert glow made them shine brightly against crisp geometrical insets. Who ever had the chance to contemplate the beauty of a ship's bridge while in Alert condition? The klaxon had stopped, having done its job of waking the dead, leaving only the red glow and wildly flashing CONDITION: ALERT signs. I suddenly wondered about Sarda. Had

Mornay snatched the opportunity of the call to battle-stations and somehow overtaken him? Taken him by surprise? Sarda knew humans better than Perren did, but Mornay was clever and abrupt in her methods. I pushed my thoughts through the deck platings and deep into the ship. *Don't trust her.*

"Spock," the captain asked, "how long till they can take us into warp?"

The first officer tilted his head, piercing me once again with a contagious confidence. "It will take them approximately seven minutes to adjust their tractors, compensate for our bulk, and balance their combined engines for warp speed."

Behind me, the captain spoke urgently. "Bones, I've got to have Scotty on the job. I don't care how you do it."

McCoy sounded strung out. *Jim, what do you want me to say? It'd take me half a day to calculate the right dosage of this antisomnial for a man Scotty's age, weight, and physical makeup. Now, I'd love to put him on the bridge, but it's not going to happen because nothing, nothing is going to make me pump this explosive into his system.*

"I'll be right there. Kirk out. Spock, take the con. Keep me posted on those ships." He said all this on the fly to the turbolift, and I got the distinct impression that *nothing* was bloody well going to get in his way. Not all crucial starship decisions, it seemed, are made from the bridge.

"Mode of resistance, Captain?" Spock asked at the last minute.

"None till I get back. Get on those repairs. I want full shields and photon torpedoes."

The lift panel whispered shut.

Spock turned to me. "Switch to forward visual."

I punched buttons. The screen melted and solidified again to show us the fantails of both Klingon cruisers, coordinating their energy to tow us along. Spock nodded thoughtfully, but said nothing about it. Instead he moved around the gangway toward the weapons console.

"Commander, if you will assist me, please," he said. He swung onto his back under the defense subsystems monitor and peeled off the panel.

To get to him I had to step past Perren. The young Vulcan's face was sallow as he stared at those Klingon ships. He wasn't even aware of me as I passed him. As much as *Enterprise* was disabled because of me, those Klingons were out there because of him. Come to think of it, everything was because of him. He knew it, too. It shone in his eyes and the set of his lips. Not exactly regret, though. Perren wasn't the kind to regret too much. Had his plans gone as he intended, transwarp would not have been at such risk. The Klingons knew we had it, no doubt. Gelt would have told them. And even if he hadn't, information like that spreads faster than Troyan bullet-bacteria. Now wasn't the time to be searching for blame.

Take your own advice, girl, my inner guardian warned.

"As I feed these synchrotron pulsors through the system," Spock was saying, "confirm connectivity with the graphics on the scanner above."

"Aye, sir. Go ahead." One by one, we fed and confirmed each patch in, trying to cram a week's repairs into a few minutes. The end result would be power for just a few photon shots, but those were better than nothing. Small talk kept trying to squeeze out of me, and I kept mashing it down. All I needed now was to be asking Spock a gaggle of stupid questions. My nerves were whining like the *Keeler*'s rigging. My hands were cold, and I had to use the head—oh no! Not now. *Please,* not now. Heroes never go to the bathroom! Horatio Hornblower didn't, Superman didn't, Cyrus Centauri didn't—but I did. Which proved who was a hero and who wasn't. As Spock

235

worked under the console, I finally asked, "Uh, sir? Permission to step updeck?"

He paused, then resumed working. "Certainly."

I dashed into the bridge head, and by the time I dashed out again, the Romulans had arrived.

Yep, there they were. I *knew* I should never have gone to the head.

Red Alert was whooping again, signaling intrusion into our immediate space, and Spock was clawing for the intercom. "Spock to Captain."

"Kirk here."

"Romulans in the area, Captain, three ships. Light fighters."

"Maintain Alert status. Enable the Engineering control board. We've got partial staff back in engineering, Mr. Spock. Put them to work impulse-drive integrity. I'm on my way."

He would never know how much his last four words meant to us, or at least to me. Spock rose to his full height, eyeing the viewscreen with Vulcan fierceness. We watched, unable to take action, as three Romulan ships looped in front of the Klingon cruisers and fired on them. Lancets of red energy cut hard into the Klingon screens. Without a pause the Klingons returned fire, cross-secting space with blue beams. Several of those missed entirely, but a few hit the Romulan birds and scored damage. Smaller ships had smaller shields, and the Romulans were vulnerable that way, in spite of superior maneuverability at sublight. They veered off and circled for another attack.

"Why are they firing on each other?" I wondered. "They're allied, aren't they?"

Spock raised a brow. "Transwarp is bigger than their alliance," he said.

Like animals protecting their kill, the Klingon ships turned in space to keep between the Romulans and us. Even as they did, I caught a glimpse of color in the high left side of the viewscreen and pointed ridiculously at it. "Mr. Spock, look!"

He stared for an extra moment, then moved to his scanner and shook his head. "Unidentifiable. We have no cataloguing of that configuration." He straightened and watched the new ship reel in to fire on the Romulans, then attempt to cut the Klingons off from us. "I daresay," Spock murmured, "we are in scramble."

Cosmic scramble. An intragalactic, military feeding frenzy. The phrase had come a long way since, in Rex's quiet cockpit, I'd first heard it glide out on Spock's resonant voice. Once, it had meant little to me. Now it spelled gruesome danger. This kind of battle would be far from neat, far from a simple two-sided dispute. And we were sitting in the middle of it, stark helpless. We were the nested egg about to be fought over by every form of alligator.

The feeling was devastating—to be put on hold like this, to be an ignored piece of torn meat, while others fought around us. Shots of light energy in bright colors splintered around us. *Enterprise* rocked in the ebb of energy bolts that passed too near us. The Klingon ships continued to tug us along, distracted now by the other ships, bolts of enemy fire keeping them from launching into warp speed. For the moment, at least. It bought us time.

The unidentified ship cut across our bow, giving us a sharp, shocking view of its forked hull and fierce colors. We hardly had time to blink before two Romulan birds sliced by us so close that I stumbled back into the command module, and Perren swayed backward into the bridge rail.

"Take your helm, Commander," Spock said, his tone rising and lowering as though he was reading a fairly interesting café menu. His eyes strayed resolutely on the screen action.

I maneuvered in that general direction, letting my hands lead me along the command module, unable to pull my stare from the battle. I winced as the Romulans sliced through the screens of one Klingon vessel and disabled it, only to dodge into green plasma blasts from the unidentified ship. The Klingons then took their own revenge, firing hard on the nearest Romulan wing.

The turbolift opened behind me, stealing my attention. The captain appeared, then Sarda, on either side of a gray-faced apparition of Mr. Scott. I held my breath in empathy. Scott looked ill and in pain, probably the effect of whatever the doctors had to do to wake him up and get him on his feet. The captain and Sarda supported him heavily, brought him across the bridge, and eased him into the chair at Engineering. Mr. Scott pressed his hands hard on the console. I could almost feel the effort going into his concentration as he assessed the ship's available energy.

Sarda moved across the upper deck until we were side by side, but on different levels. A brief glance told me he was all right. It felt good to have him here. Until now, I hadn't let the emptiness take hold.

Kirk pressed Scott's shoulder in mute reassurance and looked at the viewscreen. "Situation, Mr. Spock?"

"Unchanged. Three Romulans, two Klingon cruisers, and one unidentified vessel, all counterattacking. One Klingon cruiser is damaged but functional. They have not as yet fired on us."

Kirk nodded. "Piper, have you got an opinion?"

I blinked. Piper who?

His asking constrained me to find an opinion even if I didn't have one. So I invented one. "I'd say . . . concentrate on the Romulans and the unknown ship."

"Based on what?"

"Based . . . on Klingon tendencies."

"Explain."

Deep breathe, let out slowly, start talking. "Klingons are like grizzly bears. They attack straight on, with sheer brute force. Even though they're a threat in firepower and ruthlessness, they're predictable. If we just watch them, we should be able to tell what they'll do next." I stopped to lick my lips, which had dried up when I realized that Mr. Spock had stopped his scanning and was also listening to me, and Perren had turned my way too. Another deep breath. "Even though the Romulans have lesser weapons, they understand the concept of subtle attack. Things like sneaking and bluffing. They're cunning. It makes them dangerous. I'd watch out for them. I'd even disable them if I got the chance."

"Spock?"

I tensed, waiting.

"I concur," Spock said.

"So do I," was the captain's response.

Before I had a chance to exhale, Kirk demanded, "Disable them how?"

It's not as if he didn't have ideas of his own. He was testing me and using my reactions to test himself. Evidently he was as curious about what made me tick as I was about finding out what drove him. But couldn't it wait for a better time? Sir?

Trying to push ideas through the whiskerbugs infesting my brain, I shrugged and said, "Maybe . . . use their distraction with each other . . . launch someone in a shuttlecraft or one of the attack sleds and make for open space to get a distress call out to Star Fleet . . ."

"They'd be caught in traction by one of those ships and taken prisoner."

"Yes . . . of course . . . sorry." And on top of being a bad suggestion, it wasn't even the answer to what he'd asked.

Luckily, James Kirk wasn't James Kirk for nothing. He took his good question and my bad answer and combined them into a wild card. "Shuttlecraft," he murmured, watching the interplay of ships before us. "Spock . . ."

They exchanged a long look—not a word, just a look.

Spock nodded. "Excellent," he uttered. Had I missed something?

Stepping down to the navigations console beside me, he tapped through to the automation of the hangar deck and computer-moved one of the shuttles into launch position. As he worked, the only sounds were the whirr-beeps of electrical cooperation and the muffled, strained voice of Mr. Scott as he fed orders through to the few engineers back on duty below decks.

"Shuttlecraft *Columbus* ready for launch, sir," Spock said then. "Automation system locked in."

The captain nodded his acknowledgment.

Why was he taking me up on a stupid suggestion? And an empty shuttlecraft at that . . . of course! A decoy. Make the enemy waste their time following an apparent escape. Like I said, he wasn't James Kirk for nothing.

"Go ahead, Mr. Spock," he said, calmly watching the enemy ships wheel and fire on each other like dancers in some erotic alien ritual. As if to give my analysis life, the small Romulan ships were using supreme strategy, working together against more potent enemy vessels, coordinating their attacks then retreating to the rim of the solar system to regroup and attack again, from different angles. The Klingons were unable to tell where the Romulans would dive in upon them next. The only surplus danger was that unidentified ship. The Klingons had their hands full trying to maintain their pull on *Enterprise* and the unnamed ship knew how to use that. Its forked hull lanced past us several times, that green plasma ray cutting deeply into the Klingon shields, only then to swing around and potshot the Romulans into falling out of formation. All the while we continued slowly moving toward the outside of the solar system, where, once clear, the Klingons might be able to take us into warp speed. Another clutch of guilt caught me by the heart. Tangled motivations looked for excuses in my head. Silent, I watched the battle tighten before me.

A small white speck appeared at the corner of the screen. It drew my attention. The shuttlecraft—veering away for open space. As Kirk had anticipated, the unnamed ship and two Romulan wings turned on their tips and angled after it in a strange race. Because they were closer in the first place, the Romulans overtook the shuttlecraft first. Pulling it against its own thrust, they drew it up alongside and tucked it under one wing, then warned off the unnamed ship with a volley of particle-beam fire.

The unidentified vessel peeled away, barely dodging the milky white gauze of particle beam, leaving the Romulans to their catch. They drew the shuttlecraft in tight to their hull. Not large enough to bring the shuttlecraft on board, they made good their possession with magnetic couplings on their ship's underbelly. When the shuttle was firmly attached, Captain Kirk said, "Now, Mr. Spock."

Sarda and I both looked at Spock at the same moment, after a questioning glance proved that neither of us knew what was happening. As Spock's long finger leaned on a toggle. It flipped.

The entire left side of the viewscreen lit up. Blue-white particles spun through space, then redoubled as a matter/antimatter explosion bubbled inside the first. The Romulan ship was memory, nothing more than scattering bits of fibercoil melting and dissolving in a pyrotechnic bloom.

I came halfway out of my chair. "Wow!"

Sarda's cool gaze washed over me, and I got the feeling that only my yip of delight kept him from an embarrassing smile. He probably saw how ridiculous I looked and decided to interiorize that grin pulling at his upper lip.

Spock bent over his readout screen at the library computer. "One Romulan ship obliterated . . . another slightly disabled from impact fallout."

"Good, Spock, good," the captain murmured.

Victory earned us a slap on the wrist. The third Romulan ship flashed by us at attack angle and lay open the skin of *Enterprise*'s forward half-shields with a shot full of revenge. The bolt crumpled our shields and burst through with just enough remaining energy to send us staggering. I was thrown out of my chair altogether, and Sarda careened backward, barely missing Mr. Scott, who was clinging to his board with whatever strength he had. When the bolt faded and the ship stopped shuddering, Sarda was picking me up and Perren was picking himself up. Kirk and Spock, darn them, were already up.

Kirk was holding tight to the bridge rail, his eyes ablaze with satisfaction. I felt it too—that rare sense of triumph that came from outthinking an enemy when the enemy already had an upper hand. It was worth that spanking they'd given us. Suddenly I understood the captain's advantage. He knew what I had forgotten. None of these ships dared destroy *Enterprise*. We had what they wanted.

"I think they're annoyed, Mr. Spock," the captain crowed.

"Yes," Spock agreed. "They do seem . . . vexed, Captain." With that, he returned to his readout screen.

That comforting thought left only the possibility of being dragged into Klingon space, or being accidentally blown to bits by wild shots, or being boarded by the enemy, or—

Spock straightened abruptly and glared at the viewscreen. "More ships, Captain! Veering in from various directions in open space," he said, his tone edged with surprise.

242

Kirk raised his voice. "Scotty, where's that shield power?"

Mr. Scott turned slightly, even that an effort since he was standing up—leaning, really—and running a protosensor rod over the board. "Nearly there, sir . . . up to 83 percent." His eyes narrowed in discomfort, and he was breathing heavily. "Working on impulse thrust—" He slipped and collapsed forward over his console. By the time Captain Kirk reached him, he was wiping his face with a blanched hand and pushing himself up.

The captain took him by the arms and steered him back into his chair. "Scotty? Can you make it?"

Scott fought for his part in the play, forcing his eyes to meet Kirk's without a flinch, in spite of the pain showing in his face. "Aye, sir . . . those spine-headed pirates'll not have this ship if I can help it." The promise drained him, but he pulled on an inner sturdiness and straightened under the captain's grasp.

Even in the midst of trouble, Kirk found a personal moment to pat Scott's arm. "Good, Scotty. We need you."

"Captain, forward deflector power is impaired," Spock reported. "Unlikely to regain."

"Identify those ships," Captain Kirk ordered.

"Attempting to do so."

I leaned toward Sarda, who still had a grip on my arm, and said, "We're trying to get photon capacity."

"All right," he said simply, and moved to the weapons control console on the upper deck. Mirroring that, I dashed back to the helm and drifted into my chair. At least it *looked* like we were helping.

"Come on, Spock," the captain urged. "I want to know who I'm up against."

Spock nodded, very slightly, then gave voice to what he was seeing on his monitor. "Tholians, sir. At least four. Sensors are unsure. And at least three more vessels . . . checking design catalog to identify." He moved across his computer, arms sweeping the board as he tapped into the fabulous memory system. Even in that short time, the cuneiform shape of the Tholian ships had become clear on our screen. Behind them, other vessels appeared, all different—claviform, turnip-shaped, biform, full-orbed, all different colors. When Spock returned to the monitor and the blue light once again washed his features, the answers were there. His brows went up. "Captain, they are Klingons. However, not Empire-sanctioned vessels. One is of a configuration currently being used by the Rumaiym, a racial tier of the Empire."

Captain Kirk moved to the deck below Spock, drawing the two of them together into that intangible bubble they shared when I looked closely. "Analysis, Spock," Kirk softly invited.

Spock tilted his head, observing the action in space, then turned his gaze downward to his captain, as if they were alone. "It's not surprising that sections of the Empire might attempt to gain a bargaining weight within the power structure. In fact, if current intelligence is accurate, we are seeing agents of at least four Klingon strains: Klinzhai, Rumaiym, Wijngan, and if I am correct about that triformed vessel, the race calling themselves Daqawlu—the Remembered."

With a dry nod, Kirk commented, "Oh, they'll be remembered, all right."

"Obviously the Klingon Empire is not so unified as they would have us believe."

"Obviously. Well, we can't keep feeding them shuttlecraft. We'll have to come up with something else." Kirk circled the command module, giving me a clear view of the harsh determination that brought his brows together and tightened his lips. His words hummed with bottled ferocity. "I don't like being the pawn."

I cast a brief glare at him, but broke it off before he saw it. *Neither did I.*

Kirk spun suddenly, and I braced for a reprimand.

But it was Spock he caught in his net. "You told me about a transwarp accident while you were aboard Piper's ship."

"Yes," Spock acknowledged. "Quite unsettling."

"Unsettling enough to disable those ships?"

Spock hadn't thought of that, judging from his expression. As he added up the elements, Sarda, Perren, and I turned to watch, and wait.

With a nod of contemplation, Spock said, "Possibly."

Kirk inhaled deeply. "Describe it."

"I believe improper imbalance in the matter/antimatter flow through the holding chamber caused the trilithium to degenerate. The result is not thrust, but dimensional warp. Am I correct, Mr. Sarda?"

Sarda shifted his feet and nodded. "You are, sir."

The captain gripped the rail harder. "Can it be repeated?"

"Repeated in what form?" Spock asked.

"If the transwarp mechanisms were patched into the *Enterprise*'s defense system, could those conditions be duplicated?"

Spock held the hot potato for a few seconds, then tossed it across the bridge. "Mr. Sarda?"

Sarda dropped his gaze as he contemplated his safety equipment and, knowing him, about a thousand other alternatives. He hated having his inventions used for military offense, but it was that or imprisonment behind Klingon lines. His innermost struggles shone faintly behind his eyes. I tensed, wishing there was some way I could help him. For a long self-conscious moment, our eyes met. Perhaps he drew strength from me, for he straightened and faced the captain. "It could be done," he said. "We could not, in fact, prevent it from happening, considering the condition of the *Enterprise*. Rather than the defense system, the mechanisms would have to be connected into the propulsion system, the warp drive itself, then expelled through the sensory in order to do what you require with any control. However . . . I do not trust myself to a task so complicated. At least, not alone. The dangers to ourselves, with an untested system—"

"I'll help." I was on my feet already. Kirk and Spock looked at me. Ridiculous! What I knew about transwarp would fit under a fingernail. Then, in an instant, I knew what I *could* do. I rounded on Perren. My words were potent as sharp wind. "You'll help too."

Perren's narrow features paled, but his eyes grew intense.

"You know what I'm talking about," I pressed. In my periphery, Kirk and Spock waited, knowing when silence was the key to winning.

"Yes," Perren murmured. "Yes, I must." He approached Captain Kirk. "You must let me. I can cut installation time by two-thirds. I beg you, allow it."

Kirk glared at him, partially in threat, partially in disbelief, partially in that special way he had of cutting through the thoughts of others. Put his ship in the hands of a traitor? Even now, Perren's face was backed by a tangle of enemy ships firing on each other, haloed by the fluorescent sparkles of direct hits.

I couldn't stand it. I couldn't let the doubt dangle. I rushed around the command module in a move I hoped was dramatic and arresting, until I was nearly at Perren's side, and faced the captain. "Sir, you've got to let him. He means it."

Kirk's glare carried a definite how-do-you-know as it snapped to me, yet he said nothing. I knew I'd better be right.

"How long?" he demanded.

Perren tensed. "Roughly . . . seventy minutes. An estimate only, of course."

A commanding hand swept from Perren to Sarda. "Both of you, get to it." The hand folded into a point,

246

and swung straight at me. "Piper, I want you down there too."

I swallowed a lump of liability. "Aye, sir. I understand."

A brief glance from me sent Sarda toward the turbolift, Perren close behind, and I brought up the rear guard, deliberately not picking up one of the discarded phasers in a vote of faith for Perren. Kirk noticed, and raised a brow at me as though he knew what I was thinking. No real surprises there, though. Gambling was part of the game—sometimes the wiser part. We both knew it.

I reached the back of the bridge and was about to join the Vulcans in the turbolift when a crack of energy struck the port side of *Enterprise,* and rocked us hard. My shoulder, with the rest of me behind it, rammed into the frame of the turbolift, and I managed to catch myself and hang there until the ship stabilized. In the wide viewscreen, the unidentified ship streaked out from the underside of our primary hull and vectored out into space toward the Klingon cruisers.

The captain moved toward the helm console and turned briefly to me. With deliberate poise, he said, "Hurry."

The Engineering deck was disturbingly quiet, jarred only by rumbles of energy from outside that told us the enemy ships had opened fire on us and the Klingons who possessed us. Perren, Sarda, and I were resolutely silent as we gathered Perren's equipment and carefully—so carefully—followed the directions Spock fed through to us on how to dismantle his elaborate isolation field around the transwarp mechanism itself. The mechanism made little engineering sense to me; it looked like something out of a child's coloring book, a quincunx contraption with several arms and a central core of funnels and circuitry.

Evidently that was the reaction chamber for the tri-lithium. I didn't even try to understand it.

Perren and Sarda worked feverishly to wrestle the various attachments into the central feeder unit for the ship's energy/matter matrix restoration cowl. Okay, so I didn't understand that either. It didn't matter, as long as *they* understood. Even with their combined Vulcan strength and a few good shoves from me, the installation of transwarp into a damaged warp propulsion system was the work of more than three people. I didn't bother asking what this or that was, especially if, by some miracle, it happened to fit. I followed their directions through the most muscle twisting sixty-two minutes of my life. It seemed more like six minutes.

Finally the work dwindled down to minute delicate adjustments and all I could do was watch. It was as though Perren and Sarda had fallen into a different language; though I was watching, their science was so specialized that I might as well have been a thousand solar systems away. My thoughts began to drift, jarred each time the ship shook under us from enemy fire. I held on to a nearby pylon and tried to keep hold of my self-control. The frustration was building again. I hated having to just watch.

I started thinking about the enemies out there. Tholians, Romulans, Klingons of every breed, and that persistent forked ship whose configuration we couldn't pin down. Living beings, tangled in a web of power grabbing. Each had a history and a goal of his or her own. And so did I.

Without pausing between thoughts, I suddenly blurted, "What's going to happen? When we implement this, what's the effect?"

Only when both Vulcans paused at the same time did I realize I'd forced them to face something they had been trying not to think about. Not only face it, but put words to it.

They exchanged a disturbing glance. Perren gripped

the micropincer he was using. "We . . . have never postulated the effect of an accidental imbalance. Our efforts, of course, have always been directed toward canceling out or circumventing any such occurence, with the hopes of eventually preventing them altogether. We take great care to stabilize the integrity of the trilithium before funneling matter/antimatter through the field core."

Spock's face filled my mind, completely unbidden. Perren, so unlike him, was turning logic inside out to avoid simply saying that he didn't know. Suddenly I longed to hear those words; there was something reassuring about the honesty in the phrase *I don't know*.

Anger boiled up in me and I snatched Perren's arm. "I've got to understand! You've got to give me some idea of what it's going to do to those ships out there."

Perren jerked away. His eyes flashed with the onslaught of my emotions coursing through him. Long black hair waved when he pulled his arm free. I went after it again, but Sarda caught my wrist.

A swell of perception washed through me, cooling my nerves, running up my arm, and spreading through my body. The anger didn't go away, but like the distortion of transwarp flux, Sarda had turned it outward and away from Perren. For a moment he took it upon himself, seeing perfectly well that I was reaching the limit of my patience with Vulcan ways. He slowly absorbed my need to understand, and with his grip forced me to comprehend what could be foretold and what couldn't be.

Seconds passed, long ones. Sarda broke his gaze from mine only once.

He nodded briefly to Perren, who collected himself with difficulty and went back to work on the microcircuits. When the triad of conflict faded to the two of us, Sarda turned back to me.

"Piper," he began, "even we do not fully comprehend why transwarp works as it does. It is not meant to be a weapon."

Though I knew how deeply he believed that, I pressed, "I'm in the command line. I've got to have some concept of what that thing's going to do to other life forms. The captain has to know."

"We would tell you, if that information could be gained without actually using the imbalance." Glints of blue and yellow light from Perren's snapping panel flickered in Sarda's bronze hair and in his troubled eyes. Guilt gnawed at him. Would he ever have peace from it? "The wave effect," he tried again, "is a reality solvent. We may liken it to pouring water on a sand castle. The sand remains, but . . ."

The transwarp contraption trilled to life, singing an electrical song, and saved him from having to find the words for the terrible vision he saw. For a moment we simply watched the equipment whirr and glow and hum.

Sarda's expression filled with omen. "We cannot allow hostile hands to possess this."

"And we shall not," Perren agreed, that rebellious thorn surfacing again.

My opinion stuck its neck out again. I couldn't stop it. I glared at Perren. "You should've thought of that a long time ago."

Sarda watched me, silent.

Perren retreated to his work. The instrumentation whistled and chirred happily under his hands. Even poorly hooked up, fed into a damaged system, the transwarp mechanisms showed the effort of years of work.

"I can complete the calibrations," Perren said. "Correlating the flux ratios of transwarp drive with the sensors must be done from the sensor control room."

Sarda gathered the necessary computer disks and said, "Contact me there when you're ready to begin."

"Very well," Perren said. "It may take several more minutes to make the correct calculations."

Sarda only nodded. He knew all that, apparently. As he stood up, his amber gaze caught fast to my own and I felt that wash of telepathy again. Was I really feeling it, or had I learned to imagine it as I came to know him better? He'd never confided in me about whether or not these mental waves were normal for Vulcans—if he even knew. I hadn't asked, and a good thing too. He might be supremely embarrassed if my feelings were induced by his inability to control that inherited telepathy. He seemed so different from Spock, as different from Spock as Spock was from Perren— Sarda, even more different from most Vulcans who came to Star Fleet. Very few of Sarda's fair-haired clan ever roamed from their home planet, yet he was here, rare, and of great value to me. As we stood together over a mechanism that might either save or destroy us, I found myself hoping he never would learn to control the soft inner communication.

"Where will you be?" he asked.

My answer was deceptively simple. "Where I'm needed."

"I know you will do well."

"Thank you. For everything."

His expression remained stoic, but he dropped his eyes, then raised them again. "And I thank you," he said, almost whispering.

"Good luck," I responded.

Before we got into a chain reaction of thank-yous, he wisely dipped away and left the area. I lingered there long after he was gone.

Below me, Perren drew my attention when he paused and put a hand to his lips. I knelt down. "Something?"

His brows came together in contemplation. "This arrangement must be coordinated from the bridge, at

251

the engineering subsystems monitor. If you can do that, I can monitor and adjust the intermix according to your readouts from pulse to pulse."

"I can do that," I told him. I could do it, if only I knew what he was talking about. Let's hear it for blind optimism.

Perren's face went blank for a moment, then twisted in confusion.

"What's the matter?" I asked.

He shook his head. "I'm unsure about the sensor output system. I can correlate the thrust ratios for warp drive, but I do not know how to adjust them to run through the sensory."

It sounded like a bigger problem than I could solve—surprise, surprise—and I bit my lip before making a wild assumption. My feet were tingling when I stood up. "I know who does. I'll contact you when I get to the bridge."

I started toward the exit. Before reaching the door, though, I remembered my charge from a higher authority—a trust I wouldn't betray.

Perren saw me turn, saw the tangle of emotions in my face, the sensation of being torn between two distinct duties. Even though I said nothing at all, the problem was obvious.

He read my hesitation—even I couldn't say if he read it correctly—and paused fine-tuning the transwarp to seal his credibility with a promise. "I give you my word."

The throb and hum of *Enterprise*'s sensor system trying to accept the new energy of transwarp became the pulsing of some great heart. I absorbed Perren's promise. *Think like a Vulcan.*

With my tone, I charged both of us to fulfill the vow. "I accept your word."

The hangar deck was cool with freshly circulated air, sweet with the lingering odor of the antisomnial. I

252

swung around the corner of the alcove where the Arco sleds were anchored down, and was only superficially surprised to see Sarda there, kneeling beside Scanner. He'd evidently decided to make good use of those extra few minutes Perren said he had. He was holding Scanner in a sitting position against the attack-sled's folded solar wing.

I knelt beside Scanner, but my question was for Sarda. "What are you doing here?"

His gaze was penetrating. He didn't want to explain. "Deviating."

That was all I was going to get, too.

Scanner's face was clammy as I touched it and turned him to me. "Scanner? Look at me. Are you okay?"

He blinked past the pain left over from artificial sleep and unnatural awakening and moaned. "If this is life after death . . . I'll take death." He folded over, and only Sarda's grasp kept him upright. When he raised his head, his face was pale and his eyes glazed. "You got . . . trouble upstairs."

Good. Sarda had been filling him in, probably trying to distract him from his own discomfort.

I took him by the shoulders. "Scanner, listen to me. We've tied the transwarp into the warp drive and we've got to correlate the thrust ratios with sensor issue. Can you tell me how to do that?"

"Aim it . . . you mean?"

"Yes, aim it."

"Yeah . . . oh, worm guts . . . they killed me, Piper." He let his head sag back against the solar wing. Pinch-faced, he fought the gaspy breath of nausea and cramps. Sarda and I shared a glance of penetrating empathy and waited.

"We'll get you to sickbay," I promised.

"Can't y'just . . . bring sickbay down here?" Scanner closed his eyes tight. When they opened again, some of the color was returning to his face, as well as

253

his wits. "Yeah . . . that transmitter on the bridge . . . a dead jellyfish could work it. Y'all can do it easy."

"Gee, thanks. How?"

"Same way you aim sensors, except . . . push the impulses through weapons override . . . even if the safety system says you can't."

I frowned. "It'll burn out."

He took a choppy breath. His cheeks flushed with heat. "You can't stop that. It's all there is. That crazy transwarp hookup won't last long anyway. You might's well force a human heart to breathe air." Cramps took hold of him again, piercing all three of us and making me realize what Mr. Scott, with his hands full of starship, was going through. Scanner pressed his arm under his ribs. His free hand made a loop toward Sarda. "Tell her, Points."

Sarda's lips flattened, a strange reflection of his hand on Scanner's arm as it gripped tighter. He felt responsible; I sensed it simmering. "Probably true," he admitted.

Obviously, none of us had possessed the courage to say it before this. The captain's plans suffered as I waded through the truth. *Enterprise*'s systems were sturdy, but not meant to funnel the shared energy we would soon demand of them, the hazardous intermix with its deliberate imbalances. In perfect condition, possibly—but not with the damage I'd inflicted. The Klingons were towing us closer by the minute to the system's edge where, at warp speed, they could easily rush us into their home territory. Time now worked against us. All we had was this one chance. Mutual disablement.

"I'll tell the captain," I said. "We'll make it work somehow."

Scanner managed a weak smile. "I was hopin' yawl'd say that."

"Sarda, can you manage with him? I've got to get back to the bridge."

254

Sarda nodded. "I'll contact you from the sensory."

I started to get up, but faltered when Scanner caught my sleeve. When I looked down, he said, "Don't let the bastards beat us, Piper."

My hand caught his and squeezed. "You count on it."

Comforted, he slumped back against the solar wing.

I didn't stay to help Sarda get him on his feet. The bridge of *Enterprise* was waiting—and all the clocks were ticking.

Make it work, make it work, make it work . . .

Chapter Twelve

"Risk is our business."
—Return to Tomorrow

THE BRIDGE WAS organized chaos. Captain Kirk was leaning over the helm, his medieval costume incongruent with the geometric surroundings, doing the jobs of ten. The scarlet lights of Alert status were distorted by blasts of color energy from enemy ships as they swung by, lashing out at each other, and catching us in the crossfire. Iridescent damage on the nearby Klingon cruisers lit up our faces. To my right, Mr. Spock was bending over his readout hood, its blue light on his face clashing with the scintillas from the main viewer. He had to hold on to the edge of the console to keep on his feet as enemy fire cut at our battered deflectors. He and the captain were alone on the bridge.

As I came out of the turbolift, a strange thought flushed over me. Getting to the bridge hadn't been easy, and I'd been thrown down at least twice as the ship was rocked by battle turbulence. I'd had to ignore the groggy, nauseous crewpeople just coming around after having had their lives risked for them. When the turbolift doors opened, it occurred to me that precious few of those people were authorized to come to the bridge. Yet here I was, privileged to be at the hub of decision, alone with Captain Kirk and Commander Spock.

Kirk spoke into the intercom, correlating something

I couldn't hear clearly, and Mr. Scott's voice came back up at him through the com system. I looked toward the engineering panel, confirming to my jarred senses that he wasn't there anymore.

"Nominal but coming back slowly," Kirk was saying. "Good work, Scotty, keep it up." Fighting from inside a cage, he adjusted the navigational controls and *Enterprise* pivoted against the Klingon tractor beams until we had a clear view of a Romulan ship veering toward us, with one of the cuneiformed Tholians close behind. Instantly Kirk struck a firing launch. Space filled with bright red-orange lancets. Phasers! They'd gotten phasers working! And the captain was using them to keep the enemies busy out there, protect our weakened deflectors, and complicate the Klingons' effort to protect their prize—us—while they also tried to beat off attackers who were determined that if they themselves couldn't have us, nobody could. Including the Klingon Empire.

The pastel Tholian vessel swerved to miss our primary hull, one of her wedges blazing with melted hull material. The Romulans cut upward on short notice and fired their particle beam at us, but the Klingons fired and detonated the particle beam before it reached our screens. *Enterprise* rocked and whined in the dispersing waves. I caught myself on the bridge rail and managed to stay upright.

From one side, Spock's voice overlapped the snapping of tangled voltage as *Enterprise* trembled back to life. "Port side Klingon cruiser is keeping in contact with the other cruiser, Captain," he was saying, his hand to the com receiver in his ear. "Distorted . . . they are attempting to contact their Empire or other Empire ships . . . I believe to request help that . . . may be on stand-by already, if I decipher these transmissions correctly."

"Cut off their broadcast. Make sure those transmissions get scrambled. They can tow us," the captain said to the screen, "but they'll have to do it alone. Scotty, ready secondary phaser banks."

"Secondary banks are dry, Captain. I'm trying to funnel in some power. It's only a matter'a time before the hull in D-section ruptures and that'll be the end of our reserve. We've taken too many hits there, sir." Scott's voice held the timber of a man possessed.

But I was staring at Spock. Just last year I'd finished a top-of-the-line course in computer cryptography and I blasted well knew that with the new wave-maze technology the Klingon Empire had developed, we couldn't possibly tie in to their transmissions. Professor Eufinger had made that indelibly clear. But there was Spock, blithely doing the impossible.

Well, Eufinger had always been a cretin anyway.

The captain's voice shook me awake. "What's the status on the transwarp appliance?"

I had to clear my throat. "It's tied in, but . . . a little shaky. We have to correlate from here to the engine room and over to the sensory. Perren's standing by, and Sarda should be in the sensory any minute."

Kirk left his station and approached me swiftly on the lower deck, shooting me full of the moment's urgency. Even though I was standing over him, the sense of eminence he radiated was staggering. I felt drawn to his presence, even comforted, in spite of the battle blazing on the screen behind me. "Do you know what to do?" he asked.

"It's been explained to me, sir," I said, obviously avoiding the real answer.

He seemed to like that response even better than if I'd told him I knew all about it and understood it perfectly and could pull it off without a hitch.

"Go," he said. We crossed by each other as he went to join Spock.

The engineering subsystems monitor was sluggish under my hands. The functions override and critical

258

regime indicators took too long to respond. Oh, well . . . I didn't know for certain what they meant anyway, so let them take their time. I tapped the com through to engineering. "Bridge to Perren."

"This is Perren."

"I'm at station. Hold while I tie us to Sarda."

"Acknowledged."

Another tap. "Bridge to sensor broadcast."

A few seconds passed. I was about to call again when the breathless response came. *"Sensory. Sarda here."* He'd been running.

"I'm feeding the coordinates through to both of you. Keying weapons cross feed now."

"Acknowledged. Drawing power to transwarp."

"Broadcast ratios are confirmed, Piper. Standing by."

My eyes drifted closed. I inhaled and turned. "Captain? We're ready when you are."

Kirk's expression pasted me to my controls. "Target the Klingons who have us under tow. I'm going to move us up into their tractor to tighten the range. We'll go for a short incursion first." He skipped the steps altogether, going from Spock's side back down to the helm, and introduced the controls to their heading. Beneath us, *Enterprise* whined against the strain of impulse power fighting the tractor beams to push forward into them. Not as impossible as trying to pull away, but not easy.

"Aye, sir. Targeting." I had to force my fingers to move. Green lights on the board blinked, confirming that Sarda was receiving the coordinates.

"Romulan ships moving in for another rush on the Empire cruisers," Spock reported.

"Just as well," the captain muttered. "All right, Piper. Ready transwarp flux . . ."

"Range is uncertain," Sarda warned. *"There may be an echo effect. Brace yourselves."*

I held my breath, waiting for the captain's next

259

word, as the two Romulans vessels wheeled into near space. Echo effect? Did he mean—

"Execute!"

I leaned on the emissions toggle. The controls went wild.

Enterprise's electrical noises drooped out to long howls. My arms became elastic. I felt my knees fold in the wrong direction.

The edge of flux—we still felt it, even though the waves were deflected outward at the attacking ships. The flushback twisted reality around us. I heard Kirk's voice as he shouted something to Spock, but the words made no sense. Still, I clung to the sound.

While Sarda's safety systems directed the actual flux at our enemies, the dimensional distortion couldn't be controlled. It fed back on *Enterprise,* engulfing us in the same peripheral effect we'd felt aboard Rex. If this was the fallout, what was it like out there, in the main stream?

The ship lurched and bolted to starboard, then righted.

My arms came back. The queer feeling subsided abruptly, leaving us all breathless.

"Status, Spock!" Kirk demanded.

The answer took too long. "Tractor beams have released us." Spock's report carried a ring of triumph. "We are free to maneuver."

He turned to the main viewer. We all did.

The scan of immediate space was horrifying. Partially dissolved ships floated by us, dismembered, or spliced together wrong, completely rearranged—when a Tholian ship drifted past with a Romulan wing protruding from the side of its hull, I had to look away.

Spock, still staring at the screen, stepped down to the captain's side. Together, with expressions frighteningly alike, they watched what we had done. The area looked like an interstellar junk yard. The only vessels left maneuverable in immediate space were one Rumaiym ship, the unidentified ship, and . . . *Enterprise*.

Far off at the edge of the viewer, there was movement. The remaining Tholians, their hatred of disorder apparently stronger than their desire for transwarp, cashed in their chips and retreated at high speed. So did the ships Spock had identified as Wijngan.

The first ship left to move on us was the Daqawlu vessel, a streamlined yellow and black ship made mostly of curves. It gathered speed gradually, then faster, and fired full disruptors.

Enterprise rocked under us. I felt myself hitting the floor, my hip smashing the edge of the engineering console as I went down. In the corner of my eye I saw Kirk dive for the helm control. Impulse power hummed up from the lower decks, and the starship tipped away from the Rumaiym beams.

"Shields four and seven down completely, Captain," Spock shouted over the combined din of disruptor fire and impulse rumble.

Kirk struck an intercom button. "Kirk to Engineering. Scotty, divert all available power to photon torpedoes."

"They're too weak, sir," Scott's voice filtered up from distant decks. *"I'll need four minutes to recharge. Buy me that time and I'll give you disruption potential."* He sounded better than he had when he'd been on the bridge. Typical, for Scott, health was directly related to proximity to the engines.

The arcuate Daqawlu ship had vectored out into deep space and was diving on us again at attack speed.

"All right," Kirk growled. "We'll do it the hard way. Piper, enable the flux. Execute on my mark."

The yellow and black ship swooped toward us. Her phaser port glowed faintly with gathering energy.

"Now, Piper."

Had someone said something?

"Piper!"

I flinched, drawn abruptly back to my role in this awful drama. "Oh . . . aye, sir . . . enabled."

"Execute!"

I bit my lip, and fed the impulses through as Scanner had instructed.

This time the dimensional flux wasn't as distorting. Had it lost its power? Were we drained already? A wash of nausea, loss of vision, dizziness . . . and it was over. I blinked, and worked to focus on the viewscreen.

Before us, the Daqawlu ship shimmered briefly as reality short-circuited. They fell out of attack pattern, turned belly-up, and swept to one side of us. The ship left our viewscreen, then veered back in and came to a stop at a respectable distance. There seemed to be no other effect.

Kirk moved around the helm module, his eyes fixed on the drifting enemy vessel. "Spock? No effect on the ship?"

I'd never seen Spock hesitate. This time, though, he did. When he moved to his scanners, it was with a distinct force of will. Slowly, he said, "Confirmed . . . the ship is intact." He straightened then, his saturnine features limned with empathy, gaze rooted to the Daqawlu ship. "But there are no life forms aboard."

The captain turned sharply. "You mean . . ."

"Whatever happened during that flux," Spock confirmed, "it took them all with it."

Astonishment filled the captain's face. He stared at the screen. My nausea returned, and I was surer than I'd ever been that he and I were nursing the same thought. It was easier to kill an enemy than condemn him to eternity between dimensions.

Involuntarily, we moved toward the viewer. Only a step or two. Enough to seal the horror.

Water on a sand castle.

We were shaken from our stupor by the Red Alert

262

klaxon as it whooped to life again. My heart hit my boots. It couldn't be. It *couldn't*.

The captain looked at Spock. Feeling it, his first officer lifted his head from the scanner hood and somberly confirmed, "More ships, Jim." His nitaglase eyes shined in the Alert's red glow as he uttered words more awful than plain information could be. "Battle cruisers of the Empire."

Go through it all again? We couldn't. *I* couldn't.

Kirk struck the comlink. "Scott, weapons?"

"Best I can offer is 70 percent range on photons, sir," the engineer reported stiffly.

From another side of the engineering deck, Perren's voice interrupted through my monitor's intercom. *"We do have remaining power for another transwarp flush. Shall I enable?"*

Damn him. That meant I had to report to the captain. I hated myself. "Captain . . . transwarp is standing by."

"Man your post," Kirk snapped. "Ready photon torpedoes."

With a burst of energy, I smacked the comlink and said, "Stand by, Perren. Do not enable. Repeat, do not enable." I swung around the chair to the weapons station and went after the photon controls, steeped in resurging faith for the man on the lower deck. My fingers tingled on the triggers, stiff with both relief and anticipation. We were back on familiar territory—my kind of ground, and his.

"Captain," Scott hailed. *"I canna guarantee that photon capacity. Energy was drained severely by those flux beams. I'm rerouting power through impulse reserve."*

"Speed it up, mister," Kirk demanded, suddenly fierce as he dragged his senior officers together and made them stand in the fire with him. "We're at battlestations. I want fighting capacity."

The intercom crackled. *"Aye, aye, sir."*

"Piper, man the exterior scanners," the captain ordered, sending me dashing around the bridge to the dynoscanners at the opposite side. While I was moving, Kirk spoke into the intercom. "Mr. Sarda, report to the bridge immediately."

I almost passed out when I heard that. We were going to be together—right when we needed to be. I was glad for that—and for the fact that Captain Kirk refused to use the transwarp flux again.

"Piper, report the range of those ships."

The scanner light flickered with numbers. I squinted into it. "Point six-zero light years and closing."

A few moments of silence gave us no comfort. During that time, the captain took the helm himself. "Spock, divert more power to impulse drive for the best speed out of the area."

"Very well," Spock said. He crossed to engineering and played with the controls as fluidly as if he'd accepted a challenge to play chess. Yet this time, I knew he was deliberately hiding a deeper concern. It showed, if subtly, in the way he moved.

I peered into the space scanners. The three Empire cruisers moved in on one monitor. Hope sank as I watched them grow nearer, the schematics of their configuration flashing on two other monitors. And on the scanner at my right a distant flicker showed me we were finished. More ships on the way.

I watched the monitor, hypnotized. Four equidistant points of starlight bloomed against black space. Only my training kept me from sinking into a chair and waiting for the end.

"Captain," I murmured, "four more."

Our eyes connected.

Anything he would have said to me was drowned in the hiss of the turbolift. Sarda glanced at me, a fulfilling glance, if fleeting, and took in the conditions we faced.

"Sarda, take weapons control," the captain ordered.

Sarda nodded, but said nothing as he hurried to his station.

Though the captain surely knew there was nothing left to try against the odds coming at us through open space, we both knew we would try anything to keep surviving. Beyond our own survival was the scientific integrity of the Federation. We would destroy ourselves to preserve that.

I watched the scanner. Behind the Klingon battle cruisers, four new points of light became ivory pearls, closing at warp speed.

"Scotty, I want those photons, now!" Kirk made no attempt to hide the urgency.

"Working, sir. I can give you 78 percent range, and two-thirds power."

"It'll have to do. Sarda, target those new vessels."

"Targeting."

"Range," I rasped. "Two-hundred-eighty-thousand kilometers and closing." Damn it, did we have to keep doing this?

"Stay sharp." Kirk's voice was bracing.

In my scanner the four ivory jewels separated like exploding fireworks, preparing to surround us. They were closing fast, all teeth bared. As they peeled away from one another in classic formation, their shapes flattened into graceful disks and grew limbs. Sound caught in my throat. I choked it out.

"Captain, hold your fire! Starships!"

All eyes struck the viewer.

"Spock, confirm!" Kirk snapped.

Spock hung a receiver in his ear and fingered his controls. He met the captain's disbelieving gaze. "Confirmed, sir. Commodore of the Fleet Lyle Craig aboard U.S.S. *Hood*—"

The captain burst to his feet.

Spock went on, his voice strong now. "Captain Jarboe on the U.S.S. *Yorktown* . . . Captain Andreoni on board *Exeter,* and Captain Long with the destroyer *Majestic.* Commodore Craig suggests we sit back and . . . watch the nickelodeon." His brow rose over the unfamiliar word.

But it wasn't unfamiliar to the captain. His face was alight with triumph as we watched the starships move in around us, and saw the sudden action of the surprised Klingon cruisers. Kirk slapped the command console with both hands and roared, "Advise they are welcome, Mr. Spock!"

"With a capital 'well,' " I whispered. *We made it work, Scanner. Rest easy.*

The United Federation of Planets dumped politics on the floor and moved in as if to a trumpet carillon.

Three Klingon battleships wheeled to meet four Federation starships, and we could nearly taste the surprise. From our Alert-darkened bridge, we watched as the starships took on the battle cruisers and the destroyer *Majestic* peeled off after the unidentified ship that was still haunting us. Two of the Klingon vessels suddenly moved in on *Enterprise.* They were going to use us as a backdrop—a safety net.

Kirk saw it. His sharp words cut through my fascination with the screen. "Piper, take the helm! Plot a course astern, z-minus thirty degrees. Lock and execute. Give them a clear field to open fire. Sarda, arm photon torpedoes. Wide dispersal. Fire!"

I should have known he wouldn't just sit back and watch the nickelodeon, whatever that was. Jim Kirk would fire a bologna sandwich out the photon tubes if he had to, but he'd do *something*.

Photons burst through inner space, blasting a Klingon ship out of our way as *Enterprise* descended gracefully out of the center of battle. The Klingon ship pivoted away, its hull dazzling with crackles of energy, and nearly collided with the nameless forked ship as the latter reared away from our fire. We could nearly taste their rage.

Cut free from us and roaring like teased animals, the Klingon ship recovered and whirled around on an imaginary axis, bringing its full disruptor banks to bear on us. A bright glow opened on their firing ports, and the bolt streaked toward our bare port hull. Instinctively, we braced for an impact that would tear the skin right off the ship.

But the cavalry was still here. From the top of our viewer came a gleaming ivory disk, immense and instantly blanking out the whole screen. Massive call letters flashed by, black against the creamy plated hull, and we heard the thunder of disruptor fire striking full shields. *Hood!*

The other starship flooded past our viewer and was gone almost as suddenly as she had appeared. She'd taken the bolt on her own shields, leaving us intact to move downward and out of the way. Now she was turning on the Klingon who had attacked us, slicing hard into the damage we'd done, redoubling it.

We descended into a clear spaceway. *Hood* and *Yorktown* moved in over us, taking our place among the clutter of ships. They opened fire. The Empire cruisers cut away suddenly, swinging after each other in retreat, and disappeared into light speed.

Exeter was chewing Romulan bones. By now, there was nothing left of the Praetor's ships to return to his distant Neutral Zone. Even the dangerous forked ship, after firing three final shots on *Yorktown* and learning what it was like to have a starship turn on it, turned on a pointed hullfoil and streaked into open space. *Majestic* wheeled after them, nipping at their heels.

"They did it!" I shouted. At least one foot left the deck. From opposite sides of the bridge, Sarda and I shared a penetrating gaze. His relief was plain. He slumped back on the weapons control console, surveyed the screen, and looked at me again. Against my flight suit, I raised a thumb in silent tribute. Perhaps it was the space between us, or the red dimness of the bridge, but I thought he almost smiled.

Kirk rested a hand on his command chair, but said nothing. That was all right; he didn't need to say anything.

Spock was standing near communications, receiving a message. "Sir, *Hood* is hailing us." His voice was soft now with that charismatic smoothness that said the danger was over and we had survived in high style. "Commodore Craig reports this sector is clear. He and Ambassador Shamirian are awaiting your reply."

Kirk's cheeks grew round with a repressed grin. He pounced on the intercom. "Ben! You old sea gypsy. You're late."

"Now, Jim, you know as well as I do what it takes to round up four starships. Pardon my saying so, but Enterprise *looks a little ill around the mainmast."*

"Don't worry about my ship," Jim Kirk countered, pleased with himself. "We're still in one piece."

"I never worry about you, Jim."

Another voice interrupted now. *"Jim, this is Craig. Don't ask me how you stayed in that one piece in the middle of a scramble. I'm impressed right down to my birthday suit."*

"That's one I owe you, Lyle."

"Deduct it from the three I owe you. What else can we do for you while we arrange to tow you to starbase?"

"We have a medical emergency here," Kirk told him. "We need as many medical personnel as you can spare, a damage control team, and a skeleton crew while my crew recuperates."

"You've got it. Patch me through to Leonard. I can tie in my ship's surgeon and let them share details. No sense in us captains horning in."

"Thanks again, Lyle."

"Glad to help, Jim. Craig out."

The captain settled into his command chair and surveyed the bridge before turning to Spock. "Mr. Spock," he said, a definite lilt in his voice, "secure from Red Alert. Patch our sickbay through to *Hood*."

"My pleasure, Captain." Another lilt, clear as bells. The bridge lights came back on.

Within an hour we were under tow, this time toward home territory. *Yorktown* and *Hood* were towing *Enterprise,* and behind us, *Majestic* was towing Rex. *Exeter* had stayed behind in the Ciatella Star System to make sure the area was secure. Starbase Four had been alerted and was preparing its space dock to accommodate a heavy cruiser. Breathing time.

And that's just about all I was doing: breathing. And gazing in disbelief at the beautiful starships ahead of us as we rolled through open space. When Captain Kirk appeared in my periphery, I hardly noticed.

"Everything all right, Commander?"

"Hm? Oh . . . yes, sir, of course. Everything's fine," I said, trying to convince myself. I wasn't used to this. I kept waiting for things to start going wrong again. "Captain . . ."

His eyes narrowed. "I thought so. What is it?"

"Sir . . . what's going to happen to Perren? I mean, what do we do with a Vulcan? Lock him up and throw away all that brilliance? He did help us . . ."

"Yes, and I'm sure the Judicial Committee at Star Fleet Command will take that into consideration. I'm going to submit a recommendation that he be remanded to the custody of his home planet. We'll let the Vulcans decide. That's equitable, I think. Don't you?"

This time I couldn't stop the nonregulation sigh of relief. "Yes, sir, I sure do."

He stayed by me for a few minutes. Together we watched the elegant starships as they towed us along. Finally, he urged, "What else?"

I looked at him. He was watching me carefully, his head at a slight angle. How did he always know?

But he did know. I made no more attempts to hide it. I looked once again out into space. "That unidentified ship . . ."

The captain nodded, and clasped his hands behind his back. He thought about it for a moment before answering. "A blemish on the art of war, Piper," he told me. "You don't always get the comfort of knowing."

At least he understood. It made me feel better. The sniggering doubt would always remain, but at least it was a shared doubt. Now only one question remained.

"Sir, how did you get out of trouble at Starfleet Command?"

He resisted a grin and tipped his hat. "Trouble is only a minor annoyance when you've engineered it yourself. And don't worry. The assault charges against you were dropped due to extenuating circumstances."

"Before I ever laid a hand on those security people, I'll bet."

Now he did smile. Then he said, "You'd win."

I shook my head and sighed. The captain watched me passively.

"We've got a lot of cleaning up to do," he said. "Go to your quarters and get some rest."

"My quarters, sir? But I thought—"

"You're still officially assigned to my command." He paused then. "*Banana Republic* or not, *Enterprise* is still your home ship."

Swelling in the compliment, I hardly knew what to say anymore. I let my hips rest against the bridge rail and, finally, I relaxed in his company. "I seem to be thanking you a lot lately, sir."

A little shrug softened the soldier in him. "And we don't thank you enough. It evens out. Go on. Get some rest."

I flexed my shoulders. "Aye, sir. I will."

"Oh, and Piper—"

"Sir?"

"The Annual Atlantic Wind Ships Race is coming up. I need crew. Interested?"

The deck of *Enterprise* felt as if it was surging on a wave. "Just try setting sail without me," I said.

"Wouldn't think of it. Good night, Commander."

"Fair weather, Captain."

Chapter Thirteen

"A little suffering is good for the soul."
—The Corbomite Maneuver

SICKBAY WAS A ZOO. Several doctors, nurses, and orderlies had beamed over from the three ships escorting us and were preparing to beam back to their own ships with groups of our ill crewpeople. All four sickbays were hard at work trying to ease the aftereffects of the heavy drugging. Some people were on their feet. Others were still unconscious. Many still hovered in between. Sarda was here already, apparently for the same reason that brought me here before following the captain's suggestion to rest.

Scanner was one of those in-betweens: still in bed, but the light had returned to his eyes and the whip to his tongue.

"Piper! You daughter of a snake. How are yawl?"

I tweeked the forefinger that waggled at me and said, "You don't want to know. Are you all right?"

"Naw, I died. I'm just here as an example of what not to do."

Sarda offered a straighter answer. "Merete estimates he will be duty-fit in a day." The sentence sounded awkward until I realized I'd never heard him call Merete anything but "Doctor." Sarda had changed. Not for the human, but for the better.

Scanner tugged at the lapel of my flight suit. "So how's it gonna feel carryin' a rank of full Commander?"

I backed off a step. "Oh, no, not again! Not a chance, not a prayer! Maybe they'll promote you, but they're not going to do that to me again, not for a long, long, *long* time! I'll resign first!"

"Okay, okay . . . forget I mentioned it."

"You'd better forget you mentioned it, because if Star Fleet gets any bright ideas I'll know where they came from."

"Hey, this is me forgettin'." He held his hands up in surrender.

Luckily for him, a roll of laughter from a group of recovering crewpeople distracted me from my reaction to that unsavory idea. "What's going on over there?"

"Oh, nothin'," Scanner said. "Really nothin'."

I looked at Sarda. A Vulcan version of a shrug tightened his shoulders. "Judd has evidently rigged some holographs into the patients' lounge, to entertain the crew as they recuperate. I have not as yet seen them, but they seem to be efficacious."

"Are you telling me," I began, "that we actually have a visual record of Scanner's idea of entertainment? What is it, Scanner? Old Laurel and Hardy tapes? Films of test flight crashes? What?"

"Ain't tellin'." Whether he wanted to tell or not, his cheeks grew rosy.

"This I've got to see."

"Piper, it's dull, I'm telling you!"

"Sure. I know a setup when I see one. Come on, Sarda."

We elbowed our way through the lump of crewpeople—easy, because most of them were still weak. Laughter is the best medicine, Confucius or somebody once said, and it showed in the blanched faces around us as health slowly returned. When we got through to the specially rigged holo platform, I saw why. I also remembered that a certain *Tyrannosaurus Rex* lover had been armed with a tricorder during a particularly opportune moment.

273

The group rippled with laughter again, in time for me to see a small holographic version of myself, engaged in a vigorous dance. Veils whipped in and out of the image periphery, as did a grasping Klingon hand from below. Veils!

Sarda's voice was fuel on the fire. "Piper, I had no idea you were so . . . athletic."

"Scanner!"

It took three strong orderlies, but eventually peace reigned again and I was forced to accept my share of it. In a ship still empty of most of its crew, I discovered what quiet really meant. It was nice, for a change; soothing. My quarters were the same as I had left them: Merete's bunk pleated and pin straight, mine a little rumpled. I never could make a bed.

That didn't matter now anyway. I planned to add to the rumples. I ordered all the lights off except the one tiny courtesy bulb in the head. Darkness folded around me, welcome as a warm cloak, and my head felt like an iron ball when it hit the pillow.

One deep breath to usher me into sleep—and the door buzzer sounded.

Ease off, guys, I'm under orders to sleep.

My voice triggered the door. "Come."

The doorway was dark, and as the panel opened, bland corridor light molded around a stock authority. "Commander Piper . . ."

I struggled into a sitting position. "Oh—Mr. Scott. Come in, please."

Still silhouetted, he moved into my lightless quarters. "Lassie . . . I'd like a worrrd wi' you."

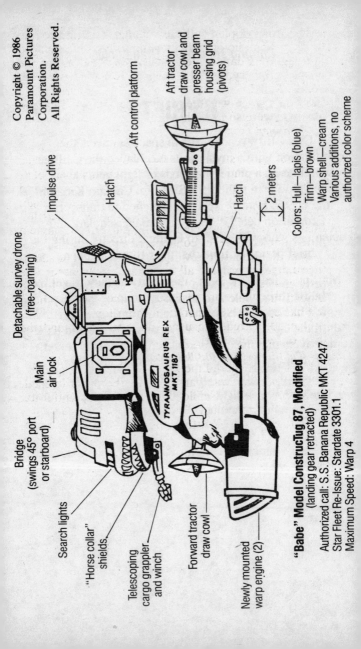

Aft tractor
draw cowl and
presser beam
housing grid
(pivots)

Aft control platform

Impulse drive

Hatch

Hatch

Detachable survey drone
(free-roaming)

Main air lock

Bridge
(swings 45° port
or starboard)

Search lights

"Horse collar"
shields

Telescoping
cargo grappler
and winch

Forward tractor
draw cowl

Newly mounted
warp engine (2)

TYRANNOSAURUS REX
MKT 11187

Colors: Hull—lapis (blue)
Trim—brown
Warp shell—cream
Various additions, no
authorized color scheme

⊢ 2 meters

"Babe" Model ConstrucTug 87, Modified
(landing gear retracted)
Authorized call: S.S. Banana Republic MKT 4247
Star Fleet Re-Issue: Stardate 3301.1
Maximum Speed: Warp 4

THE RIFT

Every fifty years, a rift in space connects the
Federation with a mysterious race called the Calligar
who live on a planet hundreds of light years away -
much too far to travel in a Starship. Captain Kirk and
the U.S.S. *Enterprise* are dispatched to transport a
Federation delegation of diplomats, scholars and
scientists who will travel to Calligar directly during the
brief period of time that the rift will be open.

Mr. Spock leads the Federation party as they travel by
shuttle through the rift just as a group of the aliens
arrive in Federation space. The meetings go smoothly
until the Calligar take Spock's party hostage and Kirk
discovers that the aliens are keeping a deadly secret.
With angry Tellarite and Andorian fleets ready to
attack the Calligar, Kirk must save Spock and the
others before war breaks out and the rift closes for
another fifty years.

STAR TREK
THE NEXT GENERATION

STAR TREK: THE NEXT GENERATION NOVELS

STAR TREK: THE NEXT GENERATION GIANT NOVELS

For a complete list of Star Trek publications, T-shirts and badges please send a SAE to Titan Books Mail Order, Panther House, 38 Mount Pleasant, London, WC1X 0AP.
Please quote reference ST51.